To: Many Blessings
From: Vaundre' McGough
2018

Back 2 Life

Vaundre' McGough

Back

2

Life

I once was blind, but now I see

Vaundre' McGough

Back 2 Life

Copyright © 2018 by Vaundre' McGough. All rights reserved.

No part of this publication may be reproduced, stored in a retrieval system or transmitted in any way by any mean, electronic, mechanical, photocopy, recording or otherwise without the prior permission of the author except as provided by USA copyright law.

This novel is a work of fiction. Names, descriptions, entities, and incidents included in the story are products of the author's imagination. Any resemblance to actual persons, events, and entities is entirely coincidental.

The opinions expressed by the author are of his own merit.

Published by Vaundre' McGough

Vaundre' McGough is committed to excellence through his work. Habakkuk 2:2 Then the LORD replied,

"Write down the vision make it plain on tablets so that whoever reads it, may run with it."

Book design copyright © 2018 by Vaundre' McGough

Cover design by Word2Kindle.com

Interior design by Vaundre' McGough

Published in the

United States of America

ISBN 13: 978-1726369213

ISBN 10: 1726369218

1. Fiction/General
2. Fiction/Drama
   18-09-11

Acknowledgements

Special thanks to Jesus Christ who is my everything. I thank my mom and dad for their inspiration as the best parents in the world. To my sister for believing in me. To my nieces and nephews stay true to who you are and be the best you can be. To my cousins all over the country. Follow your heart and follow your dreams. To my friends, life is what we make it. Life will throw the good and the bad. We go through it to get to the other side of the good. To God Be the Glory and the honor.

Table of Contents

1 The Boss--6

2 Party Hard---14

3 Iron Fist--20

4 Lawsuit--27

5 Home Sweet Home--32

6 Destroying Evidence---39

7 Girls Just Want to Have Fun-------------------------------55

8 Blue Monday---62

9 The Aftermath---78

10 In Hades---83

11 Nurse Mary---97

12 Rehab---110

13 Connecting Flights-------------------------------------118

14 The Doctor's Office-----------------------------------128

15 Lunch with Friends-----------------------------------139

16 Nathaniel Meets the Cartel------------------------150

17 Volunteering---156

18 Destination Bangkok------------------------------160

19 Taking Out Mark------------------------------------165

20 Clearing A Conscience----------------------------177

21 Wanted by Everyone-----------------------------190

22 Moment of Truth---------------------------------200

CHAPTER ONE

"The Boss"

It is the summer of 2008. Christy Billings a young 28-year-old of Hispanic and Irish descent is on top of the world as a top executive at DinoCore, a Fortune 500 Marketing Firm. She oversees fifteen individuals responsible for the marketing strategies of the company. Christy was just informed she will be receiving a bonus before Christmas due to her and her employees for a high rate in marketing returns for the company.

She sits in her boss's office, Mark Collins a self-starter Caucasian in his mid-30's with dark hair and GQ style clothes to fit his personality. Mark proceeds around the front of his desk in front of Christy. As he leans up against his desk, Christy crosses both of her legs.

Mark flips through a seven-page spread sheet his holds in his hands.

"Christy, these returns are incredible. I just can't believe you did this!"

Christy laughs.

"Come on Mark, you know my work. I can't believe your surprised at all."

Mark returns a laugh.

"I know Christy, but I'm just in awe at how you do what you do."

"Well, thank you Mark." Christy crosses her legs again in a different direction as she gestures with her hands. "So, you called me down here to tell me…what?"

"Yeah, so um, I called you down to give you a high five to you and your staff for making the quarterly, and to say you will be receiving a $10,000 bonus. How is that?"

"Ten thousand?"

Mark nods his head. "Yes, is that a problem?"

Christy's mouth widens with surprise.

"Ten thousand for me, and not my workers?"

"No, unless you want to split it?"

"No way Mark, are you crazy? That's mine, all mine, besides, I could have done it without them actually."

Mark laughs as he tosses the seven-page spread sheet onto his mahogany desk.

"Your so selfish Christy."

"Don't I know it. This is great to hear Mark. I want to thank you for putting a good word in for me with your boss and mine. Let Mr. Boykins know, I work to please,

and I will continue my hard work. He will not be disappointed."

Mark continues his praise.

"I appreciate that Christy and I will relay the message because, when I look good, you look good."

Christy agrees.

"You got that right."

Mark and Christy nod their heads in agreement.

"You will be receiving that bonus two weeks before Christmas Christy, sounds good or what?"

"That sounds awesome Mark, I love it. I can do some extra Christmas shopping for myself."

"Great. If we keep rolling the way we are, we will all get a stake in the company. That's what the boss said."

Christy smiles.

"Wow Mark, really?"

"Really Christy."

"Awesome, thanks for filling me in on that."

"No problem. I just received word from him and vice president today. They said this company will earn a net profit of 10 million by the end of the year."

"Cool Mark."

Mark changes the subject.

"So, how is your new place?"

"I love it. You should come by and check it out, great view of the lake. I've got a huge pool, a guest room, and pool table." "You think you need all of that Christy?"

"Of course. It's everything a girl like me needs."

Mark agrees.

"That sounds like something you would say Christy. Where is this place?"

"It's the hills babe, what do you expect? I'm like seven stories up."

Mark folds both of his arms curious.

"You throw any parties yet?"

"I've thrown seven parties so far since I've moved in. I can't stand my neighbors though, there always calling the police for disturbance. They are so boring, I mean if they want quiet, they should move to a forest."

Mark laughs causing Christy to laugh too.

"I'm serious Mark."

"Were your girlfriends there when they called the police?" Mark asks.

"Of course, they were." Christy pauses for a minute. "If you are asking about Leslie, yes she was there too."

Mark stares at Christy as she stares back at him.

"What?" Mark asks

"What do you mean what? Mark, I know you like her."

Christy points her index finger up at Marks forehead.

"It's written all over your forehead."

Mark gives in.

"So, okay, when are you going to hook me up then?"

"I don't know Mark, it's on you. You do know she has a boyfriend, right?"

"Yes, I know that. You have a boyfriend Christy, and that doesn't stop you from cheating."

"A girl has got to do what a girls' got to do Mark?"

Mark shakes his head at her.

"What?" She asks.

"You unbelievable sometimes Christy."

"Okay, anyway, I'm going to set it up, I will let you know when she will be over. All you need to do, is act like your stopping by to say high, and that you were in the area, then you and her can hook up. Now if you mess this up Mark, then the only way you're going to meet her again will be in your dreams sweetie."

Mark laughs.

"Okay, gosh, you're like my sister."

"How is that?"

"She's so forward with everything."

"Just giving you a little push my friend, some of you guys need it."

"Yeah, with you, it would be pushing me right off the cliff if this doesn't work out."

"Yeah, well, you won't know if you don't fall sometimes babe. I don't know what's with you guys, I mean, if you like a girl, talk to her, she won't bite you."

"That's great to hear Christy, but if this one does, I hope you will be available to take me to the hospital for rabies."

"Ha, ha, very funny."

"So, last but not least before I leave, are you going to the company party Saturday?"

"You know I'm going to the party Christy. This is the biggest party of the year!"

"That's right, hey, just don't drink so much okay?"

Mark stares at Christy.

"I can control it, don't worry about me. Hey, we are going to party like rock stars though, right?"

"Most definitely." Christy says.

As Christy stands in her business suit and short skirt that defines the curves of her body she chuckles as she sways her hips from side to side towards Marks office door grabbing the handle looking back at Mark.

"So, what do my workers get?"

Mark replies.

"Oh, well, they will get two thousand."

"They should get nothing if you asked me."

Mark with his head lowered responds.

"I would never ask you Christy."

Christy smiles.

"Good, because you know what I would say."

Mark is shocked at Christy's response as he returns to his desk.

"Christy, come on, why do you have to be so cold?"

Christy shrugs her shoulders.

"Maybe because you taught me to be that way in this business?"

Mark laughs.

"Oh yeah, I forgot."

Mark pauses.

"It's great though, seeing that you are a Pitbull with your staff. I taught you well."

"Most definitely babe."

"Thanks Christy, keep up the good work."

Christy winks at Mark leaving his office closing the door behind her. As she proceeds down the hallway towards her office, she reminisces about her level of success. Mark returns to work in his office as he laughs about Christy. He uses his office phone pressing the number nine button with his index finger. The phone rings as someone on the other line picks up the phone.

"Bill?" Mark asks.

The voice on the other end responds. It is the CEO, Giles Boykins.

"Just want to let you know, I just talked to Christy, she was ecstatic about getting the bonus." Mark says.

Mr. Boykins responds.

"Oh no, I told you, don't worry, she's in my corner, I have her around my finger, just relax." Mark says.

Mark pauses as Mr. Boykins responds.

"Trust me, if we keep feeding her money to cater to her lifestyle, she will be all in." Mark replies.

Mark pauses again as he listens to Mr. Boykins.

"So, how much longer do we have to deal with these Cartel guys before the SEC finds out?" "Okay, well, I'll take your word for it. I haven't told her about them because you told me not to."

Mark pauses again.

"Okay, talk to you later, sir, bye."

Mark hangs up the phone as he sits in his high back leather chair rocking back and forth. Meanwhile, as Christy enters the main door leading to her wing where she supervises her people, the smile on her face dissolves when she sees two of her workers mingling and talking to each other by their cubicles. The two ladies, in their mid-twenties, are Angela Harmon and Melissa Sanders. Angela is feisty and doesn't mind expressing herself for the truth, as her friend Melissa Sanders is subtler and more laid-back. As Christy approaches them, she frowns as she tears into them with her words. "What are you two doing?" The two women are shocked and surprised by her surprising entrance. Angela is the first to respond. "Were just talking, what's the big deal?"

Christy responds in anger. "What's the big deal? What is your name again?"

Angela is surprised she doesn't know her name.

"Angela, what, you forgot my name? I've been working with you for six months now."

"Don't question me! If you were important to me, maybe I would remember your name, but since you're not..."

"Why can't we talk, we're are all doing an exceptional job here from what I heard upstairs? We just made well over the initial quota in for the company."

Christy interrupts the Angela. "Who told you that? Does this look like a church gathering or something?" The words are insulting being that Angela is a Christian and she knows Christy is an atheist. Melissa tries to break the ice by apologizing. "Were sorry Ms. Billings." Christy turns her head slightly where her right ear is extended towards the two women.

"What did you just say, sorry?"

"Yes, I said sorry" Angela responds.

"I'm sorry to Ms. Billings. I will get back to work."

Christy glances at Angela, then raises her finger at her in a stop motion.

"You say sorry when you step on somebody's expensive shoes."

Angela now in her chair at her cubicle with her back towards Christy, turns around in attack mode. "You know, what's your deal? I mean, we just made you look good this quarter and your beef is about us talking for a few minutes? Are you kidding me? You have issues." Christy turns her head looking down at Angela. Other workers nearby stop what they were doing. The moment is silent until Christy responds pointing at Angela. "In my office now!"

Christy briskly walks away to her office. Angela now mad, slams her papers on her desk, then rises to her feet grabbing her purse as she storms off towards Christy's office. Inside Christy's office are plush Mahogany furniture, matching a cherry oak wood desk. Her office has a lot of windows where co-workers can see inside. They see both Christy and Angela arguing but without sound. Lip reading is their only option of entertaining themselves. Inside the office, Christy chastises Angela. "Don't you ever talk to me that way in front of my employees, do you understand me?" Angela stands realizing her mistake. She becomes humbled as she realizes the other employees are watching through the glass pane windows.

She wants to set an example. "Yes, it's just, we weren't' doing anything wrong Ms. Billings." Christy continues her chastising. "You were doing something wrong, not working. I want you working twenty-four seven until you get your break or your lunch. Until then, you talk on your own time, do you understand me?"

"Okay." Angela humbly responds.

Christy finalizes her insults.

"And the next time you insult me like that, you will be sorry! I will set an example with you for the other employees"

"An example? What do you mean?"

Christy scoffs at Angela's remark.

"Oh, you really don't want me to go there."

Angela stretches her arms out to release the tension building up in her emotions.

"Okay, I just said I was sorry, may I please go now?"

Christy stares at Angela and responds.

"No, you stay until I tell you, you are permitted to leave."

This makes Angela's emotions explode like a volcano. She folds her arms with her lips quivering as she watches Christy turn around with her back towards her. She then makes her way to her desk to have a seat. Sitting in her leather chair crossing her legs, she smiling as she watches Angela stand in front of her like a little child just disciplined by her mother. Angela does everything in her power to remain humble knowing her coworkers are watching her every move.

"Be calm" her inner spirit speaks in a whisper as she tries to avoid eye contact with Christy knowing it will intensify her suffering. But her spirit commands her to look Christy in the eye. The two eye each other for a couple of minutes. Angela lowers her head because the pain becomes too much to bear. Her eyes fill with tears as tiny drops of water fall just as it would from the sky. The reaction is everything Christy needs to feel empowered towards her as she releases her chains of bondage.

"You may go now."

Angela not making eye contact with Christy, quickly turns around and storms out of her office to the women's bathroom across the hall. She enters the first stall pushing the door open. She crashes her frame onto the toilet seat of the stall. Her purse crashes to the floor with its contents inside sounding like a ton of bricks. She sits on the toilet with her feet turned inward to support the weight of her body in emotional pain. She cries immensely as her sniffles echo inside the bathroom.

As Christy thinks about her dominated victory over her employee, she happens to glance out the corner of her eye and notices all her employees staring at her mesmerized by her lack of human dignity. This enrages her even more. She hops out of her chair storming towards her office window. She yells through it loud enough for everyone to understand.

"I said get back to work!" In the bathroom, Angela finishes releasing her pain as she exits the stall with her purse. She approaches the bathroom mirror to try to touch up her damaged makeup but then realizes it is futile. As she slowly exits the bathroom heading towards her cubicle, she passes by Christy in slow motion. The two make eye contact at each other in passing as Angela rolls her eyes up at her in a non-Christian like manner. Christy smirks at the entire encounter knowing that she won.

CHAPTER TWO

"Party Hard"

Around 8 p.m. the company party is underway. The CEO, President, Vice President, Executives, and Staff workers dressed for success, are present at this gala. Angela and her friend and co-worker Melissa arrive in Angela's Toyota Prius as they pull up to the valet. Two valet attendants approach their car.

One opens the passenger door for Melissa, and the other for Angela. Both ladies exit the vehicle wearing long elegant dresses underneath their coats. Behind Angela's car is Christy in her convertible two-door dark blue colored BMW with a royal blue colored convertible top.

She exits her car wearing a long bright red dress with matching leather shoes as the tip of the shoes expose themselves. Christy tips the valet attendant ten dollars. He is star struck at Christy's appearance. Angela and Melissa notice Christy right away. As they make their way to the sidewalk, Christy briskly walks past them making herself noticed. Angela whispers to Melissa.

"I cannot stand her." Angela says. "I noticed." Melissa responds.

Christy enters the building with her high heel shoes clicking across the marble floor. as she struts her way towards the ballroom with her red purse in hand, many co-workers greet her as they mingle in the furor of the building. The men are all dressed in tuxedos while the women are wearing star studded dresses you would see at an Oscar Red Carpet. Momentarily, Angela and Melissa enter the building.

They see other co-workers from their department walking over and began mingling with them. The demarcation between management and employees, is obvious. Later the gala begins. A couple of hours pass and everyone present is having a good time. The President and Vice President of the company congratulate Christy for her exceptional work. Mark sits next to her. He becomes jealous of the attention she's getting and decides to drink more than usual. His excessive drinking causes him to say things he shouldn't.

"So, check this out everybody, this girl comes over to my house. I open the door and say, what are you doing? She says what? I say, how did you get to my house? I never told you where I live. She says, you gave me the key and address to your house last night you Moran. I say, oh."

Mark laughs aloud.

He takes a drink as he continues his tirade. All the President and VP become uneasy as they look at each other.

"And that's just one girl. I think I was with three girls that night. I hope I didn't give them keys to my place either!"

Christy becomes annoyed as she leans in whispering to Mark.

"Stop it, you are acting like a fool Mark."

He glances at Christy and laughs aloud. Everyone at the table except Christy. She leans over to him.

"Mark, I think you've had enough." Christy says.

"What? No Christy, I think I've only had very little."

"Oh really, Mark? How many drinks have you had?"

Mark glances down at his drink, then breaths his alcoholic breath at her saying…

"Yes. One after another Christy my love."

The table is silent until Mark bursts out with laughter. Christy rises from her chair and storms off. Mark watches her leave.

"Guess she's headed to the lady's room."

Mark pauses. "Hey Daniel, we are really cooking those books, aren't we?"

The Vice President is alarmed at the question.

"Cooking the books? What are you talking about Mark?"

Mark glances around the table.

"You know Daniel, come on. You're in charge of it."

The Vice President replies… "Really?"

"Yeah, you told me, we have the green light and that I needed to make sure Christy was on board."

Mark pauses for a second. "I tell you, she's really loved in her department. Did you know her team despises her?"

Mark laughs aloud. Daniel interrupts him as he prepares to stand up while buttoning his tuxedo jacket.

"Hey Mark, walk with me to the restroom."

Mark takes another drink.

"Why, I don't have to go."

Daniel the VP stands at his table giving Mark a serious look.

"I think Mark, if you don't go, after this event is over, you will wish you had."

Mark realizes the severity of the moment. He sets his drink down on the table, adjusts his tie, then rises from his chair. The eyes of the President, Chairperson, and Co-Chairperson watch Marks every move.

"Yeah, I think your right!

The Vice President proceeds to the men's room with Mark following behind him. Meanwhile, inside the lady's room, Christy touches up her makeup. Suddenly, the door to the lady's room opens. In walks Angela and Melissa. Angela stops in her tracks seeing Christy standing in front of the mirror.

Christy's eyes connect with hers from the angle of the mirror. Angela looks away as she approaches the mirror. The bathroom is silent with the three women inside of it. Melissa stands next to Angela as she fixes her hair.

      Melissa strikes up a question. "So, what are your plans for the weekend Angie?" Angie, occupied by the presence of Christy, is distracted as the words enter her ears for her brain to translate. When finished hearing everything, she reluctantly responds. "Oh, I'm going on a women's retreat with my church." "Oh, that sounds fun." "Yes, I think it will be. We're all looking forward to it." "So, where are you going?" Angela asks. "To Stone Mountain, with family." Melissa says. "Sounds interesting, I want to join you the next time you go again." Angela replies. "Oh, sure I would love your company." Melissa says. Christy ignores them both as she finishes her makeup and leaves.

Down the hall in the men's room, the Vice President Daniel steps away from the urinal as it automatically flushes. Inside one of the stalls, Mark is throwing up from his excessive drinking. Two co-workers leave the restroom looking back to where the throwing up sound is coming from.

 Daniel adjusts his tie in the mirror as he frowns. Mark finally exits the stall exhausted. He steps up to the counter to wash his hands avoiding eye contact with

Daniel. The sound of the toilet automatically flushing increases the moment as Daniel glances over at Mark washing his hands.

Angela grabs the counter with both hands as she breaths hard. "Melissa, it is so hard for me to contain myself when I am around her. I can't believe I am acting this way." "Calm down Angie, your human, and you have human emotions that need to be checked like all of us do from time to time, that's all.

Ask God to help you when that moment comes. That's faith, right? What does the Bible say, pray for your enemies?" Melissa asks. "Yes, it says that, but I would like to kill my enemies first, then ask God to bless them wherever they're going so I can get on with my life." Melissa burst with laughter as Angela finishes her makeup laughing along with her.

Mark immediately sobers up.

"I'm so sorry Danny, I got out of control out there."

Daniel becomes sarcastic.

"Hey, don't worry about it Mark, I'm your boss. I could have fired you at the table and this moment we are having here would only be a dream."

Daniel turns and steps closer to Mark as he dries his hands.

"You know what a fool is Mark?"

The question confuses Mark as he glances back at Daniel through the mirror.

"No, not really."

"It's someone who speaks before they even know what they are saying. Don't you ever do something like that again. You're lucky Mr. Boykins was sitting at another table, mingling with his guests."

Mark takes a deep breath as he tosses the wrinkled paper towel into its home, the garbage. He slowly glances at Daniel. "What can I do to make this right?" Daniel stares at him. "I want your entire bonus deposited in my account by Friday. If it's not there by 11 A.M., you will resign, or I will fire you." Mark stammers with his words. "My whole bonus Daniel?" Daniel gets angrier. "Did I stutter?" "No, no, I just wanted to make sure that's what you said. It's yours by tomorrow, no problem." Daniel turns around to check his himself in the mirror. He finalizes everything

adjusting his tie again, then exits the restroom leaving Mark to lick his wounds. Mark stares at himself in the mirror. Later, the party ends, and people begin filing out of the building. Angela and Melissa are

outside mingling with other co-workers. Christy exits the building with another executive. She makes eye contact with Angela staring her down. Melissa notices the moment.

"What's with her, why is she so evil?"

Angela responds. "I don't care."

Christy stands on the sidewalk waiting for the valet attendant to bring her car to her. All the big wigs leave in their Rolls Royce's and Bentleys. As Angela and Melissa walk down the steps with two co-workers towards the valet, Christy twists her body around flinging her purse. It hits Angela in the face as she approaches.

 Angela quickly reacts. "You hit me!"

 "What?" Christy asks with a startled response.

 "You purposely hit me with your purse!"

Christy turns her head away from Angela looking for her car.

 "Give me a break, I'm not thinking about you."

Several people still present, notice the commotion.

Angela replies. "You're crazy and out of your mind!"

 "I'm crazy? Look at the way you are acting. If I hit you, it was an accident." Christy responds.

 "Then apologize," Angela demands.

 Christy responds under her breath, "Yeah right! What, you want to fight me or something?" The comment shocks Angela. "What?" Christy retorts. "You heard me, what are you going to do about it?" As people approach the situation, Angela responds, "You're crazy." Someone intervenes. "Is everything okay here?" Angela is eager to respond until she notices Christy's facial expression in the form of an "I dare you" look. Christy's car pulls up driven by the valet attendant.

"No, it was just a misunderstanding, that's all." Angela responds.

Christy smiles then walks towards her car. She turns around looking at Angela. "You know, I never liked you," Angela says.

"Is, that, right?" Christy responds.

"Yeah it is,"

"Well you know what Angela?"

"No what?"

"You just made your job with me a lot harder. You have a blessed night!"

Christy hands the valet her receipt and another expensive tip as she stares at Angela while entering her BMW and driving away. Melissa stands in front of Angela. "What did you just do? Your life will be total hell from now on." Angela realizes what she's done. "Don't remind me." Christy stares into the sky. "Oh God, please help me."

CHAPTER THREE

"Iron Fist"

The next day at work, Angela walks in to her cubicle. Melissa is already seated at her desk. Melissa whispers to Christy. "Get ready." Angela is confused. "At what?" "Christy is on a rampage, she was yelling at Peter and Gabriel about how messy their work station was. I think this is an intro to what she wants to do to you." "Well, I prayed about it so, I'm not worried at all." "Good for you" Melissa responds. Melissa turns around in her chair with her legs, rolling her chair with her feet up under her desk. Angela sets her purse on her desk and removes her coat placing it around the back of her chair, and calmly sits down.

      She turns on her computer, waits for it to warm up, then she types in her personal password. Angela is happy to begin her day. She works hard through the day processing different assigned accounts. Her work is successful until Christy appears standing over her from behind. Melissa notices as she begins breathing hard waiting for Christy's wrath to begin. Angela, deep in her work, notices Melissa staring at her. As she types, she asks Melissa a question. "What's with you Melissa, why are you staring at me?" As Angela continues focusing her eyes on her computer screen, she decides enough of the suspense. She turns to Melissa.

Melissa has a pale look on her face. "Melissa are you okay?" Angela asks. Melissa's eyes turn back to her screen but glances up in the air giving Angela a signal to look behind her. Angela glances behind her. She is startled seeing Christy standing over her. Christy, looking down at her responds. "In my office now!" Christy stands off to the side waiting for Angela to move at her command. Angela stops her work. She logs off her computer while grabbing her purse. She stands up and follows Christy to her office. In her office, Christy walks behind her desk shielding Angela away from her. She hovers over her desk like a judge standing giving orders in a courtroom.

"So, do you have something to say to me?" Angela is confused at the question. "What are you talking about?" "You know what I am talking about." "No, I don't." "Talking, making accusations about your boss is an immediate dismissal." Angela twists her lip up. "I didn't say anything about you, I have no idea what you're talking about." "I have witnesses." "What? What witnesses, from where?" "The bathroom at the gala last night, a female employee was in one of the stalls. Should I recite what you said?" "Go ahead, if it floats your boat." Christy begins to recite word for word what Angela said about her reading from a sheet of paper that she picks up from her desk.

"It is so hard for me to control myself around her. I can't stand her. It would be easier if God killed my enemies instead of blessing them, then I could move on with my life." Angela pleads her case. "Okay, so I don't hear your name in any of that, I could be talking about anyone."

"Oh, it's about me Angela, and everyone in this department knows what you said. I was the only one in the lady's room with you and Melissa that night." "Well your wrong Ms. Billings, and it would not be good to spread lies like that around to other employees unless you have concrete proof." "I said I have witnesses, weren't you listening?" "Do I need Mark Collins in hear?" "Mark is not going to help you. Do you understand the severity of this situation? I can fire you right now. Do you understand?" "Over what, a lie?" "You want Mark to help you, okay, let's go to his office right now." "Fine." The two women exit Christy's office and proceed upstairs to Marks office.

      Minutes later, Christy and Angela walk in standing in front of Marks office door. Inside, Mark is busy working on his computer. Christy stands behind Angela. "Go ahead, knock." She knocks on the door. Mark glances up to see who it is. He recognizes Angela and Christy through his side window. He motions for them to come in. Upon entering, Angela quickly pleads her case to Mark pointing at Christy before she can respond. "Hi Mark, I have a problem with her, she is accusing me of something I didn't do saying I was talking about her behind her back. She is threating to fire me." Angela takes a quick glance at Christy, then back at Mark. "Christy, what's going on?"

Mark asks. Christy smiles responding in a humble manner as if Mother Teresa were talking. "Good morning Mark, as you can see, one of my employees who has given me so much trouble, is conspiring to turn the rest of my employees against me." Angela quickly responds. "That's a lie!"

"Hey, calm down Angela," Mark quickly responds. "Mark, I cannot have this, it's becoming such a burden to work with her. Time after time, she has exemplified a stubborn attitude that is tainting my department. This behavior is infecting the rest of my staff." Mark glances at Angela.

"Angela is that true?"

Angela responds instantly.

"No, it is not true. Mark, listen, she is lying. The day I started working here, she has been a dictator to me and everyone in the department. We work hard, and that's why we were able to achieve high numbers for this quarter, but part of that was because she threatened all of us, that she would let many of us go if we didn't do a great job." Christy shakes her head. "Mark, you know that is not in my character. I give my staff leeway to be who they want to be, but also to do their jobs in a timely fashion." "Oh my, Mark, she is such a liar. I cannot believe how she's talking right now, so calm cool and collective. If you could see her when she's dictating her Hitler regime over us, you would be shocked!"

"Christy how long has this been going on?" "For a month or two now with her. The final straw came when she said derogatory words against me in the lady's room at the gala last night." Mark turns to look at Angela. Both Mark and Christy wait for a response from her. "What?" Angela says. "Did you make any comments towards

Christy in the restroom that were demeaning towards her?" Angela is silent. Christy, knowing she has the upper hand stares at Angela waiting for a response. Mark does as well. Angela feels trapped in a corner like a racoon. "Well, she's been so rude to me and everyone in our department. She speaks to us like we are twelve years old." Mark and Christy say nothing. They wait for a yes or no from Angela. Angela finally gives in. "Okay, yes I did, I'm sorry but, it's because the way she is towards all of us. I wouldn't come to you with this concern if it wasn't true?" Mark thinks for a moment. Mark quietly asks a question. "Angela, why didn't you come to me when this first started?" "Why me? She treated us all like crap. I didn't want to be the only one."

Angela pleads to Mark. "Mark, no one in our department is brave enough to address this but me, so I had to come here now." Christy is enjoying the moment. "See Mark, everything is about her. I recommend that she be let go." Angela says. The room is silent as Mark lowers his head to ponder over his thoughts. Mark acknowledges Angela's concern as he nods his head up and down. "I see." He pauses for a second. "Well Angela, I was unaware that this was going on over there." Christy's demeanor changes. Her momentum of feeling she has Marks favor shifts, as she feels the life being drained out of her.

Mark pauses for a second time as he sighs.

"So, everyone in that department feels the same way about this Christy?"

"Yeah for sure. She is totally a…"

Angela's mind scans trying to find the right words to say without being offensive.

"A dictator is the only word I can think of right now, and that is being subtle."

"That's cute Angela." Mark says.

"Just two days ago, I was talking to another coworker, and she stormed in yelling at the both of us, just for talking," Angela says.

"Who is the other coworker you were talking to?"

Angela pauses for a second.

"I'd rather not say."

Mark stares at Angela as she continues talking.

"So, I asked her like what's the problem, we just surpassed the quarterly mark for the year in sales. It's obvious we are doing our jobs."

"And what did she say?" Mark asks.

"She chewed me out, like ripped my heart out in front of everyone. The least she could have done if she had a problem with me was to address me privately in her office."

"Everyone is anxious around her," Angela says.

Mark stands to his feet walking around his desk towards Angela as she remains standing with her arms folded. "Well first off, you guys are doing a superb job in your department and since you did make the quarterly mark in sales, I congratulate you for that." Mark begins to fold his arms in front of Angela. "Now, in regard to Ms. Billings." Christy lowers her head as she awaits her fate like a child caught fighting on the playground. "I know she comes across aggressively at times, I've noticed it myself. It's part of her personality, but that does not excuse what she does or how she treats people. She just needs to tone it down a little." Angela leans her head forward.

"A little?" Angela asks.

Mark laughs. "Yes, I hear you Angela." Mark pauses for a moment. "But with our policy here Angela, the rule states, you are not allowed to speak derogatory towards your superior." Christy raises her head in confidence." You were required to fill out a complaint and submit it to me, then I am required to hold a meeting with the two of you individually, then together, then present my findings on the matter." Angela's confidence diminishes as she feels her momentum leaving her body. "I have to uphold the policy Angela, and since you did not do that, I don't want to do this, but I am going to have to let you go."

Angela's face appears in total shock as her shoulders drop feeling the weight of the situation on her shoulders. Mark continues. "I'm sorry Angela. You can still fill out a dispute form and submit it to human resource. I will do what I can to see if you can get your job back." Angela's eyes begin to water. She tries to contain her emotions. "Any more questions" Mark asks. "No, nothing from me

Mark," responds Christy. Mark turns to Angela. "Angela?" Angela at a loss of words, shakes her head no. "Okay then, Angela you may pack your valuables from your station, and leave. If you have any more questions, I will do what I can to answer them."

Christy smiles at Mark. "Thank you, Mark, for resolving this matter." Mark nods his head in agreement. "Okay, you two may leave, thank you for coming." Angela with her lips quivering, turns around head lowered, and briskly leaves Marks office. Christy and Mark watch her storm out of his office. Angela rushes back to her station to clean out her desk. In Marks office, he addresses Christy. "What's wrong with you Christy, she is one of our best workers?" "What do you want me to do Mark? If I have a problem, I'm supposed to bring it to you, right?"

Marks shakes his head in disagreement as he walks back around behind his desk. "You really messed this one up Christy, now I have to make this stick, so she won't come at us with a lawsuit, and the fact that we are cooking the books, we can't afford any eyes on us right now." Christy is alarmed at Marks comment. "Cooking the books?" Mark realizes his mistake. Christy grills him. "Mark, what are you talking about cooking the books? I thought we were in the black? Are you telling me something I don't know?" Mark glances up at Christy but avoiding eye contact. "You keep your mouth shut, you understand me?"

Christy is silent. "Do you understand me?" "Yes Mark, I understand." "I will clean this mess up for you, if you can keep your mouth shut. I'm working to start my own company when this company goes under, and I want to bring you in with me if you can keep your mouth shut. This is totally confidential." Christy's arms relax by her side as she sighs with grief. "Okay. The secret is safe with me Mark."

"Good. That's all I want to hear. I am always there for you Christy, I need you to know that. Now, I need you to be here for me. You would do the same for me, right?" Christy still shocked, finally responds.

"Oh yeah, sure."

Mark scrambles through papers on his desk in a panicked demeanor.

"Thank you for taking care of this." Christy says."

Mark extends his hand to shake Christy's. Their hands shake as Christy presents a fake smile.

"Okay," Mark says.

"Thank you." Christy responds.

Christy quickly leaves the office. She rushes over to the lady's room. As the door closes, she composes herself thinking about her future. After a moment, she stares into the mirror looking at her own image searching for answers.

The next day at work in Christy's department, everyone is hard at work. Christy sits in her office thinking. Suddenly, a knock is heard at the door. In walks

Angela looking broken down. Christy is surprised to see her.

"Why are you here, what do you want?"

Angela stands with her head down as she begins to speak.

"Hi. Ms. Billings, I just wanted to apologize for talking about you at the party Saturday night. I was wrong."

Christy responds.

"Well you should be."

"Yeah, I am. And when I accused you of trying to hit me with your purse, I was wrong then too."

Christy's eyes stare through Angela.

"I hope you don't think by apologizing, that you will get your job back."

Angela's eyes look like a desperate puppy looking for a new home from the pet store. "Oh no, I'm just coming to you doing the right thing. I'm a Christian, and I should know better. I was totally out of order with the way I acted."

"Um, okay, yeah, just so you know, the Christian thing does not work for you, so you should give that up."

The remark appalls Angela. "Ugh, okay." Angela pauses for a moment. "Well I wasn't trying to impress you with me being a Christian. You could be one too, if you gave God a chance." Christy laughs aloud. "For your information sweetie, I'm an atheist, I don't need God, if anything he needs me, and you can print that in your little Bible." Angela defends her belief. "You know, you were created by someone who loves you." Angela says.

"Yes, my parents," Christy laughs responding. "It's okay Ms. Billings to know, you're not the greatest person in the world, and that you never will know everything there is to know."

Christy stands up behind her desk with both of her hands on her hips. "What makes you think I need your God, Angela? What can he possibly do for me that I have not done for myself? I have a great job, a house on a hill, a convertible BMW, tons of money in the bank, a boyfriend that thinks the world of me, and bosses that praise my work. Babe, I have the entire world in the palm of my hands. You know that phrase in the movie Scarface, "The World Is Yours? Yeah, that's me honey." Angela clears her throat before she speaks again. "Okay, I'm sorry I bothered you. I just wanted to say that all is forgiven on my end for the way you've treated me and what I said about you. I want you to know, I pray for you every day, and I hope that God continues to bless your life in a way that your heart is open to receiving his salvation into your life." Christy stares at Angela.

"Is there anything else?"

Angela becomes shy.

"Well yeah, I do want to offer you a peace treaty invitation to my church. I can swing by your place and pick you up if you would like. My pastor is a great teacher of the Bible." Christy becomes offended as her body language expresses it all.

"Excuse me, but I am not interested in going to any church with you! I thought I just made that clear to you when I told you I was an atheist?"

Angela feels insulted.

"Excuse me?"

"You heard me."

The room becomes silent.

"But Ms. Billings… I was not trying to offend you or anything, and I just thought you would like the fellowship."

Christy becomes enraged.

"Listen to me okay! What part of everything that I just stated to you, gives you the impression that I want to go anywhere near a church with you?"

Angela is shocked even more.

"Oh wow."

"I know you're an atheist, but how can that be that you don't believe in God? I mean, you are acting on a belief in someone you don't believe, but that belief that you have has everything to do with faith which is connected to God because you are acting on a belief?"

Christy becomes angry.

"I'm calling security!"

Angela glances around the office.

"That's the problem with you people, you think too much about someone who does not exist! Don't think, just get out of here!" Christy demands pointing towards the door.

Angela proceeds down the hallway towards the elevator. Someone shouts her name. Angela slowly turns around and sees her friend Melissa walking fast towards her. "Hey you. I

"Okay, okay, I'm going..." Angela says.

called you last night, why didn't you return my call?" "Oh, I'm sorry Melissa, I forgot." Melissa stares at Angela looking her up and down. "It's okay. Well, you look good today. How are you holding up?" "I'm holding. I just came up to apologize to Christy." "To get your job back?" Angela is appalled at the question as her neck snaps back. "No!"

The outburst shocks Melissa. "Okay, then why? You know how she is." "Because it is the right thing to do. I can't live with that on my conscience even though I can't stand her. I have to have peace, even if it kills me." Melissa laughs at the thought of that happening. "I like that Angie, I never looked at having peace that way." Angela presses the "L" button for Lobby on the elevator. The oval light "L" illuminates. Melissa leans up against the wall next to the elevator. "I miss you. It's so boring around here now, no one makes me laugh. Everyone is like a robot. You know, you kept us all relaxed when you were around, we could be ourselves."

Angela is surprised.

"Really?"

"Yes really."

"Wow, I didn't know I had that impression on you guys. I thought most people here couldn't stand me most of the times."

"Oh, no girlfriend, you were the life of the party for our team. We looked up to you, still do." Melissa says.

Angela feels the peace in her body as every muscle relaxes.

"Thank you, Melissa, I needed that."

Melissa leans in and hugs Angela. They embrace each other's friendship as the elevator door opens. Angela enters the elevator.

"I will see you later," Angela says.

"Okay, call me, so we can hang out," Melissa replies.

"I will this time, promise," Angela says.

Melissa smiles at her as the elevator door closes taking Angie to the Lobby area of the building. Melissa proceeds back to her station. Four hours later, Angela arrives home to her apartment. As she enters inside, her pet cat Oscar greets her at the door meowing.

"Hey bud," Angela replies.

Angela walks over to her couch and crashes on top of it. She drops her purse on the floor. Oscar runs up to her smelling her feet and hand. Angela stares at the ceiling wondering what will she do next? Panning her apartment, it is fully furnished and decorated with the décor of a young female adult in her mid-twenties. She grabs her remote control turning on the television set. The local news is on. She quickly turns it off. Her cat Oscar looks up at her. "What Oscar, that's bad news. Besides, I just experienced it at my old job. We don't feed on depressing news in this house remember?" Oscar stares at her not understanding. His tail wags back and forth waiting for her to play with him. Angie's seen that look before.

"Not now buddy, I need time to unwind. Give me about ten minutes." Oscar meows, then walks away.

CHAPTER FOUR

"Lawsuit"

The next day, Christy enters Marks office. She sits down while Mark finishes his conference call. "Okay Jack, great talking to you. I will fax that information over to you ASAP." The voice on the intercom responds. "Sounds good Mark. Talk later, bye."

"Bye Jack."

As the conversation ends, Mark spins his chair around facing Christy.

"Hey Christy, what's up?"

"Mark, what's going on?"

Mark shuffles some papers on his desk.

"Well, I wanted to do a follow up with you about the firing of Angela Harmon."

"Okay?"

Christy's fishes for answers.

"So, what's the problem?"

"Well, for starters, her lawyer just called our office. She has filed a major lawsuit against us."

"What? Well, I'm sure your guys got this covered right? This should be a cake walk."

Mark stops shuffling the papers on his desk as his eyes glare up at Christy.

"Really, Christy? Is that your assumption?"

"Well, what do you want me to say Mark?"

Christy turns around and sighs as she places her right hand on her hip. She turns back to face Mark. "Mark, she has nothing!" "Oh?" asks Mark. "She has a lot Christy. She's also claiming that you infringed on her religious beliefs!" "Her what beliefs?" "You heard me Christy. She said you told her you don't need her God." "I didn't say it like that Mark!" "Oh no?"

Christy thinks for a minute. "No, well not like that exactly." "Exactly," Mark responds as he pauses for a moment to calm down. "I told you Christy, we don't need this right now. Couldn't you have said something nice about God. What, don't you believe in God or something, almost everyone does?" Christy has a serious look on her face. "I have a right to

believe what I want to believe. I believe in me, I trust me, I love me, and I am the only one that I see when I wake up and look in the mirror. That's what I believe!"

Mark thinks for a moment.

"But you were insulting Christy, it's the way you said it, and that's probably why she went on with this lawsuit."

Mark sarcastically responds.

"I believe in God."

Christy gets mad.

"Well good for you Mark. I don't believe in God, angels, heaven or whatever. I am an atheist, and that's all I have to say about this."

Mark laughs.

"Wow Christy, I didn't know you were an atheist. Do you believe in Hell then?"

"Okay, Mark, that's not funny, now this is personal but to answer that first question, hell no. Is this corporate policy to ask me whether I believe in God or not?"

"No, just…I just didn't know you felt that way."

"That's my right, isn't it?"

"Yes, it's also Angela's right to express her religion. Christy, don't you want to go to heaven when you die?"

"I'm in heaven Mark, I'm living the life that everyone wants to live. I'm living the American dream. What more of a heaven could that be?"

"Oh yeah, sure, just like its Angela's freedom of religion to believe in God." Christy is confused. "She said she's a Christian, that's different from religion."

"So, what Christy, it's still the same way you feel about not believing, she feels about believing."

"Okay, so what's your point Mark?"

Mark becomes angry.

"My point is just what I said, and, if there is a deposition about all of this, I need to know that your firing of her was a legitimate reason to cover our behinds because if I keep her fired, this has to stick if it is going to work. This company does not have time for this. I told you what's going on with this company."

"Yes, it was a legitimate firing Mark, you were at the meeting. She wasn't doing her job when she was supposed to be doing it, and she talked about me behind my back. If she talks about me, then the entire department talks about me, and the company does not make its quota, then you'll fire me. I'm not having that." Mark raises both hands. "Okay Christy, calm down, you were right on this one." Christy stares at Mark before responding. "I know I was, that's why I'm always right. Look Mark, she's been a thorn in my side since she got here! Always smiling and laughing, making the other workers too relaxed to do their work. She's always spreading this God loves you stuff. I've had it up to here with her."

"Yes Christy, but she also helped us make over the quota this quarter. She's the best we hand. Does that not sit well with you? This girl is a genius at what she does. She has a gift." "Well when I open her present, I see nothing but trouble Mark." Mark is silent. He leans forward on his desk as he reads over Angela's profile. She graduated with honors at Cornell. Volunteers at nursing homes, and

Children's Hospitals." "What are you Mark, her cheerleading squad. So, what! Who cares what she does on her off time. She is in total disregard to our policy that a worker is responsible for respecting the one in authority, that's me."

"Yes, I hear you Christy, but I'm getting heat from Mr. Boykins upstairs about this lawsuit coming just when this company is about to go under. How can we pay her when we are about to close our doors?" "That's not my problem Mark." "It is your problem. Your problem is whatever my problem or this company's problem is." Christy defends herself. "I'm not going down for this if that's what you mean. I know this companies secret." Mark is surprised at the comment. "What did you just say?" "Nothing." "Are you saying you would throw me under the bus for this Christy?"

"I'm saying, I have your back if you have mine Mark."

Mark lifts the lawsuit letter, shaking it in his hand at Christy. "We go way back Christy, I can't believe you would say that. You're like a sister to me, but your also cut throat. If you hang me, I will definitely hang you." Christy shrugs her shoulders as she sighs while rolling her eyes. "Well I guess we have something on each other then." "You know Christy, I like you, but your so stuck up." "Excuse me?" "You heard me. You treat people like crap sometimes." "Well yes, because most times they are." "See what I mean?" Mark replies. Both take a breather to digest the moment. Christy is the first to reply. "Okay, so where do we go from here?" "Human resource says they will get back with me. We have two options, settle out of court with her, or give her the job back." Christy's face looks grotesque of the thought of the second choice. "You are not giving her, her job back Mark." "Christy, you are not in any position to tell me what I need to do right now. Remember, you work for me." Christy quickly responds. "I work for DinoCore." She pauses a beat. "Well at least for now since they are in the red from what you are saying." The words from Christy's mouth quickly grabs his attention.

"What are you doing? Don't go there."

Mark's face is stoic. Christy sighs as she leans over onto Marks desk with both hands firmly placed in position like a track runner for the 60-yard dash. "Oh, honey I would not only go there, I would get an interview with CSPAN, CNN, HLN, and MSNBC if you don't give me what I want." Mark sits back in his chair with his head down. "I trusted you Christy to be silent about that information." "Well, you picked the wrong person for that." "Obviously." Mark pauses. "Okay, what do you want?" Christy laughs. "I don't want her getting her job back Mark, I just told you. If she gets her job back, I'm telling everything, and you'll be lucky to get hired as a Real Estate broker."

"Then you had better make it look good Mark, because I have CSPAN on speed dial on my phone.

Mark sarcastically smiles.

"Okay Christy, you win."

Christy stands straight up from Marks desk folding her arms.

"Christy, you're something else, you know that?"

"Tell me something I don't know Mark?" she responds.

Mark responds.

"Exactly."

Mark pauses.

"Okay, I will make this stick. I have to write up a report so, you have to give me more ammunition telling me as far back as when she was hired, the things she's done that go against her work environment." Christy laughs. "Oh, I have tons of stuff, even if I have to make something up." "Okay, give it to me by the end of the day. The boss upstairs will need an update. Christy, you do know, this company does not have the money to pay her for a lawsuit." Christy responds as she turns to walk away pulling out her cell phone and lifting it up over her head.

Mark pauses again.

"Listen, I do this, and you have to promise me, you will keep your mouth shut?"

Christy stops at Marks door, turns around, and crosses her heart.

"I cross my heart Mark and hope to die."

"Most people hope you would die."

This insults Christy.

"What?"

"Just joking." Mark says.

"Make sure I get that information before you leave today Christy."

"Oh, you bet I will."

Christy opens Marks front door.

"Oh, by the way, I'm having a party at my house Saturday. Leslie will be there. Her boyfriend is out of town. Now is the time to make your move if you want her."

CHAPTER FIVE

"Home Sweet Home"

Saturday rolls around and Christy is sitting outside with her friends by her pool at her fancy upscale home overlooking a beautiful lake. Her lawn is fully manicured and patio furniture set present glistens in white color to appear radiated by the sun. A young man in his 20's stands in front of her custom-made fire grill sizzling hot dogs, barbecue ribs, T-Bone Steaks, and Chicken wings on it. "Dave" he is called, also serves Christy's friends drinks at the bar. Twenty people in total are present at the party. Music plays in the background as everyone enjoys a good time. Her best friends Cheryl and Leslie, sit with Christy in their swimsuits taking selfie photos of themselves with their cell phones and posting the pictures on their Facebook pages.

Christy hops off the patio lawn chair, and hurries over to a group of guys that just arrived. She takes a group photo with them hash tagging it "A Girl just wants to have fun!" Later in the day, the girls sit drinking lemonade. Leslie talks about her boyfriend problems. "Jeremy is getting on my last nerves you guys. He's always doing guy stuff and never paying me any attention." Cheryl and Christy giggle together. "Yeah, I know the feeling," Cheryl responds. "That's a bummer "Les," Christy says. "So, what's up with you and Jay,

Christy?" Cheryl asks. "Oh, it's the same ole same ole. He's a drag too sometimes. I need some excitement, so you know I do what I have to do to get it." Cheryl and Leslie laugh together as they respond simultaneously.

"Like what?"

Christy shrugs her shoulders.

"You know...I always have a guy on the side, every girl should."

Leslie voices her opinion.

"But you've always talked about being with one guy and one day getting married having kids, what's with you?"

"I still do, but, I figured, why not have a little fun until the right one comes along right? Besides, he's probably doing something I don't know about. They all do, right?"

Cheryl disagrees.

"Not my Stevie. He is totally committed to me for sure."

Christy doesn't believe Cheryl.

"How do you know?"

Cheryl commands, "I just know."

Christy badgers her.

"But how? Are you with him twenty-four seven?"

Cheryl thinks for a moment.

"Well no, no one can ever be with someone like that."

Christy slumped down in her lawn chair, quickly sits up leaning forward at Cheryl.

"Then how do you know?"

"I don't, I just know! We don't keep secrets, and we tell each other everything. That's more than enough for me. You can't be more honest than that, right?"

Christy sighs as she sips on her lemonade through a straw as she sets her glass down on the table.

"Well you do what you feel you need to do Cheryl, miss goodie too shoes, but I need excitement right Leslie?"

Leslie agrees slightly.

"Well yeah, I guess."

Cheryl gives Christy some advice.

"Just be careful Christy."

"Be careful about what?"

"If Jay finds out about this other guy, he might go crazy."

Christy laughs.

"Jay? My Jay?"

She pauses for a second.

"No way. He's like a baby kitten."

"Yeah Christy, but when a guy is confronted with another guy, that's like putting two lions in a cage and a lamb which would be you in the center of that cage telling both lions dinner is served."

Christy turns to Leslie whispering in a low tone.

"What is she talking about, I told her I'm in control of this. Nothing will happen."

Leslie giggles as she sips on her lemonade through a straw as well.

Seconds later, Mark from Christy's job appears at her front door. Someone lets him in. He is escorted to the backyard where the party is. Upon entering through the patio window, Christy notices him standing there. She leaps off her lawn chair running towards him. "Marky!" Mark smiles as the two hug each other. "So, glad you could come! Hey, I want you to meet my girlfriends." Christy grabs Mark's hand leading him over towards Leslie and Cheryl like a little child leading her father. "Girl's, I want you to meet my boss Mark Collins. Mark, these are the girls, Leslie, and Cheryl I told you about." Mark becomes bashful as Leslie stares at him after sipping on her lemonade. Leslie interrupts.

"Nice to meet you Mark," both ladies reply together. Christy ushers Mark to a chair surrounding an oval shaped table near the girls Leslie and Cheryl. Mark plops down on the chair. "Do you want a drink?" "Yeah, sure, I'll have a coke." Christy laughs. "A Coke?" Mark laughs in return. "Yes, I stopped drinking." "Since when?" "Since the party don't you remember?" Mark gives Christy a look that reminds her of that night." "Oh yes, I forgot. That's a good Mark. I support you with that, but for me, I'm going to drink today until I fall over my own balcony babe." Christy brings Mark his Coke, then sits back down with her girls. "I would love to see that. It would definitely make You tube, that's for sure," Cheryl says.

Leslie eyes Mark. "I like that you are showing discipline in that area Mark, that's a good thing." "Thank you, Leslie, I'm trying, but it's not easy. Drinking is like being thirsty, your mouth is always feeling dry." "Well, I'm taking a college course about addictions, and drinking is one of the leading causes of domestic violence and abusive relationships. Statistics show, men who abuse their soulmates, only intensify the situation when alcohol and drugs are involved." "I agree Leslie. I remember when I would get drunk, I would say things I shouldn't say, do things I normally wouldn't do. It's like I became someone else." Cheryl is curious about Mark. "So, Mark, do you have a girlfriend?" "Me, no. Just acquaintances." "Ah, I see. Leslie is available if you're interested." Leslie interrupts Cheryl. "Cheryl?" Cheryl is surprised. "Well it's true isn't it? I just thought he should know Leslie jeez, relax." "We were also talking about cheating Mark; how do you feel if you were cheated on by your girlfriend?" Mark is caught off guard. "Well I…" Leslie interrupts saving him. "Leave him alone Cheryl, gosh! You, and this cheating stuff. What is with you?" "Nothing really," Cheryl defends. Cheryl rises from her chair. "Well, I need some food." "Good idea," Leslie replies. Cheryl leaves Mark and Leslie alone.

"You have to excuse my friend Cheryl, she is really tripping today." "Oh, that's okay. Those are some great questions she's asking though," Mark says. "Really?" "Yes. I mean, cheating is not always a good thing and I would not do it if I were dating. My thing is this, if you don't want to be with someone, you should let that person know and give them the common courtesy ending that relationship." Leslie is charmed. "I like that." "Well, I've never been with someone that I adored. I thought I did, but I didn't, so I never led her along." Leslie agrees. "You're right." She pauses. "So, what are you going to do about it?" "About what?" "Love," Leslie asks. Mark ponders over the question. Meanwhile, at the bar, Christy flirts with a guy from her old high school who now plays professional football in Florida. "So, when are we going to hook up Alex?" "When you come to one of my games Christy." "Okay, send me a ticket, and I will be there." "Okay, you're on. I'll be playing here on the 18th." "I'll be there. You have my address, right?" "Oh yeah." Christy grabs her drink walking back towards her hangout spot.

She meets Cheryl who arrives with a plate of food. They both notice, Leslie and Mark are nowhere to be found. Christy's mouth is open wide.

"No, she didn't." Cheryl says.

"Yes, she did," Christy responds.

"I cannot believe she did that."

"Calm down Cheryl, they could have gone for a walk."

"Oh yeah, sure." Cheryl says as she bites into her food. "You started all of this."

"What?" Christy asks.

"Don't what me. You set this up Christy."

Christy lowers her head as she smiles like an evil demon. "You should be ashamed of yourself Christy. Leslie is a good girl. She's got problems with Jeremy, but this isn't the answer." "Oh, Cheryl shut up, I bet you tried hooking them up when I walked away. Just because you're not happy, you shouldn't pass that on to your friends." "What's that supposed to mean Ms. Goodie two shoes?" Christy's pride rises. "It means I have everything going for me, I'm making more money than I've ever dreamed, I have an expensive home, a hot car, two men that love me, I am on top of the world, and I'm loving every minute of it. You should join me."

"Christy we are the best friends. You don't have to act stuck up like this. I'm worried about you. You're becoming hard to be around."

"Don't worry about me, worry about yourself. Life is great for me. It's the way I want it, and the way I like it, and it's going to stay that way until I say otherwise."

"I wish you could hear yourself speak," Cheryl says.

Christy laughs aloud.

"Hear myself speak? Why on earth would I do that?"

"Because if you listened to yourself, you could hear how much pride is gushing out of your soul, that's why."

"How long have we've been friends Christy?"

Christy's eyes look up into the clouds thinking.

"Since fourth grade?"

"Christy, ever since you got this job, you've been obsessed with yourself, and it's driving me up the wall."

Christy responds sarcastically.

"That's a bummer Cheryl."

"I'm serious Christy."

"About what?"

Cheryl is serious. "You're so out of control, and you can't even see it."

Christy laughs.

"No way! Your just jealous Cheryl!"

Some of Christy's patrons notice the commotion.

"Of what?" Cheryl responds.

"Of what I have?" Christy points all around her home.

"I'm supposed to be proud of you, not jealous of you Christy. I should be inspired by you to do what you do, but in a humble way." "So, what am I supposed to do? Make you happy?"

"No, but not be a thorn at the expense of losing your soul? I mean, come on. What are we living for Christy? To have a great job so we can buy things that we think will make us into somebody we were never meant to be in the first place? I think we were created to live to love and that love we share changes the hearts of the people around us to do the same."

"Okay Cheryl, what you are saying, is just noise. I tell you what, you come do my job and then give me a report at the end of the week at what your results are. You would quit in a heartbeat."

Cheryl responds shaking her head no.

"I doubt that."

"Really? Are you kidding me, you wouldn't last a day?"

"Yeah, well, I love you Christy. I love you more than you love yourself, but I can't do this anymore with you."

"That's your fault you're not happy Cheryl! What, am I supposed to do, feel guilty because I do what I do to get what I want?"

Some of Christy's guests slowly leave to avoid the confrontation before them.

"No Christy, that's not the point. I can't do this anymore because of what you have become." The bragging, the flaunting in people's faces like you're something and they're not, that's the problem."

"If I'm flaunting it, it's because I got it!"

Cheryl stands grabbing her purse wrapping it around her right shoulder as her plate of food sits unwanted. "I have confidence Christy, that you will become a better more loving person like you once were, but I think you will have to suffer a bit to get there."

"Suffer? Oh, give me a break! You know what Cheryl, you're the problem and you always have been."

"I love you Christy but, money is not everything. I think family, and close friends, along with good health is the bread winner of them all."

Christy sits in her chair with her legs crossed nodding her head arrogantly. "Don't forget about God." Cheryl is shocked at her response. "What did you say?"

"Thanks Cheryl, I'll try to remember that nugget. You can go now." "Did you say God?" Christy remains silent.

"Yes, God should be in our lives Christy. Thank you for adding that," Cheryl says. "I was being sarcastic Cheryl! If that's what you believe, believe that too, but for me I'm god of my life. I control what I do, what I say, and how I feel. To me, that's what makes me a god."

"You need help Christy."

Christy gets mad.

"There is no God Cheryl!"

"Christy, for your information, you didn't create the air you breathe, the planet you live on, and the people around you. You did none of that."

"I didn't need to, I have more important things to work on," Christy says.

Cheryl raises both her hands having enough of Christy.

"Okay, so, I am leaving now, I pray for you and hope for the best in your life."

Christy responds sarcastically.

"I will pray for you too Cheryl and hope you pull your head out of the clouds and into reality."

Leslie and Mark appear from inside the house. Cheryl storms off walking past them both. Leslie turns around shouting her name.

"Oh, my God Cheryl, what just happened?"

Christy raises both of her hands as she sits in her lawn chair. Leslie turns to her staring.

"What?" Christy asks.

"Like what? Cheryl just left mad. You didn't see that?"

"Yeah, but she won't be leaving alone, there are several people leaving too. But you my friend, should be thanking me."

Leslie is surprised.

"I do not know what you're talking about."

Christy is offended.

"Leslie, I just hooked you up! You should be thanking me!"

Leslie is confused.

"Thanking you for what?"

Christy stands to her feet, stares at Leslie, then storms off as Leslie and Mark stare at each other. "I think you'd better go Mark." Mark feeling trapped like a deer in the headlights, agrees. "Yeah, well, can I call you." "No Mark, I don't think that would be a good idea." "Okay," Mark says as he calmly lowers his head walking away leaving Leslie alone with no one to talk too.

CHAPTER SIX

"Destroying Evidence"

That Sunday, several workers of the company DinoCore, sit in offices shredding important documents containing a paper trail of the company's finances. Mark is among them wearing jeans and a polo shirt. The Vice President Daniel instructs Mark about a pile of documents on a table. "Mark, these files right here must go to the shredder. These are files dating back from 2007." "All of these?" Mark questions. "Yes," Daniel replies. "You shred them to the point that you can't read anything, got it?" "Yes, I got it." Mark grabs the files with both hands scooping them up off the table exiting the room. Other workers enter. Daniel instructs each one of them which files need to go to the shredder as they leave the room.

Mark makes his way down the hall to a room on the far end of the building. As he approaches the room, he hears paper shredding along with the machines humming as they digest their paper food. Mark enters the room setting the files on the table. He glances around at the workers busy shredding the documents. Consumed in their work, they don't even recognize Mark standing near them. Mark observes each document fed into the machine in groups of three. On the other end, the files ooze out like French fry sticks. Mark clears his throat to get their attention.

One worker glances over at Mark. "Leave it right there, I will get to it, thank you." Mark waits for a moment. The worker continues feeding the machine. Mark tries talking over the sound of the shredding machines. "Daniel says, these need to go in asap." "What?" Mark points at the stack of document. "Daniel said, these need to go in next." "Who's Daniel?" "My boss." "Who are you?" "District Manager with this company," Mark says. "Well, those will have to wait in line. We were instructed by Mr. Boykins to do these in the order that they are placed on the table." "He told you that?" "Yes, he did." "And who are you?" Mark asks. "I'd rather not say, but, I can tell you, I'm like a ninja. You see me, then you don't." Mark nods his head. "Oh, okay, I'll tell Daniel what you said then." "You do that, thanks." Mark turns around slowly walking away out the room.

As Mark makes his way down the hall, he runs into Daniel. Daniel stops Mark with his hand stretched wide. "Are they shredding the stuff I gave you?" Mark gives Daniel a puzzled look. "Well no, they said, they were instructed to shred some other documents first already on the table." Daniel becomes angry. "No, no, no! I gave you specific instructions Mark, to tell them to shred the documents I gave you!" "I know Daniel, but…" Daniel ignores Mark as he rushes past him towards the room Mark came out of. Mark stands in the hallway listening to Daniel's tirade. "Hey, I am telling you right now to shred these documents!" The young man's voice is heard slightly. "Mr. Boykins said…." "I work for Mr. Boykins. He told me that these documents must be shredded first, then those files!"

The machines continue shredding as Daniel speaks louder. "I am giving you a directive! Shred these now!" The young man's voice becomes timid. "Okay, okay." Daniel storms out of the office walking towards Mark. "That's what you should have done." Daniel walks past Mark back into his office. Mark stands in the hallway with his head down as he leans up against the wall. An hour later in his office, Mark is shredding his own paper trail. In his hand is the complaint form Angela filled out and gave to him. He glances over the document, then tosses it into the shredder. Next, he grabs Christy's folder stating all the complaints she has towards Angela. He stores the folder in a special place in his drawer. Suddenly, Mark's phone rings. He answers it. "Hello?" Daniel responds. "We have a meeting asap in the board room." Mark responds, "I am there," as the call ends. He grabs his cell phone and sport coat leaving his office making his way down the hall towards the board room.

Making his way to the board room putting on his sport coat and opening the door to the meeting room walking through. Inside the room are older men in their late fifties, a couple in their sixties, all casually dressed. Two younger men twins to be exact, in their early thirties, are also present seated next to each other like a television rerun. These two men are unknown to Mark. Mark proceeds around the large Carmel brown wood table taking a seat. He makes eye contact with the two young men. Next to Mark, is Daniel, then Richard Baker President of DinoCore, Edward Sable Treasurer of DinoCore, and Peter Teller from the Human Resource Department. Moments later, the office door opens. In walks the CEO of the company, Giles Boykins. A man in his early seventies, bald on the top with white hair in the back wearing black thick rimmed framed glasses. Mr. Boykins takes a seat in his jogging outfit at the head of the table.

Mr. Boykins makes a slight grimacing sound as he slowly seats himself into the comfortable leather high back chair. Everyone at the table sits silent waiting for their leader to speak. "Good morning everyone. Let this meeting come to order. As you all are aware, I asked that you come in this morning because we have a significance of extreme importance before us." He pauses. "This company, in which I built from the ground up back in 1976, when businesses were booming all over the place and the Stock market had incredible gains totaling 52.42 points closing at 900. The money was so good, I bought a huge boat from my first return in my company."

The tycoon pauses for a moment. "Nowadays, everybody is scared to invest. From the housing market crash in 08' to jobs leaving overseas, it makes it harder to convince people to invest. It's easier now to convince them not to invest." Mr. Boykins laughs at himself. "I took pride in building this company from the ground up, as should any man. But the times have changed, and I haven't changed with it obviously. It's hard to fix something that is not broke, and these young investors today don't know that taking risks takes precise observation. You can't get ahead of the horse, it's just not smart you know?" He pauses. "People want a return before the return happens. Because of this, I am forced to do things I would not normally do. I played out of bounds, and when you do that, you end up all over the place." He pauses. "So, before this boat sinks, we are liquidating all assets to this company started tomorrow. Now don't worry, you will all still get your bonuses, I will make sure of that. But to ensure that everything we talk about in this room remains confidential, I am demanding that you all, except for my nephews to my left, sign this form admitting that you will adhere to the confidentiality of this meeting."

Mr. Boykins nephews stand simultaneously as they proceed to grab papers from the table, passing it to everyone seated along with a pen to sign. Mr. Boykins clears his throat as his nephews wait for everyone at the table to sign. Mark glances over the contract. To his left, he makes eye contact with Daniel. Daniel whispers with his lips. "Are you going to sign or what?" "Yeah, I want to read what I'm signing first, don't you?" Daniel feels insulted. "Just sign the darn thing Mark, and don't forget about my bonus okay?" Mark says nothing as Daniel signs his contract. Seconds later, Mark does the same. After about seven minutes pass, everyone at the table has signed. Mr. Boykins nephews collects all the contracts.

    Mr. Boykins speaks. "Good. Now, the company will remain afloat for the next couple of months. My nephews will be here in my absence." He pauses. "Now, I hope you all have a rainy-day account as I do. In this business, you must have some getaway money on hand. I cannot give you any recommendations based on what will take place soon, so, please use your own discretion when applying elsewhere." Mr. Boykins stands to his feet. "I wish you all well and thank you for your services here at DinoCore. You've made this company what it became. Oh, Mr. Collins, I would like to have a word with you in my office please." Mr. Boykins leaves the room with grace followed by his nephews.

Mark glances at Daniel as he stands to his feet walking out of the room. Mark continues to sit for a moment gathering his thoughts as everyone else disappears from the room. Mark finally stands and makes his way to Mr. Boykins office. As he enters, Mr. Boykins nephews stand next to him. One on his left, the other to his right. "Have a seat Mark," Mr. Boykins says. "Is it okay if I just stand Mr. Boykins?" Mr. Boykins pauses for a moment. "No Mark, I think you need to have a seat for this one." "Okay sir." Mark has a seat.

"Mark Collins, you are one of my favorite employees by far. You came to me as a young vibrant man with a no holds barred type attitude. You made your own waves and those waves carried this company all the way past margins I never dreamed." "Thank you, sir." "Don't thank me yet." Mr. Boykins opens a file with a picture of Christy inside along with her resume and other information. "Christy Billings, you recommended her to this company am I correct?" "Yes sir." "She too made waves just like you, until this lawsuit came up out of nowhere." Mark squirms around in his chair as he sits trying to straighten his posture. "Now Mark, this lawsuit is something I told you we don't need. If something like this gets out before we close the doors, the doors will remain open until this is settled. This is going to attract a lot of attention. Do you see where I am getting at Mark?" "Yes, I do sir."

Mark clears his throat.

"I am taking care of that."

"How Mark?"

"I've destroyed the paper trail of Ms. Angela Harmons complaints with this company sir."

"And? You think that's going to stop the lawsuit?"

"No sir but it will slow it down until we close the doors."

Mr. Boykins is silent as his nephews stare at Mark.

"That's not going to cut it Mark," Mr. Boykins says.

Mark looks confused.

"Then what would you have me to do sir?"

The office is silent.

"I think Ms. Billings should have an accident."

"An accident?"

"Yes Mark, an auto accident."

"Auto sir?"

"Yes, and Mark, if you keep asking me with the same question I ask you, I'm thinking either you don't want to do it, or you don't understand the English language."

Mark nods his head.

"I understand Mr. Boykins. What do you have in mind?"

"One of my nephews can better explain. I'm not an auto mechanic."

The nephew to Mr. Boykins left responds.

"Braking mechanism."

"I see," Mark responds.

"Cut the brake line, and she's done," The nephew says. "But you must do it five minutes before she leaves work. The fluid will drain, and when she hits the highway, she's done."

Mr. Boykins makes eye contact with Mark. "Can you do that Mark?" Mark swallows his fear as he clears his throat.

"Yes sir."

"Good."

Mark continues to stay seated as Mr. Boykins glances at Christy's picture. "She was a very beautiful girl." He pauses, then glances up at Mark. "That is all Mark." "Yes sir." Mark stands to his feet and proceeds towards Mr. Boykins door. "Oh, and Mark?" Mark stops, turns around to answer. "Yes sir?" "I want it done by the end of the week." "Yes sir." "Enjoy the rest of your day

Mark." "Thank you, sir." Mark opens the door exiting the office. Once outside, Mark gathers himself almost collapsing by the weight of the responsibility given to him as he leans up against the wall to regain his strength taking several large breaths. A door opens down the hallway. Mark quickly stands straight up straightening his sport coat jacket to look confident. The Treasurer Edward Sable walks by him. "Enjoy the rest of your day Mark." "You too Ed." Mark watches Edward walk down the hallway towards the exit to go home.

The next day, Christy's boyfriend Jay Casey drops by her place. Jay is two years older than Christy. Christy opens the door standing in her grey tank top, and gray sweat pants with her bare feet exposed to her white marble floors as she greets him with a hug. "Hey you!" She says as Jay stands in the doorway wearing a checkered button-down shirt, and white shorts with checkered penny loafer shoes. "Hey," Jay says. He enters as Christy walks over to her couch plopping down on it. Jay follows her taking a seat next to her. "So where have you been all day?" Jay asks. "Oh nowhere. Just running errands, then I came back and crashed here." "I thought you were going to drop by my place? When I got off work, you weren't there." Jay thinks to himself. "Oh, because, Larry said he saw you at the game downtown." "The game, what game?" "The Falcons game." "You know I hate football Jay, so why would I go to a game?" "You know we were supposed to hang out together?" Christy stairs at her T.V. screen in the living room. "Huh?" she says. "You forgot?" Asks Jay.

"Well yeah, after running around paying bills and stuff, I totally forgot. You know girls multitask, so we have a lot of things on our minds at one time. It's easy to forget something." Christy pauses. "Babe, I'm sorry, I tried calling you while I was out, but your phone went straight to voicemail?" Jay pulls out his phone searching his "recent calls column." Christy's eyes stare down at Jay's phone as he searches for her call. "Well, I don't see your call in here. It should be in here if you called," Jay says. "Do you check your phone periodically? Christy asks. "Yeah I do. Let me see your phone?" Christy is hesitant. "What?" "Let me see your phone?" "You don't trust me?" Christy asks. "I want to see your phone Christy and see your call lists." Christy pleads standing up from the couch. "No! I can't believe you don't believe I called you. Maybe I did dial the wrong number, so what?" Jay grabs Christy's hand and she quickly pulls it away from him. "What are you doing?" "By the way, they did a lousy job on your nails babe," Jay replies.

I stopped by my mom's house, we talked like for hours." Jay interrupts her. "You and your mother don't get along, why did you go there?" "She's still my mother. What's with the third-degree Jay?" Jay lowers his head. "I don't believe you called me Christy. Why do you lie so much?" "Jay, come on, I'm not lying! I ran errands, then came home. Don't ruin the time we have right now, please?" Christy stands on her tip toes to kiss Jay to calm things down.

"Christy, if I did this to you, you would go crazy."

"No, I wouldn't."

"You wouldn't?"

"No."

"Why do you lie so much Christy? Just answer me that."

"What are you talking about Jay? I'm not lying."

"These games. You don't ever keep your word, you are never where your supposed to be, what's your deal? "It's like you've been acting weird lately, what's going on?"

Christy laughs. "I don't get you."

"Don't get what?" Jay responds.

"You!" Christy stares up at him. "You are so insecure."

"I'm insecure?"

"Yes you! Who else is in this room Jay?"

"Are you seeing someone else Christy?"

Christy is appalled at the question. "What?"

"You heard me Christy!"

"Me cheating, on you? Get real. If anything, I should be asking you the same thing."

"What are you talking about, I've been nothing but honest and the best boyfriend you ever had."

"Oh, I wouldn't go that far Jay. You're a decade away from an Oscar for that role."

"Just answer the question, I can be a man about it."

"Okay, you want an answer?"

"Yes."

"Okay."

Christy, looking up at Jay straight in his eyes.

"No Jay, I am not cheating on you."

Jay sits back down on the couch. Christy grabs Jay's face with both hands kissing him.

"I love you and I'm sorry for missing our appointment today, okay?"

Jay melts as he stares into Christy's eyes.

"Okay, I forgive you."

"Thank you." Christy says as she kisses him again.

Jay shrugs everything off as he glares at the T.V. grabbing the remote control turning to the Sports Center channel. Christy moves in closer to him.

"So, are we good now?" Christy asks.

"No, I'm cool," Jay says.

"You're cool?"

"Yeah."

"You don't sound cool."

"Oh, I'm supposed to sound a certain way to be cool now?"

"Yeah, like not be so tense when you say it like your lifting weights or something." Jay laughs.

"Get out of here Christy."

"Are you hungry?"

"Yeah," Jay says.

"Okay, let me fix you something."

Christy hops to her feet heading towards the kitchen as Jay shouts...

"Fix me some steak, asparagus, and brown rice."

Christy laughs aloud from the kitchen.

"I'm not fixing that."

"Why not?" Jay asks.

"Because Jay, I don't know how to cook like that!"

"Well you should."

"I'm going to fix you hot dogs and chips."

"Awe come on Christy, you and your friends had that at your party."

"You mean my party you couldn't make?" Christy asks.

"Yes, that party. I want some real food. You better start learning how to cook especially if you going to be my wife."

Christy sticks her head out of the kitchen area into the hallway.

"Excuse me?"

"You heard me."

"What are you talking about, marriage?"

"Yeah, I've been thinking about taking our relationship to the next level," Jay says.

"Okay, like don't I have a say in that?"

"Yeah you do, by saying yes."

Christy laughs obnoxiously.

"Oh, my gosh!"

Jay stands to his feet walking towards the kitchen.

"What, you're not ready to go to the next level with me?"

"This is way too fast Jay," Christy says.

"Christy, we've been together for two years now."

"I know, and we still don't know each other," Christy says.

"What's there to know?" Jay asks.

"For starters, everything," Christy says.

"Like what?"

Christy's mind scans for answers.

"Like, I don't even know your favorite color."

"You are serious right now Christy? My favorite color?"

"Yeah."

"Who cares what my favorite color is?"

"I do Jay."

"Why, do you plan to buy me a suit or something because if you are, my favorite color is orange, and I don't think they even make orange suits unless you're a profession is a pimp?" Christy laughs again while she places two hot dogs on her George Forman grill. "See, I did not know orange was your favorite color. Mine is yellow if you wanted to know." "Okay, since we have our favorite colors out of the way, is there anything else you would like to know about me?" "Yeah, like, what's your favorite food?" "I just told you that five minutes ago." "The steak thing?" "Ugh yeah?" "Okay, mine is Lobster, with steamed veggies, and mashed potatoes." Jay sighs under his breath. "What else?" "Jay!" "What?" "You're supposed to be interested in this stuff," Christy says pleading. "Christy I'm sorry, I don't find this stuff amusing. I find us getting married having kids, and our careers with a yacht sitting behind our big house and four cars in the driveway." "Four cars?" "Yeah, my Mercedes, my red Ferrari, my Range Rover, and your BMW." "Why do you have to have three cars Jay?"

"Because guys have a lot of cars." Jay walks back towards the living room. "Who says?" "All the guys." "Well you're not having all of those cars." "Yes I am." Christy leans out of the kitchen shouting. "No, you're not!" "That's money we can have put away for expensive vacations and stuff." Jay sits back down on the couch. "So, you're ready to go to the next level then?" Christy explains herself. "I'm saying, if we did get married, you didn't let me finish my sentence." "Come on Christy, it's either yes or no?" "It's or right now Jay which means, I need to think about this." "What's there to think about?" "Ugh the happily ever after thing." "Well I'm in. You need to let me know something soon or…" "Or what?" "Or just or." "Well that's two "OR's Jay, at least we have something in common." Christy pauses for a moment. "Are you're planning to break up with me or something because I'm not going to wait forever Christy if that's what you're thinking?" Christy leans back in the kitchen and continues cooking Jay's food.

That Monday, at work, Mark is busy in his office as Christy enters.

"Hey Mark."

Mark glances up at her.

"Oh, hey Christy."

"So, did you enjoy yourself at my party?"

Mark continues working.

"Oh yeah, I had a great time, thanks for inviting me."

Christy stands in front of his desk waiting for a reply.

"Okay, that's it?"

"Well yeah Christy, I mean, what else do you want me to say?"

Christy sits in one of his office chair crossing her legs.

"For starters, you can thank me for hooking you up with my girl Leslie, and give me all the juicy details, like where did you two run off to earlier?"

Mark stops working.

"Hmm. Let me think. I just said thank you for inviting me, and nothing happened, but she did give me a tour of your house before she told me to leave."

"What?"

"Christy, maybe you forgot the display you put on yelling at your friend Cheryl and making all of your guests uncomfortable?"

"Mark, that's just the way I am sometimes, don't take it personal, I know it's Monday."

"I just got a lot of things on my mind Christy," Mark says.

Mark continues typing on his computer.

"Like what?" Christy asks.

Mark remains silent.

"If you're worried about me snitching on you to the media about this company going under, don't worry I won't. I just needed some leverage on you about this lawsuit thing with Angela."

"I'm not worried Christy, this company will no longer exist in a couple of months anyway, who cares right?"

Christy's eyes widen.

"A couple of months? I thought you said by the end of the year the doors would close?"

Mark realizes his mistake.

"Look Christy, I'm busy right now okay, could you come back later?"

"No Mark! What do you mean two months from now? You lied to me Mark!"

"Everybody lies in this business Christy, come on."

Christy is silent for a moment.

The non-reply causes Mark to look up at her.

Christy presses for answers.

"What are you not telling me Mark? Was there a meeting about this or something?"

Mark is silent.

"Mark!"

"Okay Christy! You're so demanding, yes there was a meeting yesterday."

"Why wasn't I told?"

"It was only for the big wigs, and the people under the big wigs. You're under me, so to them you don't count."

Christy presses for more information.

"Okay, so, what happened at the meeting?"

"The CEO, Mr. Boykins informed us, the company will close in two months which I just told you."

"What else?"

"What else what?" "There has to be more Mark, I know you can't keep a secret any longer than a politician telling the truth. You have the emotions of a woman."

"Thanks a lot for that information Christy, I will be sure to inform my doctor of that the next time I see him, so he can put that on my medical record."

Mark stands up from his chair walking over towards the picture window that has a view of the street of Downtown Atlanta below. He lowers his head. "It's over Christy. Everything I built for twelve years. I had a stock in the company. That's smoke now. Mr. Boykins said all the assets will be distributed and sold away. We will still get our bonuses though, at least you will."

"What, you won't?" Christy asks.

"I owe Daniel my bonus for that drunken outburst I created at the party."

"Wait, I was there when you were acting a fool. What else did you say when I left?"

"You don't want to know."

"So, Daniel threatened you to pay him your bonus or what, he would fire you?"

Mark turns his head looking at Christy.

"Yes, something like that."

"That's wrong Mark, he can't get away with that." Mark smiles sarcastically.

"He did."

The office is silent as Christy thinks to herself. She offers a suggestion. "I can threaten him about what I know with the company and tell him if he doesn't back off you, I'll go to the press."

"No Christy, it's deeper than that."

"What do you mean?"

"I mean, this company going under is the least of our problems at least for me and Mr. Boykins."

"I still don't understand what you are trying to say Mark."

Mark is silent for a second.

"We have some clients who are let's say, on the up and up."

"I still don' read you," Christy says.

"They are in the illegal drug business out of El Paso, Texas and Juarez, Mexico."

"What?"

"Yeah."

"Who?"

"The Cartel Christy ran by Felipe' Morales better known as "The Shadow."

"Mark, you've got to be kidding me."

"I wish I was. They've invested a lot of money in this company, and we've been laundered it for them."

"This is crazy Mark. Why would Mr. Boykins do something like this, why would he take a risk with this company, does he know how much trouble he's in?"

"He does now. It's all greed Christy, nothing less. The more money the company makes, the better the company looks to investors," Mark says.

"You said you and Mr. Boykins, what do you have to do with any of this?" "We used two separate accounts with the Cartel, one with the company, and one with me using a dummy company name." "Okay, so..." "So, not only are their monies with DinoCore gone, but the one with the Cartel too." "How can that be Mark, you just said the dummy company is separate from everything." "It is, to a certain degree. The dummy company represents real account transaction connected to the market. So, when the market tanks, everything with that company tanks, and we are left with nothing but garbage." Christy stands to her feet. "You're crazy Mark, if they find out their money is gone, they will skin you alive!" Mark approaches Christy to calm her down by grabbing by both arms. "No, listen, they won't know! For all they'll know, the company is fine. Do you think Cartel people check the stock market?"

Christy shakes her head. "Yes, I do." "Christy listen, I'm taking what's left of their money and starting my own company in another country, and when everything cools down, I will set up shop back in the states while I'm still in another country and you can run it. You won't have to worry about getting another job, you and I can go on living our rich lifestyles as if nothing ever happened." Mark stares into Christy's eyes. "This is the only way out Christy, I got you okay?" Christy's greed takes over accepting the offer. "Okay, then, what about the lawsuit?" Mark steps away from her. "Oh, I took care of that. I shredded all of the documents you gave me, and Peter from Human Resource is going to hold up his end, so everything is good."

Christy's eyes look around the office thinking.

"Okay, well, that's some good news then. Two months huh?" Christy says.

Mark agrees.

"Two months, and we start a new life."

"What about the SCC?" Christy asks.

"Oh, Mr. Boykins says, the books will be squared away. He will give something back for each investor, it won't be what they had, but it will be something, so by that time everything is sold off, the public will just think our boss to a huge loss from the economy, sold the stock of the company, closed the doors and retired."

Christy glances at Mark.

"And you think the public will believe that?"

"Yes, why wouldn't they, I said they will get something back for their investment with us. Bernie Madoffs clients lost everything, this is a different scenario."

Mark doesn't believe Christy is convinced by the confused look on her face.

"What Christy?"

"Something doesn't seem right."

"What?"

"All of this Mark!"

Christy rises from her seat.

"This is our secret right Christy, I mean, I did my part for you and this lawsuit and you are going to have a job after all of this is over."

Christy begins walking towards Marks door.

"Yeah, sure," She says.

"Christy?"

She stops at the door turning the knob.

"Everything is good Mark, I should get back to work. See you around."

Christy opens the door walking through it on her way out closing the door behind her. Mark stares at his door. He doesn't buy Christy's response.

An hour later, one of Mr. Boykins nephews, Nathaniel Boykins enters Marks office in his blue slim fit suit, red tie, white shirt, and brown leather dress shoes.

"Hi." Nathaniel says.

Mark responds in return.

"Hi, how are you?"

Nathaniel glances around Marks office checking out the décor.

"Good, everything is good. I just wanted to stop by and find out what time you were going to do that thing this week?"

Mark looks confused.

"What thing?"

Nathaniel, standing in front of Marks desk, stares at him.

"You know that thing we talked about Sunday, right Mark?"

Mark is still confused as Nathaniel becomes irritated as he uses his hands as a sign language.

"The girl on the twentieth floor?"

Mark realizes what Nathaniel means.

"Oh, yeah, that thing."

"Good, so you are good with doing that, right?"

"No, I'm not."

"Why not?"

"Well, for starters, she's a good friend of mine, we go way back, and two, the matter that concerns her has been taken care of, the lawsuit won't hold up without documents."

Now Nathaniel is confused. "How do you figure that?"

Mark explains. "I shredded the documents, that's how."

"Well, the boss which is my uncle and your boss says, he still wants that carried out."

"Does your uncle know what he's doing?" Mark asks.

Nathaniel raises both of his hands.

"Who cares? He just wants it done Mark."

"Well, I care, and I'm not doing it."

Nathaniel becomes heated.

"Were you or were you not in the boss's office on Sunday discussing this matter, and you were given specific instructions on what to do and how to do it?"

Mark leans back and forth in his chair.

"Listen, I know that you are young and all, and your uncle pays you to be here, but you are wet behind the ears," Mark says.

Nathaniel stands with his back straight and his arms folded as he listens to the chastisement. Mark continues his chastisement. "You have no clue on what goes on here. You just showed up Sunday! I've been here longer than you jumped into puberty. I had a stake in this company. Hard work, sweat, grinding every day. All of that will be gone in two months." Mark waves his hand at Nathaniel as if he were shooing a fly away. "You were still in Elementary School playing PlayStation when I started here, so don't come in here thinking you're a gangster trying to order me to do a hit." The office is silent. Nathaniel realizes, it's his cue to talk. "Are you finished?" Nathaniel insults Mark. "Am I finished, is that what you just said to me?"

Nathaniel leans on Marks desk with both hands staring him in the eyes. "If you don't handle this the day your supposed to handle it, with no questions asked, you will be handled." "Is that, right?" Mark asks as he laughs. "So, what, are you going to do, take me out or something? That suit you are wearing is a dead giveaway if you are a hitman. It says gangster for life all over it." Nathaniel removes his hands from Marks desk feeling the insult hit him square between the eyes. He smiles as he turns around walking away. When he reaches Marks door, he turns around looking back at Mark. "It's going to get done either way. I'll be sure to tell the boss what you just said to me being that I'm a family member and all. You do know how uncles feel about their nephews. Nathaniel glances around the office for a split second. "By the way, nice office for now." He closes the door shut.

CHAPTER SEVEN

"Girls Just Want to Have Fun"

On Sunday, Angela Harmon is in church service. As the service concludes, her cell phone buzzes. She checks her phone and sees a text message from her lawyer. The message reads… "I just wanted to keep you abreast on the status of your lawsuit. I have been made aware that the courts have not received the documents from your previous employer regarding your lawsuit. I contacted the HR department and they've informed me, they don't have any record of you filing any complaints of harassments at your job. Get back with me soon because the courts must have these documents otherwise, they will drop the lawsuit. Call me, bye."

Angela quickly texts him back…. "That's crazy, I turned those documents in a week ago!" I told you about the meeting with Mark that I had, so, I am confused that this is happening. She (Christy Billings) must have removed my files, or, the company made them disappear. Either way, I made copies, so, no worries. Angie Harmon. Bye." As everyone inside the church, disperses, Angela enters the foyer of the church. From a distance, her girlfriends Amy, Jasmine, Rachel, and Michelle approach her. Rachel is the first to hug Angie. "Hey Angie, we waited for you, when did you get here?" Rachel says. "Oh, uh, 9:30. I was running really late this morning," Angela says. "Oh, well, you're here." Rachel replies.

Angela's cell phone buzzes. She checks her phone as the other girls chat about the service. The text she receives, say, "You think this Christy Billings would do that to you?" Angela texts back. "Yes, I do, she is the evilest person I've ever met." Her lawyer texts back. "SMH. Well, okay, fax those documents that you have copies of to me, and I will get them to the Judge on Monday morning." Angela responds in text. "Will do, thanks." Her lawyer responds texting… "No problem." Angela places her phone back in her purse. "So." She says. "What have you ladies got planned?"

Amy is the first to respond. "Let's get breakfast at "Leo's." All the girls look at each other to see if that is a good place to eat. All their heads nod in unison as they all agree together for "Leo's." They all leave the church heading over to Leo's. Twenty minutes later at the restaurant, they all exit their cars meeting at the front door. As they enter, they stand bunched together waiting to be seated. A greeter walks over to them. "Hi, how many?" He asks. Angela speaks first. "There are five of us." Michelle points with her index finger making sure Angie's count is right. Angie notices her checking. "Yes, Michelle it's five, I work with numbers remember?" Michelle laughs responding, "Just making sure babe."

The girls get seated led by the greeter of the restaurant. "A waiter or waitress will be with you to shortly." All the ladies respond in unison as they sit. "Thank you!" Jasmine glances over at Angela. "So, Angie,

I noticed you looked kind of concerned after church. Are you okay?" "Oh yeah, it's just stuff about my pending lawsuit at my old job." "How is that going?" "Well, for starters, my ex-boss, God bless her soul." The ladies laugh together at Angela's sarcasm. "I found out from my lawyer that the court had not received the filings of my complaints against the company. The HR department never faxed it over to them." "Why?" one of the girls asks. "I don't know, I gave them everything, and because they were my employer at the time, they had the documents on file. They could easily turn them over to them, but they didn't." "That's crazy," Michelle replies. Angela continues her story. "I think my ex-boss destroyed the documents and probably paid someone in HR to do it." "But, that's against the law," Amy says. "I know, but there is something else going on, and I think it runs all the way up to the CEO of the company." Rachel has a puzzled look on her face after she takes out a mint placing it in her mouth before responding, "You think?"

Angela puckers her lips as she nods her head in agreement. "So, what are you going to do now Angie?" Michelle asks. "I applied for several other jobs. I haven't heard anything yet." Amy encourages her. "You'll find something. You are smart, funny, and very creative. Remember when you planned my daughter's birthday party last month, and all of my family said they had so much fun?" Angela smiles at Amy. "I do, thanks sister." A server appears. "Hello, I'm Samantha, and I will be your server today." All the girls at the table greet Samantha with. "Hi, Samantha! Samantha laughs. "Thank you for that warm welcome. What can I get you ladies?" Rachel glances around at everyone. She decides to speak for them all. "Water for starters," she says as everyone agrees. "Anything thing else to drink?" Samantha asks.

The girls glance over the menu in the drinks column at the lower right-hand corner on the back of the laminated menu. "I'll have Apple juice Samantha," Rachel responds. "I'll take an Orange Juice," Michelle says. "Um, I guess a Cranberry Juice for me to settle my stomach," Angela answers. Amy glances over at her responding, "Stress reliever huh girlfriend?" Finally, Amy and Jasmine agree on their choice of drinks. "Apple juice." "Yeah, the same for me." Samantha writes down the last notes for drinks for the girls. "Okay, that will be right up. I'll come back in a minute and give you time to look over the menu for your orders okay?" In unison, they all agree. "Okay, thanks Samantha."

"Leo's" instantly fills up with more customers coming in for breakfast. The sounds of dishes being cleaned and stacked can be heard from the back room as workers take orders from waiters and waitresses. Back at the ladies table, Amy becomes nostalgic. "I love this place," she says. The other girls look around agreeing. "Yes, it's nice." "Their Blueberry pancakes are awesome," Angela replies. "Blueberry?" asks Jasmine. "Yes, blueberry, what, is there an echo in this place?" Angela says. "Yuck Angela." Jasmine answers. "I can do a blueberry muffin, but that's as far as it goes for me." Rachel says. "Pancakes are supposed to be left alone. As soon as you start altering the originality of a pancake, you take away what a pancake really is," Jasmine responds. The rest of the girls stare at Michelle. She notices their eyes waiting for her advice on pancakes. Michelle stretches out both hands. "What?" Rachel takes her right hand rubbing the back of Jasmines. "It's okay Jasmine, we know how serious you are about your pancakes." Everyone at the table chuckles. "Yes Jasmine, don't kill us all, we don't want to die over some pancakes okay?" Jasmine shakes her head at them all.

Meanwhile on the other side of town late in the afternoon....

Jay and Christy lay cuddled on her couch at Christy's home. Christy's cell phone buzzes as Jay lays asleep next to her. Christy checks her phone.

     A text message reads...

     "Miss me, I would like to see you tonight if possible?"

Christy's eyes sway from side to side thinking how she can meet her mystery man.

     She responds...

     "Sure, name the place."

Her cell phone buzzes again.

     "Marriott 8 p.m."

Christy texts him back...

     "You're on."

Jay suddenly awakens as Christy quickly sets her phone down on her table. Jay stretches his arms, feeling rejuvenated.

Christy thinks aloud to Jay.

"Hey, sleepyhead, do you plan on spending the night here or something?"

Jay stops stretching as he glances over at Christy.

"I was thinking about it why?"

"Awe not tonight Jay, I have to get up early in the morning for a business meeting and it's going to be a long day for me. I'm like really tired."

Jay gets mad.

"So, what's that got to do with me spending the night, we'll both be asleep and have to work in the morning."

"You snore Jay. That's the point, I won't get any sleep. I can deal with it any other night, but not tonight."

"Okay, so I'll sleep in the other room."

"Next to my room? No way, you did that before, and I could hear you through the wall. I told you to invest in that mouth piece we saw on T.V. They said it's really good, and it will help you sleep better."

"Why don't you buy it for me then?"

"I will, since you won't."

"Okay, so your saying you don't want me to sleep over tonight then?" "Duh Jay, that's what I'm saying babe."

Jay smacks his lips in disgust.

"Okay, fine, whatever."

He rises from the couch flipping the blanket off his body which flies over onto Christy.

"Oh, my gosh, thanks for hitting me in the face with the cover."

"I didn't hit you in the face with the cover, not on purpose at least."

Jay looks around for his shoes.

"Are you mad at me Jay?"

"No, you want me to be?"

"No, I don't want you to be mad. Just come back over tomorrow night, that's all I was trying to say."

"Whatever Christy."

"Why do you say that?"

"Say what?"

"Like you just said whatever, I hate it when you say that word."

Jay finally finds his shoes.

"It's just a word Christy."

"Yeah, a word with meaning Jay."

Jay ties his shoes with anger pulling hard on the laces.

"Stop asking me if I'm mad Christy, I will tell you when I'm mad."

Christy laughs aloud as she watches T.V.

"Okay, that's a good one. I will tell you what, I will tell you when I'm happy, that way we'll be even."

Jay shakes his head.

"You always have to have the last word. Everything must go your way. It's like you have to win all the time Christy, no matter what."

Christy smiles.

"Yes, I do. Winners make the rules, and losers live by them. Remember that Jay."

"Am I a loser, is that what you're saying?"

"Jay, I wouldn't be with you if you were."

"Then what am I?" Christy is appalled at the question with her mouth wide open. "You should know the answer to that."

Jay stands to his feet ready to leave.

"Hey, why don't I sleep on the couch?" Christy pauses. "Jay, I'm not going to go over this with you. Just get here when you get off, and wait for me when I come back?" Christy pauses again. "I thought you had to take your younger brother for soccer practice tomorrow?"

Christy asks. Jay thinks about it and forgot. "Oh yeah," He says as he pauses for a moment. "Okay, so I'll get him, wait until he's done, then I'll come back here." Christy agrees. "That's a good plan Jay." "Okay, yeah, I'll do that." Jay walks towards the front door. Christy flips the blanket off her body, rising off the couch following him to the door. "I thought for a moment you were trying to get rid of me, like you had some other guy or something," Jay says. Christy giggles. "Yeah right, you're the cheater remember?" "I don't think so; a cheater wouldn't be thinking about marriage. I don't know what world you live in," Jay says. He kisses Christy on her cheek. "Well, see you tomorrow evening." "Okay," Christy says as Jay opens the door. They kiss each other on the lips. "Bye Jay." "Bye." Christy closes her front door and rushes over to grab her cell phone. She waits to hear Jay's car engine turn over, then she darts upstairs to her bedroom to get ready.

She gets dressed wearing a blue sun dress and grey heeled sandals as she glances over at her cell phone as it vibrates again. She grabs it reading the message... "I can't wait to see you." "Christy texts back. "On my way...." "Ok," The man replies. Christy smiles as she rushes into her bathroom to put on her makeup. Thirty minutes later, Christy is out the door and into her BMW starting the engine. She speeds off down the winding road on a hill in route to her mystery man. As she drives, her cell phone rings. She answers it. An older male voice responds. "Hey sweetness." "Hey lover. How are you?" Christy says. "I'm great, are you on your way?" The man asks. "I sure am, can't wait to see you." "Me too. What are you wearing?" He asks. "My blue dress, with silver open toe sandals." "I like it." "Well, I'm here waiting for you. I got our same room as before." "Okay, I'll be there in fifteen minutes," Christy says. "Okay, drive safely." "I will, bye." "Bye." The phone call ends.

Moments later, Christy's BMW enters the five-star Hotel parking lot. She parks next to a high-class Silver Mercedes Benz sedan with tinted windows that she recognizes. The door to the Mercedes opens, as a middle-aged distinguished man of Arabic decent in his late 40's. He approaches the driver's door to Christy's BMW as she exits her car. "Hey Emmanuel, my love," Christy says. "Hey, what's up?" "You always." Emmanuel glances up in the sky. "It's a beautiful night tonight for us to be together." "Yeah it is," Christy responds. The two enter the hotel. "I'm glad we could meet tonight," Emmanuel says. I really wish we could meet at your place sometimes." Christy thinks for a moment. "I don't know about that honey, my apartment is so small, I'd feel embarrassed showing it to you." "Why, a place is a place," Emmanuel says.

"It can't be that bad Christy. Hey, I'll tell you what, why don't I buy you place?" "What?" "Yes, I can buy you a place." "What if your wife finds out." "She would never find out. She doesn't even know I smoke, and we've been married for twenty years." "Wow Emmanuel, you're so deceptive. I will have to get back with you on that one." "Don't take too long," Emmanuel responds. "You know I'm a busy working girl, right?" "I am too, I'm a CEO remember? You could, come work for me. I've mentioned that to you several times." "Awe I don't know about that Emmanuel." "You could run my company while I start another one." "Hmmm, well, come to think of it, that doesn't sound like a bad idea Emmanuel. I will have to take you up on that." As the two of them approach the main lobby, a car speeds up to the front of the hotel screeching to a halt. Christy and Emmanuel turn around, as the sound grabs their attention. The car door opens, and out comes Jay as his Chevy Corvette sits idling. Jay storms into the hotel. "What are you doing here Christy?" Christy stands speechless, as her hand shield her eyes from the embarrassment. "Jay?"

"What are you doing Jay?" Christy hastily responds. Jay responds back in an angry tone. "I asked you a question?" Emmanuel steps in. "Christy, you know this guy?" Jay steps around Christy to address him. "Hey buddy, this is my girlfriend, this doesn't concern you!" Christy pleads with Jay. "Jay, please go home, let's talk about this later." Jay is not having it. "Who is this old man?" Emmanuel does not like Jay's disrespectful nature. "Old man, who do you think you're talking to kid? This old man has been around the block more times than you! Don't make me put you over my knee and show you!" Emmanuel, with his medium build and trimmed goatee moves Christy behind him with his forearm.

    The hostess at the counter notices the commotion. She immediately becomes scared of the situation and grabs the phone calling the police. Christy notices this and tries to intervene between Jay and Emmanuel. "You guys stop! You are about to get me in trouble, she's calling the police! I have an account here with my job, stop it!" Emmanuel stands face to face with Jay as Jay's college quarterback physic matches the size of Emmanuel. Emmanuel is not intimidated as Jay urges him on. "Come on man, do something!" Christy tries to push Jay away, but he pushes her out of the way as she falls to the ground with her purse in hand as all the items fall out of the purse scattering across the floor. Emmanuel swings at Jay hitting him square in the jaw as his head snaps to the right with the motion of his body following. Emmanuel watches Jay fall to the ground in slow motion. He walks over to Jay kicking him in the gut forcing his body to curl into a fetal position. Emmanuel finishes Jay off by grabbing his blonde hair and upper cutting him in the face. His body arches backward to the floor. The hostess screams as she rushes over to help Christy from the floor. "Ma'am are you okay, I've called the police!" Christy, in panic, responds. "Yes, I think so."

    Emmanuel approaches Jay again as Christy screams at him. "Please stop Emmanuel!" He stops in his tracks realizing what he has done as he glances around the hotel to see how many witnesses saw everything. He composes himself fixing his clothes as he glances at Christy on the ground crying. "This is all your fault Christy! "It's your fault! You're lucky I didn't peal him like an orange! Hope you two enjoy each other. "Never call me again!" Christy pleads with Emmanuel. "I'm sorry Emmanuel, we can work this out!" Emmanuel turns to apologize to the host. "I am sorry for your troubles." Emmanuel storms off to his car as he glances back at

Christy. Jay tries to stand to his feet, but crashes back to the ground.

Christy stands to her feet rushing over to Jay to assist him as he finally stands to his feet holding the left side of his face wiping his bloody lip with the arm sleeve of his shirt. "Jay are you okay?" Christy asks. Jay quickly yanks his arm away from her as the hostess stands in the background. "Don't touch me!" Jay yells. Christy pleads with him. "Jay, you shouldn't have shown up here like this, what were you thinking?" "What was I thinking? What were you thinking Christy? What's wrong with you?" Jay asks. "I have never cheated on you, not once! I could be with any girl I want, but all I wanted to be with you and this is how you show me respect? Look at you, you don't even respect yourself!"

    Christy defends herself. "You caused this Jay following me around like a stalker!" Jay is shocked by her reply. "So, what, you're the victim? Do you ever listen to yourself Christy? You're so selfish! You know who you deserve to be with?" Christy waits for the answer. Jay responds. "Yourself." Jay walks away from her still wiping his mouth full of blood. He climbs into his car still parked idling with its headlights still on. He places the car in gear and speeds off out of the parking lot driving like a mad man. Horns from other cars blow at the Corvette that cuts them off without hesitation. Christy stands alone as the hostess and two guests of the Hotel stare at her. She feels alone and humiliated by the event that just unfold as she glances at all her belongings scattered about on the floor. The next morning on Monday, Christy gets a knock at her door. The knock sounds like the police. As she opens the door, she hears tires squealing off in a distance. Looking around, she sees the rear end of Jay's silver Corvette speeding away. As she glances down at her feet, a box full of her personal belongings lay. She kneels grabbing the box and taking it inside her home closing the door behind her.

CHAPTER EIGHT

"Blue Monday"

On Monday morning Christy's appearance at work is horrible looking like a wreck. Her hair normally let down, is now in a ponytail disheveled in certain areas. She still possesses make up, but only with eyeliner stands out over the light foundation on her face. Moments later, she storms out of her office with an angry look across her face. She enters the elevator heading up to Marks office. When she arrives on the twentieth floor, she makes two right turns leading to his office. She storms in through his door. "Mark, what is going on, I thought you said you handled this lawsuit thing?" Mark ends his call, "I'll call you back, bye," placing the phone on the console. He instantly confronts Christy. "I know Christy, calm down."

  Christy, with both hands on her hip, stands in front of Marks desk. "Calm down? I just got a call from Human resource informing me the lawsuit is still on." "Okay?" "What do you mean okay? You know what, you don't even care, and I don't expect you too! You're not the one on trial here!" "Well what do you expect Christy? You messed up, and I must clean up your mess! You did her wrong." Christy turns away from Mark. "What Christy? Did you think you would get away with this or something? The girl did nothing wrong but make you mad because of her faith."

Christy turns around facing Mark. "Are you telling me you never did anything wrong Mark? Because if I recall, you did a lot of undermining things that I'm sure the SCC would love to hear about." Mark tosses his pen on his desk while leaning back in his chair. "There you go with the blackmail thing again." Christy agrees as she approaches Mark. "Oh yes, the black mail thing again. If I go down, you go down, you remember that?" "Yeah Christy, I saw that same movie." Mark pauses for a moment as he looks up straight at her. "What do you want from me Christy?" Christy shouts. "I want you to handle this like you promised you would!"

Mark looks away from her as his anger builds. "Do you want money Christy, is that it?" Christy laughs at Mark. "Money? Well if I did, you don't have any because Daniel has you're bonus you are supposed to get." Mark angrily points at Christy. "Now you're wrong!" Christy realizes she crossed the line. She rushes around Marks desk revealing her vulnerability for the first time. "Okay Mark look, I'm sorry, I shouldn't have said that, really." Mark acts as if he has some important work to tend to as he ignores her. "Mark please," Christy begs. Her sympathetic voice calms him down. "Mark, I just don't know what to do? This lawsuit, losing this job, everything. Besides, I lost my boyfriend yesterday." Christy says pleading. Christy steps away from Mark. The comment forces Mark to answer. "What happened with your boyfriend?" Christy sits down in Marks chair with her head down. "He caught me cheating on him." "Christy, no you didn't." She raises her head with teary eyes. "My world is crumbling all around me Mark and I don't know what to do. I've always been in control of my whole world and now my whole world is in control of me." Mark stands up from his chair as he approaches Christy sitting halfway on his desk. "Listen, I told you my plans. When I start my own company in Bangkok soon, you will be working again. I already have a vacant office over there."

Christy doesn't say anything. Mark grabs her hand as she glances up at him for a split second. "I'm going to do what I can with this lawsuit situation. Maybe I can bribe her lawyer?" "Oh, please don't do that Mark." Mark laughs. "I was just kidding." Mark takes his index finger placing it under Christy's chin. "Hey, I got you. Don't worry about anything. We go way back remember?" "Yeah," Christy responds. "I don't know why you picked Jay anyway. What is he driving, a Corvette? I'm driving a Maserati." "Jay was really good to me Mark. I messed that up." Mark removes his index finger from her chin as He stands up.

"So, I haven't been good to you? Remember that side deal we did that one time. You took fifteen thousand off the top and I took twenty while the company made two million on the entire deal?"

"Yes, I remember, those were the good times."

"Yes, indeed they were, and we can do it again when you come work for me, only this time, we'll make the two million because I will be the CEO."

"So, what about the Cartel?"

Mark walks around his desk sitting back down in his chair.

"Who cares, the company is shutting down. It's not like they can go to the SCC or the local police, they're criminals trying to make their criminal money legit Christy." I will be building my clientele and making a name for myself. You know how the market is internationally. It's a lot easier to move money around there, than here in the states. It's harder to trace in other countries, so we can pretty much do anything we want."

"Really?"

"Oh, yes Christy, we can clean house. Trust me when I say this," Mark says.

Christy is curious.

"And we wouldn't get caught?"

"No way."

"Well, as long as you're not dealing with anymore Cartel people," Christy replies.

"That's what I thought you would say," Mark says.

Christy stands to her feet.

"Well, I guess I will get back to work."

"Okay, and hey, everything will be all right, I promise you," Mark says.

Christy heads towards the door but turns around as Mark makes one last comment.

"I sure hope so Mark, because everything is looking bleak for me right now."

"Life is like that sometimes Christy. Look at everyone around you. No one knows what the other is going through unless they tell you. But on the outside, everything looks peachy right? It's like we are all acting in a movie we don't like."

Christy is not enlightened by Marks wisdom. "You were always an optimistic Mark, I guess that's why you've always been a self-starter." "Hey, I just know the only one that can make me happy, is me, not my circumstances. Look at us, we are about to lose the job we love and there is nothing we can do about it. So, we can either scream for help like we're on the Titanic or start making our own life rafts and get away from this sinking ship. That's what I'm doing right now and I'm taking you with me." Christy nods her head in agreement. "Thanks Mark." "No problem. I'll keep you posted on your situation." "Sounds good Mark, see you." "Bye Christy." Christy leaves his office with her head down. After the door closes, Mark takes a deep breath with a confused look on his face."

Hours later, Christy arrives at her mother's home. The house has a picturesque view with a white picket fence around it and dozens of flowers. Some in flower beds and others hanging from the awnings. Christy exits her car walking up to her mother's front door. She rings the doorbell. After a few seconds, Ms. Billings opens the door. She is shocked to see her daughter. They last talked a year ago. The family dog "Faith" a Labrador retriever, runs over smelling Christy and licking her hand. She pets Faith. "Hey girl." "Christy? Honey, how are you? What's wrong?" Christy enters the house not acknowledging her mother. Her mother is appalled. "Well hello to you too Christy. What's got into you?" Christy gives her mother an evil look as she sits down at the dining table.

"Like you care," Christy says.

"Excuse me?"

Ms. Billings, a woman in her late 50's with experiences in life, shows off her gracefulness with her grey and white hair. Christy tosses her purse on the dining table.

"Nothing is wrong Mom," she says.

"Oh, Well I haven't seen you or talked to you in a year. There's got to be something wrong! You come over here looking like you've been struck by lightning, no makeup on, and hair out of place. Have you looked at yourself lately?"

"No mom, how do I look?"

"Like a mess, and with that attitude, a mess on top of other messes," Ms. Billings replies.

Christy sinks her body into the chair.

"How am I acting mom?"

"Like a girl with a bad attitude Christy. Your body language says it all."

Christy scans around the dining room. "I see you've decorated a bit." Her mom glances at her work. "Yes, I did, thank you. Do want something to eat or drink?" Christy says nothing as she lowers her head. Her mom pauses for a moment as she takes a seat on the other side of the table. "Tell me what is bothering you Christy" Christy becomes aggravated and finally responds. "Life mom, life! Can you do anything about that for me, huh? I mean, life seems to be going great for you right now."

"Christy?" Seconds of silence goes by. Her mom demands an answer.

"Christy!" Christy immediately snaps out of her daze.

"What mom what?"

"Girl, don't you talk in that tone with me!"

Christy finally gives in to her emotions.

"Jay broke up with me, that's what!"

"That's what's bugging you?"

"Yes!"

"Well what did you do?"

"Why does it have to be my fault? Jay was boring anyway, I can do better," Christy says.

"Well, then why are you so bothered about the whole thing?"

"Because he broke up with me! I'm the one that's supposed to break up with him!"

"Well who ever told you that?" Ms. Billings asks.

"I did. I'm the one that's successful, I make more money than him, and every guy wants me."

"Christy you're sounding like you are God's gift to men or something."

Christy glances at her mom.

"I am."

"Well I raised you to be confident in who you are, to love yourself and others, but I didn't raise you to be a mean girl, stuck on yourself," Ms. Billings says.

Christy becomes angry.

"What's that supposed to mean?"

"It means I didn't raise some bratty girl that's turned into a bratty woman that's what."

Christy sits up in the chair.

"How can you talk to me like that mom, I'm your daughter!"

"I know who you are, I brought you into this world, I raised you. The good Lord gave you the air to breath and me as your mother to say what I am saying the way I'm saying it!"

"Dad would not talk to me like that."

"Well, you're right he wouldn't say it because he was never around."

"What's that supposed to mean?"

"It means he was not faithful to me or to you Christy."

"And you left him."

"I had to Christy. Why must we go over this?" Ms. Billings asks.

"Because I needed him!"

"So, your blaming me for all of your problems right now?" Ms. Billings asks.

Christy remains silent. Her mom lays her hand on top of her daughters left hand on the table.

"Honey, your father had every opportunity to show you how much he loved you even though we didn't work out. He was still your father. I gave him opportunity after opportunity to be there for you. He was never there for me, and he did you the same way. So, I had to leave him, for us." Christy feels her cue to speak now. "And then you married that wretched of a man Billy." Christy's mother lowers her head. "I did, but that was my mistake, not yours, and I took full responsibility for that." Christy snatches her hand away from her mother's hand with great force as she stares her in her eyes. "And because of your choice, he raped me," Christy says. Christy's mom tears up. Her tears remain under her eyelids.

"I know baby, and that's why I put him in jail," Ms. Billings says.

"Mom, you made a bad choice, and I paid for it right?"

"You want to sacrifice me Christy, go right ahead. I've told you I'm sorry, but you won't forgive me. When you forgive me, then you can forgive yourself," Ms. Billings says.

"Forgive myself? For what?"

"For allowing yourself to hold all of this stuff inside of you. It's been eating away at you for years Christy. I can see it on your face. It's coming from your heart and it's creating a world that you can't stand."

Christy shakes her head in disgust.

"Mom don't act like you really know me. I come over here for support, for you to make me feel better, not to belittle me." "How can I belittle you Christy when you don't even tell me what's going on in your life. You don't call me to see how I'm doing or if I'm okay. You know I live here alone. Is that too much to ask from your mother?" Christy defends herself.

"Oh, so now I'm the guilty one. You know how busy I am and how stressful my job is."

"Yes, I do honey, but a simple phone call would be nice sometimes, that's all I'm saying."

"Why do I have to do everything?" Christy asks.

"What on God's earth are you talking about Christy? You make me feel like I'm the child and you're the parent," Ms. Billings says.

Christy folds her arms like a child as she pouts.

"Unbelievable," Christy says.

"What's unbelievable?" Her mom asks.

"You mom."

"Excuse me?"

"I have a life okay? Can I live my life please? You've lived yours!"

"Yes, you have a life, you should have a life, but with God in your life it would be nice. You sure could use his help right now," Ms. Billings says.

Christy becomes enraged. "I don't need him thank you very much!" "Oh, now come on Christy, you're talking like a crazy woman on drugs right now. God knows the way you look, you could surely play the part." Christy has had enough. "I cannot believe my own mother is telling her only child how bad she looks. You're such a self-esteem crusher."

"Honey, I'm speaking the truth. Wouldn't you rather hear it from me than from one of your floozy girlfriends?" "I trust my friends thank you very much." "Oh, come on now Christy, Cheryl is about the only sensible girlfriend you have. She's the only one that has some morals and values." Christy interrupts her mother. "She's not perfect!" "I didn't say she was honey, I said she's the only one with a sense of right and wrong." Christy sits up in the chair. "You think Cheryl can do what I do? She lives in an apartment and only makes fifteen dollars an hour Mom. I make one hundred fifty thousand a year salary. I have a huge house and drive a $95,000 BMW. I can buy anything I want anytime I want."

Christy's mom responds in a calm voice. "And look at your life honey, you don't look so happy for someone with all of that going on." Christy shrugs off the comment as she leans back in the chair. "I'm just having a bad day, I'm only human." Her mom responds again in a calm voice. "It's your attitude baby, it stinks. The right person can smell it a mile away. It's not the things that make you, it's what's inside of you that makes you. What if you lose all that in one day, what would you do?" "Oh mom, you sound like Cheryl. You two should be best buddies or something." Christy pauses for a moment. "Look, I am where I am because I put in the work to be there. God had nothing to do with that. I went to school, I did the work, I got the grades, I worked hard. I did it all!" "With some help should I remind you?" "From him?" "Who else Christy?" "How do you figure that?" "He woke you up this morning young lady." "Well, I didn't ask him to, and I didn't ask you to bring me into this God forsaken world."

Ms. Billings rises from her chair pointing at her daughter. "You'd better watch it Christy, talking like that. The bible says to honor your father and mother that your days may be long on the earth that the Lord your God is giving you." Christy smacks her lips while rolling her eyes.

"Oh yeah, and where does it say that in the Bible?"

"Exodus 20:12."

"Well, I can live as long as I want. I'm in control of that," Christy says.

Her mother reaches across the table grabbing her daughters hand.

"If you died tomorrow, where would you be?"

"I'm not going to die mom geez."

Christy pauses for a moment.

"Besides, when you die, you just go into the ground anyway. Hope they doll me up when I go, I want to look good in my coffin. You'll make sure of that right mom?" If there is a heaven, I would go, I'm a good person, I haven't killed anyone right?"

"Are you Christy, are you a good person, because you don't sound like one to me. You don't want to wait until it's too late to decide where you will live for eternity."

"You're talking to me like I just killed somebody. Hello, this is Christy mom, your daughter?"

Christy stands to her feet grabbing her purse.

"You should apologize to Jay Christy," Her mom suggests.

"What are you talking about Mom? Is this about Jay?"

"It's not just Jay, it's everybody including me."

Christy makes her way around her mother towards the front door.

"Who cares about Jay? I don't need him anyway," Christy says.

"Jay was a nice guy honey," Her mom replies.

"I keep thinking about what you said, and that doesn't sound right like him to just break up with you for no reason. You did something to make him do that."

Christy is appalled.

"Did you cheat on him Christy?"

Christy's head snaps as she stares down her mother.

"What did you just say to me?"

"I said did you cheat on him, because I think you did, I can tell. Have you ever thought that maybe you cheated on Jay to get back at your father for cheating on us?"

Christy shakes her head at her mother.

"Oh, I hate you!"

Her mother stands to her feet as well.

"Excuse me young lady, you watch your mouth in my house just this minute!"

"No wonder dad cheated on you, you always think it's the woman's fault that a relationship doesn't work out."

Christy's mother slaps her with such force that it echoes inside the living room.

"How dare you say that to me?" Ms. Billings says.

Christy storms past her mother.

"I'm leaving and I'm never coming back here again! I shouldn't have come. I knew you wouldn't understand."

The dog Faith follows Christy. Her mom demands Christy come back. "Young lady you come back here!" She storms out of the front door which almost Faith in the nose as she backs away at the last-minute barking at Christy. Ms. Billings follows her to the front door. "Christy, you get back here and apologize to me right this minute!" Christy hops into her BMW starting the engine and backing out of the driveway at full speed. She revs the engine at full speed down the street. Her mother stands frozen in the moment in the doorway of her house shaking her head. Faith backs away from the door as Ms. Billings steps back closing the front door.

The next day at work, Christy sits in her office when her phone rings. It is her boss the CEO Mr. Boykins. As Christy holds the phone against her ear, an enormous amount of fear appears across her face. After the phone call ends, she glances up at the clock. She is informed to meet with Mr. Boykins in five minutes. Moments later,

Christy leaves her office heading up to Mr. Boykins office. Upon entering, she is offered to sit down. "Christy, have a seat please." Christy sits down as she taps her left foot while biting her nail. Mr. Boykins sits in his leather chair looking over several sheets of papers.

The papers consist of the pending lawsuit against the company filed by Angela Harmon. After several moment, he glances up at Christy. "Christy, I am glad you could stop in to talk to me. This lawsuit situation I have in my hand is a matter of great importance. You see, the company is going through a major transition period right now, and this, is a problem." Mr. Boykins holds the papers up so Christy can see them. "Do you understand the severity of the situation I am pertaining to here?" Christy's heart pounds per second as her mind tries to catch up with her state of fear before she speaks.

"Yes Mr. Boykins, and I am truly sorry about this. Angela Harmon has been a problem for me for quite some time. I wish I had come to you earlier to address this issue. I felt her firing was the only solution to the problem." Mr. Boykins sets down the papers and raises his right hand. "So, your saying she's been a problem since she was hired here?" "Yes sir." "Christy, this shouldn't have happened. You couldn't wait until our transition process was over to do this?" Christy responds.

"Sir, I didn't know about the transition process."

"You didn't?"

"No sir. And, I was told, this matter would be taken care of under the radar."

"In God's name, who told you that?"

"Mark Collins sir."

Mr. Boykins is confused.

"Mark told you this?"

"Yes sir. He told me, you two talked about this and the matter was handled."

"What else did Mark tell you Christy?"

"Excuse me sir?"

Mr. Boykins raises his voice. "Young lady, don't play games with me, answer the question, what else did he tell you?" Christy is silent, as she fumbles with her hands rubbing them together as if she were washing them over a sink. "I'd rather not say sir." In a calm demanding voice, Mr. Boykins asks the same question again. "Christy, if you don't tell me, I will have to release you, and you won't get your bonus. You'll be left with nothing except what you have in your bank account. It is imperative that you tell me what you know because it jeopardizes the transition process of this company."

Christy feels the pressure of her emotions about to explode. She can't take it anymore and finally gives in. "Mark told me, we had two months left in the company before everything will be sold off and that the SCC does not know about everything that's going on, but that is effective as long as we keep our mouths shut. He told me about the Cartel's money invested in the company too. He told me all of this after the meeting you had on

Sunday." Mr. Boykins sits back in his high back leather chair staring at Christy. "Unbelievable," Mr. Boykins says. "Please Mr. Boykins, don't tell Mark I told you all of this, he would kill me." Mr. Boykins stares at Christy. "That would be an understatement Ms. Billings."

Christy, unable to look Mr. Boykins in the eyes any longer, remains silent. "Is that all?" Mr. Boykins asks. "That's all he told me sir!" The office remains silent. Finally, Mr. Boykins responds. "Now, was that hard, to tell the truth Christy?" Christy, partly elated he hasn't fired her on the spot for knowing what she knows, quietly responds. "Sir?" "You told me the truth, don't you feel better about yourself?" "I guess sir." Mr. Boykins leans forward in his chair, placing his elbows on his desk. "Now, Christy, I want you to keep this to yourself what we discussed here. Mark isn't in any trouble. I just wanted to know what you knew if anything. Now that you know, you must promise me, you will tell no one." Christy stares at Mr. Boykins. "I promise," She says. "Good, very good." Mr. Boykins pause for a second. "Okay, that is all for now. I will get rid of this lawsuit situation myself, so don't you worry about anything, and I know you will keep the secret you and I discussed, wont' you?" "Yes, Mr. Boykins." "That is all, you may leave." Christy slowly stands up, and graciously proceeds towards the door.

"I will give you several recommendations for new jobs too," Mr. Boykins replies.

"Really Mr. Boykins?"

"Why sure."

"You're not mad at me for knowing what I know?"

"Oh no, as long as it was between you, me and Mark."

"Oh no Mr. Boykins, it was just between the three of us."

"Good then."

Mr. Boykins pauses for a moment.

"Thank you for coming."

Christy stands to her feet.

"Mr. Boykins?"

Mr. Boykins places the files of the lawsuit in his desk.

"Yes Christy?"

"You won't punish Mark for telling me everything, will you?"

"Oh no, Mark is fine with me."

Christy hesitates for a moment. Mr. Boykins looks at Christy and says, "Trust me."

Christy smiles assured.

"What about the lawsuit?"

Mr. Boykins thinks for a moment.

"I will have to try to settle out of court with Angela and her lawyer to keep this quiet. We don't have the money for this, but I will have to find a way."

"I'm truly sorry for all of this Mr. Boykins," Christy says.

He nods his head looking at her.

"I know you are Christy."

"Thank you, Mr. Boykins."

"You're welcome Christy."

Christy leaves his office quietly closing the door behind her. Mr. Jenkins waits awhile, then he grabs his office phone dialing his secretary.

"Get my nephew in here now," Mr. Boykins demands.

"Which one Mr. Boykins?" The secretary asks.

The question confuses Mr. Boykins.

"I don't know, the one with the scar on his ear."

"That would-be Nathaniel sir."

"Yes, that would be the one," Mr. Boykins says. Mr. Boykins angrily hangs up the phone. Moments later, Nathaniel enters his uncle's office in his silver suit, chewing his gum methodically.

"Problems, Uncle?"

Mr. Boykins mumbling in anger finally gets the words out.

"Yes, I have two problems."

"Well Uncle, that's why you sent me here right?"

Mr. Boykins thinks for a moment.

"I need you and your brother to take out that Christy Billings girl, and Mark."

"Now it's Mark?" Nathaniel asks.

"Yes, It's Mark now! He can't keep his mouth shut! He told the girl everything we plan to do. This could go public and ruin me."

"Just tell me how you want it done Uncle, and I will do the rest," Nathaniel says.

"Do the lug nuts on Christy's car, and Mark, I don't know, do it whatever way you feel you need to do it. I'm not a killer, I'm a business man," Mr. Boykins replies.

"I understand Uncle," Nathaniel says.

"Just do what you do and leave no trace. I don't want any of this coming back to me understand?"

"It will be done sir."

Nathaniel prepares to leave the office until he is questioned by his uncle.

"When?"

"Well right now Uncle if you like?"

"Yes, I would like."

"Okay, I will take care of it."

Nathaniel waits for further instructions. There are none, so he quietly exits closing the door behind him. Hours later, Christy sits in her office thinking about what Mr. Boykins said. She ponders it over in her mind while murmuring to herself. "Something is wrong. No way would someone who knows what I told him, be that nice in a situation like this." Meanwhile, downstairs in the garage, Mark sits in his car smoking a cigarette on his break. Christy's BMW sits two car lengths ahead. Mark takes frequent puffs from the cigarette to calm his nerves as he thinks about the good times he had with Christy since childhood. Mark realizes, he can't go through with the evil in front of him. He grabs his cell phone prepared to call SCC. After what seems like eternity dialing the number before he presses SEND on his phone, the sound of a wrench hitting the ground, grabs his attention. Mark raises his head to look. To his surprise in front of him, he sees Nathaniel tinkering with Christy's front wheel of her car. Mark's eyes focus intently at the scene. He thinks to himself, "What is he doing?" As Mark's left hand grabs the door handle inside his car, he opens the door exiting his vehicle. Nathaniel wipes his hands with his handkerchief, then grabs the crowbar and proceeds to walk away until Mark confronts him.

Upstairs in the office building, Christy leaves her office with her belongings in hand. As she walks down the hallway looking disheveled about the meeting with Mr. Boykins and the impending lawsuit, she approaches the elevator hitting the "LL" button for Lower Level which is the garage. The elevator door opens, and she enters as the door closes behind her. The elevator travels down several floors as the buttons above her head illuminating for each floor, 19, 18, 17, 16. Christy watches the numbers simultaneously blink on then off for each floor. Meanwhile, down in the garage, Nathaniel and Mark go at it as Mark grabs Nathaniel by the arm. "Hey! What do you think you're doing?" Nathaniel turns pulling his arm away from Mark. "Something you were given instructions to do but didn't." Mark approaches Nathaniel grabbing his arm again now looking face to face at him.

With a stoned face look, Nathaniel stares at Mark responding, "If I were you, I would let go of my arm right now before you have more problems than you can shake a stick at." Mark amazed at a young man who hasn't been around the block of life. "Who do you think you're talking to?" Nathaniel looks Mark directly in the eyes as he responds, "A dead man." Mark releases his grip from Nathaniel's arm. Nathaniel turns and walks away taking the stairs up to the lobby floor. Seconds later, Christy exits the elevator to the garage as she makes her way to her car. She glances at her car noticing Mark near it. "Mark, what are you doing?" Mark is taken by Christy's sudden surprise. He is speechless. Christy stops in her tracks, "Mark?" Mark slowly raises his head looking at

Christy. He has a solemn look on his face as he turns his head looking straight forward.

It forces Christy to ask again. "Mark, are you okay? Why are you standing by my car like this, I thought you were still up in your office or something?" Mark makes eye contact with Christy as he leans up against her car. "I might as well be after I tell you something." Christy is confused. "Might as well be? Tell me what, what are you talking about?" "I might as well be dead after I tell you this Christy." "Mark, I'm not getting you. What is going on, you don't sound, right? Did Mr. Boykins tell you?" "Tell me what?" "That we talked, and he made me tell him everything you told me." Mark has a stunned look on his face as he removes his body from leaning on Christy's car. "You snitched on me Christy? I thought we were friends?" Christy, "Snitched on you, no, I didn't do that. Mr. Boykins called me in for a meeting which you were supposed to make sure never happened! He grilled me about the lawsuit thing, and he wanted to know if you said anything about what's going on with the company to me."

Mark tilts his head back in shock as he responds back to Christy.

"And I told you not to tell anyone anything I said to you Christy!"

Christy pleads with Mark as her voice rises.

"I had to Mark, he was about to fire me on the spot if I didn't. He was scaring me. He can do anything he want, he owns the company remember?"

Mark turns away from Christy to avoid the rage boiling inside of him.

"Mark I'm sorry," Christy says.

Christy replies. Mark turns back at Christy.

"You should have kept quiet! This company is about to be no more!"

"And what would I have Mark, you company that hasn't even started, to live on? Good luck with me trying to apply for unemployment because you know what they would say to me? Young lady, you were fired, you can't collect unemployment."

"Oh yeah?"

"Yes, Mark!"

"I told you I'm taking care of you."

"No Mark, taking care of me was getting rid of the lawsuit, that way Mr. Boykins wouldn't have called me in for a meeting and I wouldn't have been forced to tell him what you told me!"

Mark turns away from Christy again. "I trusted you Mark!" Christy begins to cry." She angrily enters her car as Mark stands alone by himself bogged down by his mind. Christy turns the ignition to her BMW putting her car in reverse and backing out of her parking space. Mark realizes he neglected to stop her from driving off because her front wheel lug nuts are loose. Mark shouts at her chasing her car as she speeds away. "Christy!" The screeching sound of her tires amplifies as she turns the corner fast towards the exit of the garage. Marks voice echoes her name again. "Christy!

Minutes later, Christy makes her way onto the freeway. She presses the speed dial button on her phone for her mother's number with the assistance of the phone system inside her car. The freeway has a medium amount of traffic traveling on since it is past rush hour. Christy drives in the middle lane as she waits for her mother's phone to answer. Finally, it does. "Hello?" Christy is happy to hear her mom's voice, that same voice that talked to her when she was in the womb comforting her upon her arrival into the world. "Mom?" Christy answers. "Christy? Hi honey, I'm glad you called, I've been thinking about you." "Mom, I'm sorry for what I said, I didn't mean it." "I know honey, I know you didn't. We all say things we regret. It's okay. Where are you?"

> "I'm on the freeway, I just left work. Things are way out of hand Mom, and I don't' know what to do. Will you pray for me?"

The phone is silent on her mother's end, then finally, she responds.

> "I've prayed for you since you were inside of me, and I've never stopped praying for you. No

matter what you do, your still and always will be my child."

Christy tears up as the tears stream down her face.

"Thank you, mom," Christy says.

"I love you baby," Ms. Billings says.

Christy responds.

"I love…"

Suddenly, Christy's steering wheel vibrates uncontrollably as her car drives along the side of a semi-truck to her right.

"Christy are you there, what's that noise?"

"I don't know mom, my car, it's out of control, I can't steer it…"

Christy aggressively tries to control the steering wheel. Suddenly, a popping sound ensues. Christy's BMW begins to sway from side to side as Christy tries to steer properly. Her mom responds with a concerned voice. "Christy are you okay?" "Mom, I can't control my car!" "What?" Christy's fears worsen as her left tire pops off the front left axel. Christy's car swerves uncontrollably to the right as Christy says her final words, "Oh, my God." Her BMW drives up under the tractor trailer tires of the semi-truck next to her. Christy screams as loud as she can as the semi-truck slams on its breaks creating a billow of smoke from the trailers tires. The trailers wheels dig into the right-side door of the BMW dragging it down the freeway. Before Christy knows anything, her car turns under the trucks trailer.

Christy's mother hears everything over her phone. The trailer catches the right door of Christy's BMW causing Christy to bump her head against the driver side window of her car knocking her to the console of her car. As her body lays, the sound of metal crunching is deafening as the wheels slide against her passenger door gripping it climbing over the car like a child trying to climb out of a play pen. A huge puff of smoke appears as the tire unravels the right door of Christy's car. Both front and rear wheels of the trailer roll over Christy's like a monster truck moment. The impact shatters glass, and pieces of the BMW all over the freeway. Cars witnessing the crash in front of them, slam on their brakes as the semi-truck comes to a complete stop. Christy's mangled car remains in the middle of the freeway smashed as the moment creates total silence.

CHAPTER NINE

"The Aftermath"

As Christy's car sits still, good Samaritans run to her aid. They begin peeling away the mangled convertible top covering her body seeing her lay in a fetal position on her right side. Her upper body rests over the center console and passenger seat. Broken glass and pieces of the seat are folded over her body as her eyes remain open. Her breathing is shallow as bystander's panic shouting… "She's still alive!"

Another Good Samaritan responds. "Yeah, I see her chest moving!"

Another person says, "We got to get her out of here man. Don't move young lady, help is on the way."

"Should we move her though? What if she has broken bones or something, moving her could paralyze her."

The man thinks for a moment.

"Maybe you're right. Check underneath the car and make sure the gas tank isn't leaking. The car could blow or something. A woman in her thirty's, appears holding her cell phone in the air as she runs towards the scene.

"I just called 911. They are on their way!"

Five individuals are now huddled around Christy's crumpled BMW. The truck driver, a man in his mid-fifty's, climbs out of his truck running towards Christy's car. He is horrified at what he sees.

"My Lord! Is she okay?"

One of the bystanders responds.

"No man, she's pretty messed up. What happened?"

The truck driver raises his arms.

"I don't know, her car was swerving like crazy on my left side, then she swerved up under my trailers tires. There was nothing I could do. Everything happened so fast," The truckdriver says.

He inches closer to get a better look at the driver of the BMW.

"Awe man."

The trucker talks to Christy as if he knew her.

"I am so sorry young lady."

A bystander tries to hold everyone back to allow Christy to breath.

"Get back, give her some room to breathe."

"Is she alive?"

"Yeah, she's breathing."

"It looks like she's dead, her eyes are still open and she's not moving."

The guy glances down at Christy. Her breathing is still shallow. From a distance, a fire truck, EMS, and two police cars appear with flashing lights and wailing sirens. The man holding everyone back standing next to Christy, motions with his hand for the paramedics to hurry. They arrive at the scene.

"Hurry man, I think she just stopped breathing!"

Firefighters hop out of their fire engine truck and run over to Christy's car checking it over to make sure the gas tank is not leaking.

The lead firefighter orders everyone back. "Everybody, get back, we got this!"

A police officer questions the truck driver pulling him to the side away from Christy's car. Paramedics bring a stretcher over towards Christy's car. The freeway traffic begins to back up as police prepare one lane open for motorists to pass by. Several other police units arrive to help. Firefighters use the 'Jaws of Life' to pry away the driver side door of Christy's car. As paramedics begin moving her, they are careful in their process. Bystanders who were first on scene are huddled together watching every moment. Paramedics place Christy carefully on a stretcher with her neck secured in a brace. As they place Christy into the ambulance, her breathing suddenly stops. One of the paramedic's checks for a pulse.

"We've got no pulse!"

Christy's spirit leaves her body as one of the paramedics begins performing CPR on her at the door of the ambulance. Her spirit stands next to the paramedics watching them perform the CPR as she glances around at the chaotic scene unfolding around her. She becomes scared as she watches her limp body on the stretcher being wheeled inside the ambulance. She sees a lady with her daughter watching. They both begin crying uncontrollably. Suddenly, Christy's spirit is pulled away from the scene.

She tries to scream, but nothing comes out as her spirit continues to travel into the abyss of darkness. It seems like eternity, until finally, her travel ends as her spiritual body enters a dark cave dropping into a large shaped bowl massive in circumference. She lands on top of other spiritual bodies inside followed by many other people of different nationalities around her. The stench inside the cave is unbearable to fathom. It is a lonely place where God is not present. The heat is intense. Christy feels like she is on fire. She freaks out by the people around her as they try to free themselves from the state of bondage.

Christy begins to feel the pain from her car accident. The spiritual realm has its own variables unknown to man. This unknown place was not designed for God's creation, and many are wondering why they are here including Christy. "Why am I here? What is this place?" Christy asks. Others around her look in shock at wondering the same thing.

"God help me please!" Christy whispers to herself as the horror she sees around her, takes her breath away.

Christy's screams echo inside her head. Suddenly, her spirit travels out of the darkness and back into the light. Now present inside her body in the ambulance, Christy sees the paramedics standing over her still performing CPR as the ambulance rushes her to the hospital. A paramedic feels a pulse.

"We've got a pulse again!"

A relief consumes Christy's emotions as the EMS worker tries to stabilize her, but only for a moment as her body returns to cardiac arrest. The monitor once wavy for a few seconds, returns flat.

"We've lost her again!" The lead paramedic shouts.

Christy's spirit is drawn from her body again. Christy's spirit exits her body once again dropping her into the abyss she once came from. Her spiritual body returns inside the bowl she laid with others. Christy's mouth opens feeling the urge to vomit, but nothing comes out as the intense heat feels like it is burning her spirit all over. Christy whispers in desperation.

"Jesus, save me!"

Unable to move, Christy inhales and exhales rapidly. Her breathing becomes shallow as her body presses up against other spiritual bodies inside the bowl. The other people inside try moving as well, but to no avail. Looking down from above, the huge bowl is filled with hundreds of people all on top of each other. The moment is too horrific for anyone's imagination to grasp as Christy remains pinned between a male and female. Everyone inside is scared beyond the capacity of death. The area of this dark place is hot and unbearable as the flames around are the only light available.

    Christy tries to move realizing it is useless. A man next to her stares at her with a blank stare. Christy turns her head away from him, only to consider the eyes of a young teenage girl who is scared tremendously. The eerie sounds of screams and crying echoes in and around the bowl. The sounds of screams and agony are defining to many inside the bowl as they cover their ears to drown out the sound. Suddenly, a horrific demonic figure approaches the bowl. The creature stands 18 feet tall with the body of a wolf. It stands on its hind legs rocking the bowl back and forth. Everyone inside hold on for dear life with their faces expressing intense fear as they all anticipate what is about to happen next. As the bowl sways harder, it flips to one side as every spiritual body inside, falls out toppling on top of each other. The bodies role onto the dirt filled grimy ground. Christy is surprised as she is unfazed by the fall, but she is surprised of the pain she feels from her accident. The horrific figure leaves disappearing into the darkness.

    As Christy lays on the dirt filled floor, her pain begins to intensify as everyone fallen from inside the bowl, scatters in different directions into the darkness hoping to escape from the horror. Christy glances around and sees a familiar face from the ember lit flames. It's her high school classmate, Jessica Bender. Jessica was Christy's best friend murdered by her jealous boyfriend. Jessica still bruised and beaten from her boyfriend's violent rage, sits inside a clay cell connected to other cells with other people inside them. Jessica recognizes Christy as she stands grabbing the clay bars tightly with her hands. Christy runs over towards her.

"Jessica?" Christy asks.

Jessica squints her eyes.

"Christy?"

Christy glances around.

"What, what are you doing here, oh my God, look at you, your bruised all over. What is this place?"

Jessica looks filthy and worn down not only from the beating before she died by the hands of her boyfriend, but from this place as she pleads with Christy.

"Christy, you have to get out of here! You don't want to be here!"

Christy grabs Jessica's cell. She pulls at the clay bars.

"Jessica, let me get you out!"

Jessica yells at her.

"No, you can't!"

Christy tries to pull harder on the bars, but they are too hard and clammy to grip.

"Jessica, where are we?"

Jessica glances around to see if the wolf life figure roaming around that tormented her before, is nearby. With her eyes as wide as saucers, she begins speaking to Christy.

"Christy, I never listened to my parents when they told me that my boyfriend Jake was no good. I laughed at them when they told me to stay away from him. They would always talk to me about God and how much he loved me and that I needed him in my life. I always mocked at them about their beliefs. They told me if I stayed with Jake, he would hurt me, and he did. Jake said he loved me more than anyone, but he would always beat me and blame me for cheating on him which I never did. One day, his beating went too far, and he took my life. This is where I ended up Christy. There is no way out of here, I tried. What happened to you, that made you end up here?" Christy remains silent as she thinks about her entire life. "Christy, God never intended for us to be here when we die. We are created to be with him for eternity. But we must choose his free salvation in his son Jesus Christ. I never did, I always thought I had all the time in the world. I never believed the boyfriend I thought I loved so much would take my life, and this is where I ended up. I've made my choice."

Christy is in a daze. "That's all we had to do?" "What?" "Is accept Jesus?" "Yes, Christy. The devil lied to us all our lives making us think it wasn't important, and that we had the rest of our lives to decide, but no one is promised tomorrow. He wants us to wait until it's too late to decide, then it's over for eternity. This place is eternity for those who don't believe Christy." Christy shakes her head in disbelief. "No, I did some bad things Jessica, but I haven't killed anybody. This place should be for murderers, not normal people like me!" "It's not about whose good and whose bad Christy. That's the lie the devil says. Anyone who does not receive Christ as their savior will end up here no matter the good or bad they've done in life. We are all born into sin Christy. We inherited it from the beginning of creation through Adam and Eve, the first creation on the earth."

Christy is at a loss for words. "I should have listened to my mom. Why didn't I listen. I believed a lie I told myself for a long time. There really is a God if the devil is real. This place is evil." "The devil wants us to be here Christy to suffer with him for the mistake he made challenging God in heaven. This is his payback to God for kicking him out of heaven, to destroy God's creation, us."

CHAPTER TEN

"In Hades"

Christy continues tugging hard at the clay bars. Jessica begs her to stop. "No, stop Christy, just stop, please! You can't break them. They won't break. I've tried and tried. It's useless." Christy glances around seeing very little in the darkness. "Is there a way out of here? If I can get you out, maybe we can get out of here together?" "No Christy. Don't you understand?" Christy is confused as her eyes focus on Jessica's through the darkness. "Understand what? Why, what is this place?" Christy asks.

Jessica looks around afraid to tell Christy in fear of what will happen to her, but she does it anyway.

"You're in Hades Christy!" "What's that?" "A temporary place before hell, which is the final death when you are cast into the Lake of Fire for eternity. Christy, the only way anyone can avoid this place is receiving salvation in Christ Jesus."

Christy already in fear, steps back from the cell as her fear intensifies. She does not believe Jessica. "No, no way! You don't know what you're talking about. Hell is not real, your lying to me!" "No, I'm telling you the truth" Jessica pleads. "You're a liar, get away from me!" Christy demands.

Christy steps farther away from Jessica's cell. Jessica's words cut through her spirit like a knife with the sharpest blade ever made. "No, that's a lie." Jessica pleads with Christy. "Christy!" Christy becomes delusional. "No, I'm not Christy, this is a dream, I'm in a bad dream, I'll wake up from this, yes, I will." "No, Christy, this is for real, look around you! Have you ever seen a place like this before? Who would make up something like this?" Christy glances up noticing deformed looking insects and creatures crawling on the walls along with a monster looking figure embedded in the wall.

It begins to move inside of the wall. Christy horrified, she screams. "I'm just having a bad dream, this isn't real! This can't be real! I don't deserve this!" "It's real Christy. This is what God was telling us in his word in the book of Revelation. Every human being needs salvation in Christ to wipe away the sinful world we were all born into. After this, you will be judged, we all will be, everyone in here. Were here because we didn't believe in God, and we never received his gift of salvation which was free, all we had to do was confess Jesus as our savior, that's it and we wouldn't see any of part of this place ever, don't you get it?"

Christy stands in a dazed and confused state as she tries to understand what Jessica just told her. "Christy, we were lied to by the world, don't you get that. People told us not to believe in God, that he wasn't real, or that we had all the time in the world to choose him if whenever we were ready, or that the world we lived in would never end and when you die, you just died. It was all a lie

Christy!" Christy backs away from Jessica's cell to the point, she can no longer see Jessica, but she still hears her voice. She screams at Jessica. "Stop it, just stop talking to me, this, isn't happening to me!"

Jessica continues talking erratically, but Christy drowns her out with her own voice. "No, hell is a place for murderers and thieves, and liars. I know I'm not perfect, but who is, but I haven't killed anybody. No, the killers belong here, there, whatever, not somebody like me. I made a mark in society, I worked for a fortune 500 company. Yes, I've lied on some business deals for sure, but that was only a couple of times. I did some people wrong yes, but who hasn't?" Christy nods her head quickly in agreement with her own words. "I'm still a good person, yes." She convinces herself trying to minimize the situation she is in. "I did charitable work for my company, I volunteered at soup kitchens during Thanksgiving several times, I even gave a twenty-dollar bill to a homeless guy by the freeway when I came home from work one time, and that's all I had on me!" Christy becomes enraged now. "So, don't you stand there and tell me that this is hell. That's a lie! You're not real, none of this is real! This is a bad dream, I'm going to wake up from this any minute."

Jessica grabs the clay bars, as she pleads to Christy in a calm voice. "I'm sorry Christy. Comer here, please." Christy, hesitant, slowly walks back towards Jessica. "This is real, and you are here. I said the same things you said when I got here. My Mom and Dad who loved me so much, told me, people don't go to heaven because they are good, and people don't go to hell because they are bad. The choice comes whether we choose Jesus or deny him, that's it. His death was our gift so that we can freely live beyond our fleshly bodies when we died, so we wouldn't end up here before judgement. This place was to be for the devil and his fallen angels that were cast out of Heaven with him. We are all spirits Christy, and spirits never die, but when our flesh dies, our spirits go to Hades or Abraham's bosom, then after judgement, Heaven, or hell. That's where Christs death intervened for us after the fall of Adam and Eve when they gave our free will over to the devil. Jesus came to save us from all of this, so we could live with God for eternity."

Christy stands in front of Jessica stiff like a statue. "But, this doesn't make sense! So, you mean I'm here because I never chose Jesus and believed in him? Your telling me this all came down to a choice that I made? No one ever told me this? No, no way, you're wrong. That's crazy Jessica."

"No Christy?" Asks Jessica. Christy replies with assurance. "No!" "Remember when we used to party like crazy our Sophomore and Junior year in High School before I was killed? We were getting high, drunk, and having sex with guys we knew didn't love us? We thought we we're having the time of our lives. We could have had clean fun and saving ourselves for marriage one day. But we thought we had all the time in the world. We only cared about ourselves and our so-called friends who would agree with everything we did?" Didn't your Mom and Dad ever tell you about God and what he did for the world?" "My dad did one time before he died of cancer" Christy replies.

Jessica continues talking. "I always disobeyed my parents and did my own thing. I thought I was in love, I thought I could change my boyfriend, and that he was sent from God, and that we were going to get married and have children, but he wasn't from God, he was from the devil. He started beating me until there was nothing left of me. Do you think that was God's best for me? I don't now, but I did back then, because I never listened to my parents and my friends when they would tell me bad things about him. I should have accepted God into my heart, then I would have made the right decision and even never got into this mess. And if I even if I still died by his hands, I would not be here because God's grace would have saved me."

Christy closes her eyes for a moment. When she opens them, she turns around to a hairy ten-foot-tall grizzly looking being. As it opens its mouth, a defining growl comes out. Its sharp jagged teeth appear layered over another set of teeth extending further than its original teeth. Jessica yells out.

"Christy, run!"

Christy runs, but before she can get two steps, she is picked up from behind by the creature. She screams as the demonic wolf like figure tosses her around like a ragdoll. She hits the wall and slides down the side of it. Several other fierce looking demonic figures appear. They begin chasing and grabbing other people wondering around taking them away as they scream for help. Christy is approached by one of them. She wants to pass out, but her fears keep her alert and awake. As she screams at the top of her lungs, she hopes it would scared them off.

But it stands over her and grabs her pulling her up face to face with it. Christy kicks and screams trying to break free. She turns her head to look away from its horrific eyes sunken deep into its head. Its breath is so foul, Christy vomits from the stench. It turns around, and drags Christy away separated from the others into total darkness. After minutes which seems like a thousand years for Christy, she is then thrown into a cell made of clay and mud. The demonic figure stands outside the cell. Christy facing the clay wall, turns her back towards the creature, but its hideous breathing torments her, because she can feel it staring at her. The cell closes with a loud thud, as the creature walks away with its large scaled feet stomping in the clay muddy ground echoing a loud sound as it disappears into the darkness.

Christy gathers herself, but it is useless. The clammy mud in the web of her hands, transfers all over making things worse. She slowly turns around in her cell to total darkness outside of it. A cold wind of loneliness, brushes over her body. The feeling of it consumes her as she curls up into a fetal position crying. Christy focuses her eyes in the darkness but sees nothing. Only the sounds of agony and screams fills her ears. The echo of someone's voice is heard. "Somebody helps me please!"

Minutes pass back at the hospital as doctors work frantically on Christy's body on the operation table. CPR is continued as doctors and nurses scramble around in the room assisting the lead doctor to save Christy's life.

As Christy lays on the table, her body convulses as the doctor's give her heart an electric shock with the defibrillator machine. The monitor remains flat. They do it again. No response. One nurse gives Christy a shot with a 16-inch-long needle filled with adrenaline into her heart to jump start it. They shock her again, but nothing changes.

In hell, as Christy sits in her cell crying, rocking herself back and forth mumbling positive words to calm herself down.

"God please help me. God forgive me of my sins. God please save me."

She hears something. She stands to her feet walking towards the clay bars of the cell. Suddenly the same demonic figure that brought her there, appears. It grabs the clay bars on the cell and begins to rattle it as it growls. Christy glances up at the silhouette of the creature. Backing away from the bars into the corner of the cell, Christy mumbles the Name of Jesus. She falls to the floor and presses her head into her legs curling them up to her chest. Christy covers her ears to drown out the noise coming from the creature.

In the hospital room, the doctor orders one more shock treatment on Christy as she lays motionless. The doctor performs the shock treatment to her heart. Her body rises on the table as the defibrillation suction cups grip her skin. Back in the cell, the demonic creature opens the cage and approaches Christy roaring with its sharp teeth snapping at her. As it reaches for her, Christy is whisked away from the darkness.

Her spirit travels through the darkness, into the brightness of light onto the operation table. As the defibrillator suction cups releases its grip on her body, the heart monitor machine's screen that showed a flat line now has waves in it. The monitor begins beeping.

A nurse shout out…

"She's back doctor!"

The lead doctor smiles.

"Yes, she is."

Christy, with her eyes still open, stares at the bright light from the lamp above her. Her pupils begin to dilate bringing back color.

She blinks her eyes rapidly as she takes rapid breaths. Tears stream down both corners of her eyes. The doctors continue working on her providing her a respirator device over her mouth to help her breath. Christy continues taking deep breaths using it, as the Doctors stabilize her. The operating room is calm. The lead doctor speaks to Christy.

"Ms. Billings, you are in a hospital right now. You were in a very bad accident. Try to relax okay?"

Her eyes scan left and right rapidly as she tries to grasp the situation. Christy blinks her eyes as they fill with water. Tears begin to stream down the side of her face to her ears.

An hour later, Christy is wheeled into the intensive care unit in a room by herself. Nurses tend to her making her stable. She is heavily sedated with tubes in her nose and mouth. As Christy sleeps, she dreams, replaying the moments of her life including her childhood, teenage years, adult years, and the accident. In her childhood, she remembers being held in the arms of her late father. She visualizes him pushing her on the swing set at the park as she giggles and laughs. In her teenage years, she remembers partying and hanging out with her best friend Jessica. The two were out of control at the time as she remembers comforting Jessica when her boyfriend beat her up the first time. Then Christy remembers the day she found out Jessica was murdered by her boyfriend. She remembers attending the funeral feeling lost and alone without Jessica and her father and the anger that fueled her soul at the time. The last of Christy's dream, is the accident, and the fear she felt the moment it happened. As Christy lay on the bed, the heart monitor machine beeps as the wavy lines acknowledge her current state of life.

Weeks pass by and the doctors remove the tubing from Christy's mouth and nose. Her mother along with other family members and girlfriends Leslie and Cheryl visit Christy from time to time. Her mother sits by her side every day checking on her. Another week passes by as Christy's condition improves. The nurses place Christy in a regular room. One day while she sleeps, Mark visits her.

As he enters the room with a card and flowers, he notices two other bouquet of flowers by Christy's bed. Mark reads the card on the first flower pot. It says, "Praying for your full recovery. May God's healing power take over your body removing every hurt and pain? God bless..." Angie Harmon. The second flower pot reads. "Wishing you a full recovery," Mr. Boykins and family, Nathaniel, and Aaron. Mark frowns as he sees Nathaniel's name.

    Seeing Christy asleep, Mark decides to stay awhile. He sits down talking to her hoping she hears him. "Hey Christy. How's it going? Not to good huh?" Mark pauses for a moment. "Man, I'm so sorry Christy, I should have told you about your car. I should have stopped you from leaving, but I was too concerned about myself. I was wrong for what I said to you. I know Nathaniel did this to you, and I'm going to make sure he doesn't get away with it, I promise you." A nurse enters the room to check on Christy. She smiles at Mark as he greets her. "Hi," Mark says. "Hi, are you a relative or a friend?" "I'm a friend, we worked together." "Oh," The nurse says. "Has she been awake yet?" Mark asks. "She's been awake, but not for long. She sleeps a lot. Her body is trying to get its' strength back. She was in a very bad accident, few, or any at all survive that kind of wreck. The doctors said she had no pulse two times here in emergency." Mark is shocked. "What?" "Yes, she was gone, but our doctors kept working on her, and brought her back. Luckily for her, the organs are still functioning properly. We must keep her monitored minute by minute even though she just got out of Intensive Care. "Wow, I didn't know that," Mark says. The nurse prepares to leave. "Thank you for dropping by, I'm sure she would be glad to know you came." "Oh, thank you, we went to high School together, so we have a lot of history." "You'll have to come back early in the day to catch her awake." Mark prepares to leave the room also. "Oh, okay. I'm going to leave this card and flowers, could you tell her I came by?" "Sure, what is your name?" "Mark Collins." "Okay, I will let her know you came by." "I appreciate that, thank you, bye." Mark and the nurse shake hands. "Bye." The nurse follows Mark out of the room.

Later that night, Christy has nightmares about her out of body experience. She tosses and turns with beads of sweat forming across her forehead. She sees Jessica telling her to run for her life. Christy runs as fast as she can but seems to go nowhere as she turns her head running away from grizzly looking demonic figure that haunted her. As the creature closes in on her with its teeth snapping, Christy awakens sitting straight up in her bed. The monitor beats fast showing her heart rate. A nurse quickly enters the room approaching Christy. "Are you okay?" Christy says nothing as she slowly lays back down on her bed.

The nurse quickly approaches her propping her pillow behind her head. "You just had a bad dream huh?" Christy acknowledges her nodding her head yes. The nurse consoles her. "It's going to be okay, you're just going through post-traumatic stress disorder. It's going to take some time for you to recuperate." Christy nods her head again in acknowledgement. "Try to get some rest okay? I will check on you every fifteen minutes. I'm right outside that door so you're not alone." Christy grabs the nurses hand and responds, "Thank you." The nurse in return, pats Christ on her hand. "Okay." The nurse quietly leaves the room while Christy stares out the window. The North Star is right above the hospital window as it glistens in the night light. To Christy, this moment seems like a word from Heaven letting her know everything will be all right.

    Christy wonders how a star could be that bright shining on the earth and yet be so far away from the troubles of this world. "Who could create something like that?" Christy quietly mutters to herself as the star brightens for a quick second. To Christy, the star has her undivided attention as the moment calms her soul. Her breathing becomes serene as she drifts off to sleep again. This time, in her dream, there is a bright light. As she approaches the light, it gets brighter and brighter, so bright, she stops walking towards it. As she gazes at the light, a person in a white robe approaches her. She is unable to see him completely as he stretches his hands stretch out to her. Christy glances down at the hands. In each palm are holes with blood around the edges of the holes. Christy's eyes look up seeing the man's face. She does not know him, but believes he is Jesus. He smiles at her. Christy is overwhelmed by his presence smiling in return as her eyes tear up with joy. She knows everything will be all right. Her sleep is peaceful as the night continues into the morning.

That Saturday morning, Christy awakens feeling refreshed from a good night's sleep. A nurse greets her.

"Good morning." "Good morning." The nurse gives Christy her breakfast, checks her vital signs, then leaves the room. As she eats, she gets a surprise visit from Leslie and Cheryl. They smile entering the room. "Hey!" Christy smiles responding back. "Hey!" Leslie and Cheryl walk over giving Christy a huge hug. Cheryl stares Christy in the eyes as she sits up in her bed. "Were still friends?" Cheryl. The question confuses Christy. "Yeah, why wouldn't we be?" Cheryl plays it off glad that Christy does not remember their breakup at her barbecue party." "Oh, I'm just joking, it's great to see you."

Cheryl gives Christy a kiss on her cheek as the two girls sit down next to her bed on her right side.

"So, how are you feeling?" Leslie asks.

"Oh, sore a lot of times. I did have a truck run over me you know?" Christy says sarcastically.

Cheryl and Leslie laugh uncontrollably.

"Yeah, that will definitely do it," Cheryl says.

"Cheryl?" Christy asks.

Christy suddenly laughs holding her side from the pain of the laugh. Christy pauses for a moment. "No, all I remember is getting into an argument with Mark before I left work." "An argument?" Cheryl asks. "Yeah," Christy says. "About what?" Leslie asks. "I don't remember. I do know it was a very heated one." "Where did you two argue?" Christy thinks. "By my car I think. Why?" "Oh, I don't know. What did they say happened to your car?" "The police told me my wheel came off on the freeway."

"Your front wheel?" "Yes." "Christy, do you think Mark did that to your car?" Cheryl asks. Leslie intervenes. "I don't think he would do that Cheryl." "Why not?" Cheryl asks. "Because I met him remember, at Christy's party. He seemed like a really nice guy." "Everyone seems nice to you Leslie." Cheryl responds.

Leslie defends herself. "What would he gain from doing that to Christy, their friends and they work together." "Forget it," Cheryl says. "What's that supposed to mean?" Leslie asks. "Nothing." "No, you meant something otherwise you wouldn't have said it." "Calm down Leslie, you're in a hospital." Leslie turns to Cheryl again. "What does that mean Cheryl?" Cheryl responds in a deep tone as she stares Leslie eye to eye. "It means you may be a permanent resident in this hospital if you don't drop it. Christy is recuperating over here, you're making her upset." Christy laughs grabbing her stomach to buffer her pain. "You two crack me up!" "I'm the one keeping her alive Christy, you know that Christy?" Cheryl says. Leslie shrugs off Cheryl. "Whatever Cheryl. You think because you beat me up in high school, that you can still beat me up with your words now that I'm grown." "I can," Cheryl responds. This angers Leslie. "Oh yeah, I'd like to see you try it Cheryl, I dare you."

Cheryl calmly laughs as she glances at Christy. Cheryl points to the bed next to Christy. "She will be joining you by tonight babe. She will be in that bed right over there." Christy laughs again. As her laugh diminishes, she responds, "I don't think Mark would do anything like that, not in a million years. Funny thing though." "What's that?" asks Cheryl. "I do remember seeing him standing by my car before we argued, right before the accident." "That's weird" Leslie responds. Cheryl is curious.

"What, he was just standing there like he was waiting for you?"

"Yes," Christy says.

"What did he say?" asks Cheryl.

"He didn't say anything, he just stared at me."

"So?" Leslie responds. Christy answers.

"So, I never saw Mark go down to the garage for anything but leaving to go home."

Christy stares at the T.V. screen for a minute. "I heard your job closed its doors," Cheryl says. "Oh, yeah?" Christy asks. Leslie then responds. "Christy, it's been all over the news." "Well, I've been in a coma, so I missed that part of my life." Christy responds agitated. Leslie explains what happened. "Christy, the CEO disappeared, and they think he left the country." "Really?" Christy asks. "Christy, the Feds went to his house and both him and his wife were gone. They left behind all their furniture, expensive clothes, and their four expensive cars were still in the garage. "Wow, that's crazy," Christy says. "Tell me about it," Leslie says as she continues her babbling. "His clients lost millions the news said." "I guess I won't be getting that bonus then," Christy says. "Bonus?" Cheryl asks. "Yes, we were all supposed to get bonuses for the quarter. Mr. Boykins promised us, well, I mean all the top people that we would."

The thought of the situation takes Cheryl back a moment. "Wow Christy, that's deep. You have some money saved up though right?" "Yeah, but not much. I still have my expensive car payment, insurance and house payment with utilities." "You mean, you had an expensive car with insurance payments." Christy ponders the comment. "Oh yeah, you are right. My mind is not working on all its cylinders right now." Christy laughs at her own response. "Oh well, guess I didn't need that car anymore." Leslie waves her hand at Christy to get her attention. "Oh, you'll get another one, same style and color, I know you will. A car like that, your insurance will just write it off and get you another one." "I guess," Christy says.

The room is quiet for a moment as the T.V. plays showing the news around the world. "Are you getting any sleep?" Cheryl asks. "No, well, I did sleep soundly last night for the first time since being here, but I've been having a lot of nightmares." Leslie is curious. "Oh really, what about?" Christy is hesitant to tell. "Oh, you know, about the accident and stuff like that." "So, you do remember the accident?" Cheryl asks. Christy mind scrambles. "Well, it's hard to say what it is or what I remember. It's like you're in something, but you don't know what it is until you're in it, then you snap out of it." Leslie laughs aloud. "Girl, you sound like they doped you up with a lot of medicine," Leslie says.

Christy stares at the T.V. for a moment. "I'll tell you two about my nightmares, but I am feeling tired right now." Cheryl glances at her watch. "Yeah, well I think we'd better go and let you get your rest. I have to stop by my sister's house; she just had a new baby." "Oh, yeah, that's right, what did she have?" Christy asks. "A boy." Cheryl responds. "Wow," Christy says. "She's happy now because she wanted a son. She wants to see her son to become a baseball player on T.V." Cheryl and Leslie prepare to leave. "Tell her I said hello," Christy replies as they hug her individually. "I sure will," Cheryl says as they all finish hugging each other. "We'll stop back by on Friday," Cheryl responds. "Okay, thanks for coming by you two." "You bet," Leslie says. The two girls leave waving goodbye to Christy as she waves back at them in return.

Mark Collins is packed and ready to catch his flight to Bangkok. As he stands in his kitchen wearing a black polo shirt with matching jeans and casual Gorgio Armani black textured "Chukka" sneakers checking messages on his cell phone, it rings. He answers it. "Hello?" The voice on the other end, is his business partner Steve Messer, a computer geek. He got Marks company up and running for him in Bangkok. Steve's call is from Bangkok. "Hey man, everything is all set up here, just wanted to give you a buzz to let you know. When is your flight arriving?" Mark glances at his platinum Rolex watch with diamond studded numbers. "Seven p.m. your time." "Good, really good. All the computers are set up totaling thirty." "That's great Steve. Our employees are scheduled to report on Monday." "Yes, I heard. That's great. Our WIFI is booming bud. We will be able to access clients as far as Gilligan's Island bro." Steven laughs. "I like the sound of that man. I don't know what I'd do without you coming on as my partner, you're the man." "I know, I know, keep the encouragement coming, I'm stroking my ego right now, you should see my brush." Mark laughs aloud. "You are ridiculous."

"Hey, what about that girl named "Christy you were talking about hiring, you know the one you used to work with? Is she coming with you?" Steven asks.

"Oh, no man."

"What?"

"She got into a car wreck."

"No way."

"Yeah, a semi-truck ran over her car."

"Wow Mark, what a way to go huh?"

"No, she lived Steve."

"What? Wait, you just said she got ran over by a semi-truck. And you're telling me she lived?"

"Yes."

"Wow dude, that sounds like something out of a Die-Hard movie. Will she be coming aboard after she recovers?"

"I'm hoping because, she's got a long road to recovery."

"I bet, jeez. Well, she knows what we're doing right, I mean, you told her everything right?"

"I told her a little bit, but I doubt if she remembers from the accident."

"It's a good thing you didn't, she might accidently tell someone everything."

"She wouldn't do that, she's a tough girl. She could turn you into a muffin if she wanted to. She's hardnosed."

"Whatever you say man, I mean you should know. Can't wait to meet her when she comes on board though."

"I'm going to fill her in little by little to see where she is at after the accident." "And let's say if you tell her about our scheme, what if she doesn't go along with it?"

The phone is silent.

"She will." "Yeah man, but what if she doesn't?"

"I'm telling you she will, we go as far back as high school. I know her like a book."

The phone is silent again.

"Steve, you worry too much."

"And that's what the guy in the movie Goodfellas said, and you see what happened to him when he thought he was about to get made?"

Mark laughs on the other end of the phone as Steve continues talking.

"I want to know up front who I'm dealing with before I get whacked."

Mark laughs again as he glances down at his watch again. "Well, I will see you in a bit my friend. You're picking me up, right?" "Yeah, unless you like riding in cabs out here, or better yet, on the back of a moped. Cabs are hard to get with so many people out here." "I bet. Okay, I'll call you as soon as the wheel's touch down there." "Okay, later man." "Bye." Mark ends the call as he smiles thinking about how much money he will make in his Ponzi Scheme. He grabs his carry-on bag and one piece of luggage sliding the carry-on bag over his shoulder as he heads out the front door of his high-rise apartment in downtown Atlanta, Georgia. Mark enters the elevator that takes him down to the parking garage. Mark exits the elevator rolling his luggage behind him. The luggage wheels echo a grinding sound on the pavement of the underground garage.

Mark approaches his car, a jet black two door 2014 Maserati Grand Turismo with 22-inch custom black wheels machine faced and striped. He hits the alarm button on his alarm key pad. The alarm beeps three times along with the trunk button that causes the trunk open. Mark places his luggage inside as he grabs his thin leather jacket from the trunk wearing it. The jacket fits him like a glove. Mark closes the trunk while glancing at his watch. He enters his car and turns over the ignition as the Maserati's engine growls, then hums as the engine idles. Mark presses down on the clutch with his left foot while placing the stick shift in gear. Mark releases the clutch and drives away heading towards the garage exit.

The car cruises up to the gate monitoring system. The car stops as Mark enters in his personal code to open the gate. The steel gate opens sliding to the right side of Mark's car. The Maserati's blue halogen headlights flash onto the streets of downtown Atlanta like a black panther coming out into the night searching for its prey. All the other vehicles are plane is comparison to Mark's. Some motorists stare at his car as he enters the main street. The engine of the Maserati revs as it speeds off down the street. On that same street waiting for Mark's car, is a black Chevy Tahoe with tinted windows. It pulls in behind Mark as he approaches a red light a mile down. Mark checks both mirrors with his left foot still on the clutch, and the gear shift in first gear.

Ten seconds later, the black Chevy Tahoe pulls alongside the Maserati to the left. Mark glances at it for a quick second as he checks his cell phone. Cars cross the intersection in front of the Maserati and Tahoe. The passenger window of the Chevy Tahoe rolls down half way with Mark unaware. As he glances at his messages while looking up at the light waiting for it to change, a hand extends from the passenger window of the Tahoe. In that hand is a chrome nickel plated semi-automatic hand gun with a silencer. Mark glances to his left in slow motion.

Mark sees through his window, Nathaniel. Nathaniel smiles the smile of The Joker from a Batman movie. As Mark stares at Nathaniel, the shininess of the gun attracts his attention immediately. In reflex, Mark let's go of the clutch with the Maserati still in first gear as Nathaniel fires his gun hitting the driver's side triangular window shattering it along with the back window. The Maserati jolts forward like a tiger running towards its prey causing the car to go zero to thirty in five seconds. The Maserati darts across the intersection nearly missing passing cars as it slices through the oncoming traffic nearly getting T-Boned by one car going north. Car horns sound off as other cars approach the chaotic intersection. The Maserati speeds down the main street with Mark shifting gears like a professional as his heart tries to keep up with his fear. He checks his rear-view mirror frequently as he drives. The headlights of the Tahoe appear from a distance as the traffic keeps it snared from its target.

      Mark focuses on the road as he makes a hard-right turn on a residential street. The Maserati fish tails as Mark tries to straighten it while shifting hard into third gear. The Tahoe finally makes it through the intersection as it barrels down the street on the trail of the Maserati. Mark glances in his rear-view mirror looking for any sign of the Tahoe's headlights behind him. He sees nothing but total darkness. Mark makes a hard-left turn. The power of the Maserati under estimates Marks ability to drive it as it fish tails again spinning the car around. Now pointed in the opposite direction Mark was headed, he waits as smoke overcasts the Maserati as it appears like a night commercial advertisement for Maserati Incorporated.

Mark mad at himself for losing control of his vehicle, quickly starts the engine again, but it does not turn over right away. In Marks mind, he knows Nathaniel is on his way to finish the job. Mark turns over the ignition again, and this time the engine engages. Mark presses the clutch down with the car in gear, he spins the tires heading in the direction the car is pointed. Suddenly, the Tahoe appears turning down the street the Maserati is headed. Mark keeps his left foot on the clutch as his right foot jams on the brake. Nathaniel leans out of the window at the Tahoe approaches Marks car. Mark quickly shifts the car in reverse as it backs up speeding down the street with gun fire following behind it. The Maserati's engine revs to high performance as bullets wiz past Marks head through his windshield as both the Maserati and Tahoe wiz past the parked cars too fast to read the addresses of the houses the cars reside.

Mark ducks as pieces of glass hit his face followed by sharp projectiles. An older man looking through his picture window before getting ready for bed, is stunned by the speed of the Maserati and Tahoe as they pass by. Moments later as the Maserati approaches a main street, Mark whips the steering wheel around allowing both hands to slide over the steering wheel with finesse until its center point is obtained. At this point, Mark grips the steering wheel hard with both hands allowing his car to straighten up as he slams on the brakes. The Tahoe flies right by him. Mark shifts the car in gear like a mad man impressed with himself as is the Maserati. The Tahoe now faraway in a distance backs up and turns onto the main street Mark is on with its headlights on high beam status telling Mark, "I'm coming for you."

    Mark is fifteen minutes away from the airport. His flight leaves in an hour. What does he do? His car speeds through intersections running red lights as the Tahoe trails. The Maserati corner like it was on rails. As the Tahoe approaches the same corner, it's driver, Nathaniel's twin brother Aaron realizes he should not do the same unless he rolls his vehicle over, so he brakes hard when making the turn. Mark makes another quick left onto a residential street. "Turn left!" Nathaniel yells at his brother from inside the Tahoe. The Tahoe makes the hard-left turn as the twin brothers see the tail lights of the Maserati at the end of the block. They slow down cautiously approaching Marks car. The Tahoe halts as Nathaniel calmly steps out looking around for any nosy neighbors that might witness a murder.

    There is none as Nathaniel approaches the right side of the Maserati. He slowly pulls out his gun holding it at his side. He reaches for the door handle pulling it open as he twists his body kneeling inside the car. The car is empty, but three blocks over, Mark is running down the street with his shoulder bag. As he approaches a side street, he sees a yellow car coming with a marker light highlighted with the word Airport above it. Mark sighs with relief as he waves at the cab driver who notices him. The cab slows down pulling over towards Mark. Mark can't wait for the cab to stop as he extends his hand out to catch the rear door handle. Finally, the cab stops and Mark hops into the back seat. The cab drives away.

Back at the scene, Nathaniel, and his brother Aaron, drive away from the abandoned bullet riddled Maserati. Inside Aarons Tahoe, the two get into an argument.

"Nate, I'm not torching my truck, forget that!"

"Aaron, this truck is hot right now! We just went on a high-speed chase, you don't think anyone recognized this truck?"

"No, I don't."

"Well I do. We got to torch it."

"No, we don't, I love this truck. Why didn't we use your car?"

"Because Aaron, it's better to have a higher vehicle, that way you can't miss."

Aaron is not buying it.

"No way. You always do this."

"Do what Aaron?"

"You always use somebody else to do your dirty work."

Nathaniel laughs.

"What are we on, some talk show? You better do what I tell you to do because Uncle Boykins said if we don't get the job done were in trouble."

"Well, he didn't tell me that," Aaron says.

"You were standing right there when he said it, you moron!" Nathan says.

"I was there, but he said it to you, not me."

Nathaniel notices something.

"Hey, pull in here."

Aaron is confused.

"Where?"

Nathaniel points to where he wants his brother to go.

"Over here, right in here."

"For what?"

"Just do it!"

Aaron turns into a vacant lot on an abandoned industrial building. Nathaniel glances in the passenger mirror then quickly opens the door as the Tahoe comes to a complete stop. Aaron throws up his hands.

"What's going on?"

Nathaniel says nothing as he leaves the passenger door wide open. Aaron sits in his truck waiting for his brother to come back, but he doesn't. Aaron glances around but doesn't see him. Finally, he decides to get out of his truck. As he walks to the back of it, he sees Nathaniel standing off at a distance with his gun drawn pointed at the gas tank of the Tahoe.

Aaron mad, yells at his brother. "What are you doing?" "Run little brother," Nathaniel says as he aims and fires at the gas tank. Aaron yells at him. "No!" Aaron runs for cover as two shots ring out hitting the gas tank. The Tahoe's gas tank explodes as it buckles lifting the tires from the pavement. The Tahoe is engulfed in flames as Aaron turns around facing his brother. "Are you crazy!" Nathaniel says nothing as he pulls out his cell phone dialing three numbers. A person on the other end answers. Nathaniel responds, "We need a pickup." The person responds. "On my way." Nathaniel ends the call and walks away leaving his brother standing alone gawking at his truck now turned into an inferno. Aaron rests his hands on his knees as he bends over inhaling and exhaling rapidly shaking his head in disbelief at what his brother did.

CHAPTER ELEVEN

"Nurse Mary"

At the hospital, Christy is wheeled around in a wheelchair by her nurse, "Nurse Mary." It is a nice break from being stuck in bed all day. The two take a trip downstairs to the gift shop. Inside, Christy grabs a fluffy stuffed dog that grabs her attention. "Ooh, I like this." Nurse Mary agrees. "I like it too, it's cute." Christy's face changes to disappointment as she remembers she left her money up in her room. "Oh gosh, I left my money up in my room." The nurse pulls out a twenty-dollar bill. "I'll pay for it, you can pay me when we get back up to your room."

Christy is surprised at the gesture. "Really?" "Yes, don't worry about it." "Thank you, Mary, you didn't have to do that." "Oh, it's no problem," She says. Christy graciously receives the twenty-dollar bill and pays for the stuffed animal. The cash register attendant hands her the remaining change back. "Thank you," Christy responds. "Thank you for shopping with us," the cashier attendant replies. Nurse Mary and Christy leave the store and make their way back up to the room. Mary assists Christy back into her bed. "Thank you, Mary." "You're welcome." Christy reaches over pulling out her purse from the cabinet. She reaches in her wallet, and hands Nurse Mary a twenty-dollar bill. "You know what, you keep that

Christy." Christy is surprised by the gesture. "No, Mary, here, I have to pay you back, please take it."

Nurse Mary shakes her head no as she takes her hand pushing Christy's hand with the twenty-dollar bill inside, away from her. "No, consider it my blessing to you." "Oh, come on Mary, you take it, you might need this." Mary laughs. "You act like that's my last twenty-dollar bill I will ever have. Honey, this stuffed dog just cheered you up. You were looking sad when I picked you up. I'm glad that this stuffed animal did that for you, because I noticed you've been down lately and you need to be happy. Happiness is a choice we make every day Christy, it doesn't just fall on us. Circumstances do, but not happiness. Don't let this setback you've experienced, take the joy out of your life." Christy stares at the stuffed animal. She agrees with Mary. "Okay, your right Mary." "You have that fighting spirit within you Christy, use it." "Thank you, Mary, no one has ever said that to me before." Christy pulls the bed covers up half way over her body.

Christy pauses as she thinks. "Nurse Mary?" Nurse Mary is checks Christy's medical chart. "Yes baby?" "I don't know how to ask this question but, have you ever thought about why you are here on this earth?" Mary smiles. "Oh, no honey, I'm just happy to be here, but that is something to think about though. Do you know why you're here?" Nurse Mary asks. Christy pauses as she thinks about it. "No, I just thought you might know?" They laugh. Nurse Mary places her hand over Christy's hand. "Hey, at least we're in the same boat. I think, everyone should at least know why so they can help somebody else know why too." "I agree Mary. I've been thinking about that a lot lately. I'm trying to find my purpose here on earth after my accident. I know that after my accident, I was told I'm not supposed to be here, but I'm here." "You're a miracle honey, be thankful."

    Nurse Mary checks Christy's vitals as she stands by her beside. "I've seen a lot in this hospital. Some people come in, and never leave. Some people don't make it here at all. Your one of the few. We never know why some make it and some don't, and those that don't make it, we don't know if they would be suffering while being here from their injuries. Make the best of the life that you know because tomorrow is never promised. The best you can do Christy is treat people the way you want to be treated. You will be surprised to know that one person you were kind to can really change the way they feel about themselves." "Mary, I need to tell you this. I had this awful experience during my accident. I saw myself leaving my body and I went to this awful place. I think it was a place like hell or a place before people go to hell." "You experienced this?" "Yes, and I'm not lying because my friend Jessica was there. She said the place was called Hades. There was darkness everywhere and fire."

Mary has a concerned look on her face. "Did you tell anyone about this experience Christy?" Christy whispers as she speaks. "No, Mary, I mean if I told anyone what experienced they would look at me the way you're looking at me and lock me up in some psych ward."

Nurse Mary laughs as she lays her hand on Christy's shoulder. "No, they wouldn't honey." "Yes, they would. So, you believe what I experienced?" "I've heard of people telling stories about their out of body experiences. Christy, who am I to tell somebody that they are lying about what they experienced? That's their experience, not mine."

      Nurse Mary's eyes look up to the ceiling as she thinks about what she will say next. "What you experience, it's like something you can't explain because you've never experienced that before. No one can really understand that unless they experience it the same." "Mary, what I saw, and where I was, you don't ever want to go here." "It was that bad Christy?" "Yes, Mary." Mary notices the concern on Christy's face. "You know Christy, that's where bad people go come to think of it." "No, Mary, my friend Jessica told me, anyone who denies Jesus and his salvation go to this place. It's not because you were bad or mean, it's because of sin that we inherited from the beginning of Adam and Eve in the Garden of Eden. We inherited their sin when they disobeyed God and gave the power he gave them to rule the earth and every living thing over to the devil." "Wow, Christy, no one has ever told me that, not even my pastor at church, well, not the way you explained it."

Christy sits completely up in her bed gesturing with her hands at Mary. "That's why the world is the way it is Mary. All the bad stuff Mary, pure evil like murders, babies and kids dying, sickness, disease, pain, sufferings, floods, tornadoes, all the destructive things you can think of, is the reason we see it or experience it. This is what my best friend Jessica told me in this place. She was murdered by her boyfriend when we were in high school. I saw the bruises of the beating he gave her on her face." "And you saw her in this place?" "Yes." "Who else did you see that you can remember?" "There were tons of people, I mean so many people Mary." Christy pauses for a second. "I do remember seeing this man in a cell. He had a short trimmed black mustache with black hair and torn clothes with a swastika on it. He looked like Hitler, that's all I know." "Oh, my gosh Christy, that's scary." "I know Mary. I wouldn't tell you this if I didn't mean what I saw. It was horrible."

"This place sounds like hell Christy." "It's not though. That's what Jessica said." "So, how did you get out of this place?" "I...I don't know, the next thing I knew I was back on the operation table being worked on by the doctors. This happened two or three times I think. I've never been so scared in my life Mary. Why do you think this happened to me? Does it happen to everyone that dies, and the doctor brings them back to life?" "I don't know Christy. Have you ever been born again?" "What?" "Born again, you know, a Christian?" "No, what is that?" "It's like giving your heart to God." "Why, are you one?" "Me, no I'm not one, but my sister is." Nurse Mary pauses for a moment. "She said when she first became born again, something changed on the inside of her. In her heart she wanted to do the what was right all the time. She said on the outside she didn't feel any different. She acted the same, still slept around with other guys, but on the inside, she didn't feel the same anymore. She wanted to settle down with one guy and get married having kids. She got tired of one-night stands and so, she stopped."

"Gradually, I could see a change in her from the outside the same as what she talked about her change on the inside." Christy thinks to herself. "I kind of get what you're saying now." "You do?" "I guess." "Well that's good because I'm trying to understand what I just said myself." They laugh together. "Christy, what you experienced, and the fact that your still here, tells me, you are blessed. Hell, or Hades as you said it was not good baby. That experience, where you said your spirit went, that's associated with evil, like the devil." "What does that mean then?" Christy asks. Mary pauses for a moment. "I think that either God is trying to tell you, you need to make a major decision about your life now before it's too late. You are at the point that, the devil is trying to take your life and your soul. You need to let God be a part of your life and not him."

Christy thinks about what Mary says. "Would you?" "Most definitely honey. That experience would open my eyes quick, but it shouldn't take that for any of us. From what my sister said, God is good, the devil is bad. She said, we all need God because he created us all right? I know I do. I don't know what I'm waiting for Christy, God knows I don't want to experience what you did. Look honey, rich, poor, smart, dumb, cute, ugly, we all need God period. We are not as smart as we think we are at running our lives. If we did, we'd all be rich, in great health always, no problems, no trials, our lives would be perfect. But if you look around the world, nobody's life is perfect even though it may look perfect on the outside Christy, every day somebody's life is messed up." "That was me Mary. I had it all before my accident. Perfect job, boyfriend, home, car, money in the bank, everything. Then one day, my life changed forever. On the inside, I can honestly say I was a fraud, never happy. You know, it's tough when you're trying to control everything." Mary finishes checking Christy's legs. "How do they feel?" "They're still sore, I can feel the pain coming and going." "Do you want some more pain pills?" "No, I can tuff it out. I don't want to get addicted to them." "I understand. Well, hit that button if you need me." "Okay, hey, thanks again for the stuffed animal." "No problem Christy, he's your new roommate now," Nurse Mary says.

    At approximately 11:30 p.m. Mark arrives at the airport. He rushes to his flight while wiping the sweat from his forehead. The thought of someone trying to take his life disturbs him. He walks briskly while looking back at the entrance from where he came in, to see if anyone looking suspicious is following him. The airport is scarce of passengers arriving or planning to leave out of the airport. A loud voice speaks over the P.A. system inside the airport. "Joseph Stevens, please dial 1128. Joseph Stevens, please dial 1128." Mark removes his jacket allowing his body to cool down along with his carry-on bag from his right arm. He finally makes it to his terminal for his flight. As he approaches the front desk of Turkish Airlines, he opens the side zipper of his bag to retrieve his passport. His hand shuffles inside the compartment looking for it. He can't find it. Mark begins to panic. To get his mind off the fear that is about to attack his confidence, Mark retrieves his wallet from his back pocket retrieving his I.D. and handing it to the ticket agent. Sweat begins to form on his forehead again as Mark slowly checks another compartment for his passport. His eyes glance down inside and to his surprise, his passport awaits him.

    Mark realizes he placed the passport in the wrong compartment. He hands her the passport graciously receiving it with a smile. "Thank you. Will there be any other carry-on luggage?" She asks. "Just this bag," Mark says. "Any cargo luggage that you checked in?" Mark quickly thinks about his suitcase he left in the trunk of his car. "No, this is all I have." "Okay, your all set, your flight will be leaving in fifteen minutes." She hands Mark his ticket for boarding. He receives it in his hand as he glances around for a seat. Mark finds one deciding to sit close to be the first on board. About fifteen minutes later, the Boarding Agent announces Marks flight. "Passengers boarding Flight 248 from Atlanta to Istanbul arriving at 4:40 p.m. Thursday, with a connecting flight from Istanbul at 1:20 a.m. Friday, and arriving in Bangkok by 2:50 p.m. Your flight is ready for boarding. All passengers boarding, we would ask that you present your boarding pass to me before boarding your flight. Thank you for choosing Turkish Airlines for travel, we hope you will have an enjoyable flight." Mark stands to his feet as he glances around again looking for anyone suspicious. The coast is clear as he proceeds to line up with a long line of passengers mainly of foreign decent.

Meanwhile, on the streets of Atlanta, a patrol car with its flashing lights sits parked behind Marks black Maserati. Inside of the patrol car, the officer radios in, the license plate of the car and its owner to dispatch. "Yes dispatch, I have a black 2014 Maserati Grand Turismo with custom wheels here on Clover street East of downtown. Dispatch, the license plate number is "Echo, Charlie, David, 1153." The officer waits for dispatch to respond. "Roger car 33, that was "ECD-1153, that vehicle is registered to a Mark Collins of Atlanta, Georgia age 35." "Roger dispatch, the car is unoccupied and appears to be full of bullet holes. I'm going to do a search." "Roger car 33. Two units are in route to assist." "Roger dispatch, thank you."

On the plane at the airport, Mark takes his seat. He sighs in relief to an adventurous night he never signed up for. As he rests his head back on the head rest of his seat, he's thinking that the police officers are probably at his car right now running his license plate. Passengers file inside the plane making their way to their paid seat. Luggage compartments pop open as passengers place their carry-on luggage inside of it. Mark stares out of his window seat at the night light of the airport tarmac. "This is going to be a long flight," he whispers to himself. As Mark closes his eyes, a young lady in her mid-twenties sits down next to him on his left side. Mark slowly opens his eyes. "Hi!" the young lady responds.

    Mark slowly turns his head to respond. "Hi." The young lady extends her hand. "My name is Janice." Mark reaches his right hand towards her hand, as they give each other a handshake. "Nice to meet you," Janice says. "Nice to meet you too, I'm Mark." Janice stands up placing some of her belongings into the luggage compartment above, then she sits down again getting comfortable. As Mark closes his eyes again, Janice begins talking. "So, where are you headed?" Mark opens his left eye first as his right eye follows. "I'm headed to Bangkok." "Oh, nice, I'm headed to Istanbul to see a friend, then from there, I'm going back home to Paris then back to Atlanta." Mark doesn't say anything. Janice continues talking as the plane begins to taxi on the runway. "Have you ever been to Paris?"

Mark, trying to prepare himself for the long flight, slowly responds.

"Once, on a business trip."

Meanwhile outside, the plane is waiting for its cue to takeoff as it stops on the runway. This gives Janice reason to ask more questions.

"What do you do?"

"I was with a Marketing and Investment firm in Atlanta, now I have my own business doing the same thing in Bangkok."

"Oh, wow, bet you make a lot of money huh?"

"I do pretty good."

"Let me guess, I bet you drive a fancy car too."

"Maybe."

"A Ferrari?"

"No," Mark says.

"A Lamborghini?"

"No."

"What then?"

Mark pauses for a moment knowing his response will lead to more questions. Outside, the plane begins to take off on the runway moving at a high rate of speed. Inside the plane, the silence is killing Janice, not literally though.

"Tell me Mark, come on."

"I drive a Maserati."

Janice is excited.

"I knew it!"

Mark's eyes open wide.

"How?"

"Because you look like a guy with a lot of money."

The plane is in the air heading towards the clouds. Janice thinks for a moment as her eyes look straight ahead in a daze.

"Wait a minute. You said you drive a Maserati?"

"Yes."

As the plane levels off, Janice glances over at Mark.

"What color?"

"Black, why?"

"Because, when my cab picked me up to bring me to the airport, there was a black sports car sitting shot up on my street with its lights still on. I asked the cabbie what kind of car it was, and he said it was a Maserati."

"Is, that right?" Mark asks.

"Yes. Was that yours?"

Mark responds in a shocked tone.

"Why would you think that car could be mine?"

Janice laughs.

"The coincidence Mark. Life is like a puzzle, figuring out what the word is."

"Okay then," Mark responds as he looks away from Janice straight ahead.

"Relax Mark, you are acting very defensive right now which leads me to believe that car just might be yours."

Mark is silent as Janice continues talking.

"I wonder what that person did to get their car all shot up like that?"

"How would I know?" Mark mumbles to himself.

"You wouldn't," Janice says.

Janice unfastens her seatbelt.

"This world is going crazy by the minute huh?" She asks.

"I guess."

"I mean, this is an amazing world, but people just don't have sense enough to live in it."

"That would be an understatement," Mark replies.

"I think, if people had love for one another, there wouldn't be any violence at all, you know?"

"I hear you loud and clear. Are you a motivational speaker or something?" Mark asks.

Janice smiles at Mark.

"No, I'm taking classes on human behavior. In this book, it says, all of us have choices either good or bad. No one can make you make bad choices, we make them on our own."

"I agree with that," Mark says.

"Then we have the audacity to blame God for it, all the while the devil is laughing his butt off because we're blaming the one person who created us all."

The comment grabs Marks attention as he turns his head to respond.

"So, who do we blame for all the evil in this world?"

"The devil, who else? But wait a minute, he doesn't exist right?"

"I never thought about whether he did or didn't."

"You know Mark, the greatest thing the devil did, was convince the world he doesn't exist. He already made his choice, which is hell, he must ride this thing we call time out until he gets justice from God for all the trouble he has caused humanity. All he can hope for is taking as many people he can with him to his doom. It says that in John 10:10, the thief comes to kill, steal, and destroy us."

Mark nods his head in agreement.

"Misery love company huh?"

"You bet."

Mark turns away looking out the window.

"That's pretty scary to think about Janice."

Janice begins to close her eyes.

"We are all sheep Mark, remember that."

"Were what?"

"Sheep, I mean, that's what the bible refers to us. Sheep need a shepherd because they get lost and they do stupid things sometimes. If they don't have an over seer, they are easy prey for wolves."

"Is that right? You are a wise young lady Janice."

Mark closes his eyes as the two of them drift off to sleep.

Back in an Atlanta area hospital, Christy lays in bed watching T.V. until she is surprised with flowers from Angela Harmon walking in along with and a card in her hand. Christy sees her out of the corner of her eye. Angie stands peaking around the curtain. "Hi," Angela responds. Her presence catches Christy off guard as she sits up in her bed. "Oh, hi," She says. "How are you feeling?" Angie asks. Christy swallows before she answers. "I'm okay, thanks for asking." "I brought you a card and some flowers." Angela hands them to Christy as she graciously receives it. "Thank you."

Angela glances around the room. "Is it okay if I sit?" Christy is fixed on the flowers and how radiant they are as she realizes a question was asked. "Oh yeah, sure, sit down please." Angela sits getting comfortable in her chair as she clears her throat. "I know you are wondering why I came to see you or how I knew you were here but, I saw the accident on the news and I recognized your car and name along with your picture flashed on the T.V. screen. I immediately started praying for you." Christy instantly responds. "Thank you, I appreciated it." "Oh, you don't have to thank me, I wanted to. So, how are you feeling?" "Oh, I'm getting much better. I have trouble walking. I'm supposed to have therapy soon." Christy points to the wheelchair in the corner of the room. "I've been driven around by that thing over there."

"That's a cool machine," Angie jokes. It causes Christy to laugh. They both become silent as Christy sits straight up in her bed as she opens the "Get Well" card reading it silently to herself. Angela glances up at the T.V. screen. "This is a beautiful card Angela, thank you." "You are welcome," Angie replies. Christy places the card on the rolling cart tray next to her bed next to the flowers nearby. Angela disregards the current new on T.V. and musters the nerve to speak her feelings. "Christy, I came here to be friends with you hoping that we can put the past behind us?" Christy remains silent as the words sink into her soul. She nods her head agreeing. "I agree. I want to apologize for the way I treated you and for putting you through unnecessary injustices, I was wrong. Can you forgive me?" "Most definitely, and I want to apologize to you for responding the way I did yelling at you. I knew better, I just let my emotions get the best of me."

They glance at each other for a moment, then smile simultaneously breaking the ice of confrontation. "So, when are they going to let you leave this place?" Christy's not sure about the question. "I really don't know, they said I'm improving a lot, but I still have some little ways to go. I guess in a month maybe?" "That's not far away," Angela says. "I know, it's just a guess. I hope so though, but I still have these headaches and my left side gets numb sometimes." "So, do you remember what happened the day of the accident?" "I don't remember much; the police said my left wheel came off my car." "The left wheel?" "Yeah," Christy says. "Well, how did that happen?" "Beats me. I do remember arguing with Mark in the parking garages." "What about?" "I don't remember." Christy pauses. "Then I got on the freeway and my steering wheel was hard to control." "What do you mean?" "I couldn't keep my car straight, and that's the last thing I remember."

"Wow, Christy, you are blessed to be here." "I guess," Christy says. "No, it's not a guess Christy, you could have died." "Actually, I did?" "What?" "The doctors said I died twice and they had to revive me." "Oh, my gosh," Angie responds. "Yes, that's what I said," Christy says as she stares in a daze at the foot of her bed. "You're a Christian right Angela?" Angela softly responds. "Yes I am." Christy pauses for a moment as she turns her head towards her. "When I died, I felt myself leaving my body." Angela takes a deep breath as she swallows deeply before responding. "You did?" Christy nods her head. "I've never been so scared in my life." Christy pauses again as tears begin to form in her eyes. "I could not stop it and for me to be out of control like that was terrifying." Tears stream down her face from both eyes as if they were racing towards the finish line of her chin.

    Angie leans forward placing her right hand onto Christy's as she responds. "It's okay, you're here alive." "Angela, I could remember everything I did to everyone that was bad. My entire life was flashing in front of my eyes like a movie screen. I couldn't stop it, pause it, or speed it up. I especially remembered the things that I did to you Angela?" Angela tries to calm Christy down. "Calm down Christy please, I forgive you. You're getting yourself too worked up about this. Please." Christy wipes away her tears grabbing a Kleenex from the box sitting on her bed.

Christy continues. "I remember the coldness I felt as my body traveled through a state of total darkness into this dark place where it smelled so bad, I wanted to throw up every minute. There were things on the walls all around me."

"Things?"

"Yes, like huge spiders, centipedes, stuff you be afraid to kill if you saw them in your home this size because they didn't look like your normal insects Angela. They looked hideous. I saw my best friend named Jessica. We were in high school together. She died when she was murdered at seventeen by her boyfriend."

"What did she say?" asks Angela.

"She told me the place was Hades." "Hades?" "Yeah, a place before hell." "Oh." "Didn't you know that?" "I know about hell in the book of Revelations. I'm not aware of Hades. Really, I don't think about that much, because I don't want to go to either of those places Christy, that's why I chose to follow God." "I agree with you there Angie. Is it okay if I called you Angie?" "Yeah, for sure." Angie pauses for a moment. "So, what else happened?" Christy continues. "So, I'm down there and I remember feeling this awful pain all over my body, it had to be from my accident because I could remember the pain before I went in and out of consciousness in the back of the ambulance. Jessica was in this cage and I couldn't get her out. She was yelling at me to get out of there."

"Yelling at you?" Angie asks.

"She was so scared, and I was too. There were people all over the place screaming and yelling, begging to get out. Some were calling for their loved ones and many calling on God to save them."

Angela shakes her head as she imagines every detail.

"Christy, this is too much. Are you sure this is what you saw and maybe it wasn't the effect the accident that caused you to imagine this?"

"I know what I saw Angie. How could I make something up like this? I wouldn't even know how to create such a story. Hollywood might, but not me. This stuff is way too accurate for even me to believe."

"I didn't say you were lying Christy, it's just, well, I've never experienced anything like this, that's for sure, but in the book of Revelation things like this are described."

Christy stares at Angela's serious expression.

"I know what I experienced Angie, and I will never forget it, ever. Remember when asked me at work where would I go if I died, and I told you in the ground like everyone else?" Angela remembers and laughs. "Yes, I do." "You gave me two choices, heaven or hell. Now you were right because I ended up in one of the choices you gave me. How could that be if I believed neither of those places existed, right?"

Angela nods her head in agreement. "You are right Christy."

"Okay then, I know what I experienced was not made up. Angela, everything around us existed by someone greater than us. I mean, who created us, we sure didn't create ourselves. The earth, the oceans, man didn't create that, someone greater did, and that must be God. Therefore, you would have to have faith believing in that and you've never seen God face to face, at least not yet," Christy says. "Thank God, because I'm not ready to go just yet, I mean, I know God has a lot for me to do here." "That's what I'm trying to find out, my purpose for being here after all of this. We can't be here by accident just existing doing day to day things. God is much more creative than that right?" "Your teaching me something Christy, your exactly right."

Angela pauses for a minute. "So now you believe in God?"

"I do. I want God in my life because I really love him, and not out of fear after my experience."" Christy responds.

"That's great to hear Christy. I never wanted to push on you what I believed. I hoped that you would come to know and believe God personally for yourself.

That's what he wants for all of us." "I totally understand. He will show himself in your life." Angela hands Christy a book from her purse. The book is a devotional.

Christy receives the book. "Thank you," she says.

"This book will help you in your decision."

"Welcome back to life Christy."

Angela stands up leaning over to hug Christy.

"I'm going to go, so you can get some rest."

"Thanks for coming Angela."

"No problem, thanks for having me."

The two share phone numbers.

"I will call you and check to see how you are doing. wrote down your number on this phone. I'll stop by again to see you if that's okay."

"That would be great!" Christy says.

"You get some rest...bye," Angie responds.

"Bye Angela," Christy says.

Angela exits the room while Christy scans over the book she gave her.

Christy sits in her bed reading the book. The book tells a story about the creation of the humankind. The title reads,

"Making the Right Choice."

The first chapter reads,

"Your still here to make the right choice."

Many people have the chance to choose Christ who died for the sins of the world to be forgiven by God as he gave his life as a sacrifice for us. Why is Christ the only way to get to God face to face in his presence in Heaven? Because Jesus is his only son he sent one to die for the entire world to be free from the sin nature inherited by the world from Adam and Eve. This is documented in history. Only Jesus Christ did this. No one else died a violent death the way he did for the entire world the opportunity to be saved from eternal death.

Heaven was made for God's creation, humankind. Hell was created for the devil and his followers the fallen angels because they defied God in Heaven." Christy pauses for a moment from reading as she allows it all to sink in. She continues reading. What happened on that day the devil was kicked out of heaven, was like a teenager living with their parents. Then one day deciding to run things, telling their parents what to do, and how the house should be ran. The thought of this analogy is insane to the natural mind. Christy laughs to herself as she mumbles, "Yes, it is." She continues reading. God decided Lucifer now known as the devil had to go, so he put him out of Heaven. Lucifer was the Arche Angel before he became the devil or who we also call Satan.

His job in Heaven was Ministry of Music. He had rubies, diamonds, and all kinds of jewels under his wings and all over his body. They would clang together making harmonious sounds when he moved and spread his wings. He was beautiful. "Wow," Christy responds. He was God's creation above all the other angels with an anointing that covered the throne of God. But one day he became prideful and wanted all the attention and glory for himself. He concocted a group of followers who believed in him to follow him and possibly overthrow God in Heaven. God thought otherwise. There was a powerful shaking in Heaven beyond anything you could ever imagine.

God was so angry, Lucifer flew out of heaven like a bolt of lightning along with his followers the angels. They traveled at lighting speed out of Heaven, through the galaxies of space, past the clouds in the sky and landed with a loud boom. Christy eagerly asks herself while reading,

"Where...where did he land?"

As Christy continues reading, she finds the answer,

"Earth."

"What? No way," Christy says to herself.

She continues reading. When he landed on earth, he roamed the earth before the creation of humankind began. God gave Adam dominion over the earth and every living thing. After God created Eve for Adam because he wanted Adam to have a mate to share his life with, the devil appeared to Adam and Eve questioning them about what God told them about staying away from The Tree of the Knowledge of Good and Evil in the center of the Garden and Eve. There were two trees, but God told Adam and Eve not to touch the Tree of Knowledge.

"Wow," Christy says herself.

In that tree was the discernment between good and evil and every evil thing you could imagine. The sin nature of everything the devil portrayed when he rebelled against God was in that tree, rebellion, lying, cheating, sickness, disease, famine, murder, guilt, shame, depression, and suffering. That nature of the devil and his fallen angels were put on the earth, but they were not to be a problem because God gave Adam dominion and power over everything on the earth with Eve as his helpmate. The free will God gave them was to obey him or not obey. They never knew what was evil nor what sin was until…they chose to eat the fruit from the tree they were told not to. Christy approaches the end of the book reading intently. At that moment, sin was born into the entire world passed down to everyone. Christy is amazed the reading.

Why would they do that to us? Because they didn't know their decision would impact the entire world. Do you think if they did, they would have made the choice they did? The devil hoped for Adam and Eve to sin because he knew it would destroy them and humanity spiritually which is what we are beyond our earthly bodies. This was the devil's way at getting God back for throwing him out of the Heavens. He wanted to destroy the very thing that God created, and he succeeded until God decided to send his only son as a sacrifice to save the world from eternal death. Eternal death is spending eternity without God and God's presence living forever without him. That's why Jesus did what he did. The time to choose him is now. Don't wait until it's too late. He loves us more than we love ourselves and he wants nothing but the best for us. He wants us to know, the devil is nothing to him and he will take care of him in the end. God is love, he is good, the devil is hate, and everything that is evil."

CHAPTER TWELVE

"Rehab"

About ten hours in midflight, Mark is sound asleep. Janice suddenly opens her eyes and turns towards Mark noticing he is asleep. She glances around the plane noticing all the passengers nearby except for one, is asleep also. That person sits quietly with the small light on overhead reading a book. Janice quietly talks hoping Mark is listening and will respond. "It's amazing how quiet it gets on an airplane. I mean, it is total silence. Nothing to worry about, no drama, just silence. I think our lives should be that way, don't you?" Mark surprisingly responds with his eyes still closed. "That will never happen."

Janice smiles at Marks reply. "Why do you think that is?" "Because we live in an imperfect world with imperfect people. It's hard, practically impossible to ask for that. There will always be noise whether it is from me, you, or someone else." "But Mark, don't you want that?" "Want what?" "Peace to the point that you can still remain calm on the inside?" Mark opens his eyes. "Yes, I want that, but how could that be when you cannot control your circumstances around you?"

Janice lowers her head for a moment, then responds. "We can't control our circumstances." Mark is stoic as his comment stands on its own merit. "Exactly, that's why peace is impossible to have or try to get it." Janice disagrees. "I don't believe that. I believe you can still have peace regardless of what's going on around you." Janice pauses for a moment. "Mark, look out your window, tell me what you see?" Mark turns his head sideways to look out his window.

"I see total darkness, what's the point?" "Okay, you work in stock trading. I'm sure there have been times your back was against the wall and you didn't know what to do, total darkness. Then peace comes along and it's like turning on the light. Now you have direction, clear thinking. The darkness is still there, you just can't see it because of the light. That's what peace is. But you have a choice whether to access that peace or not."

Mark thinks hard about what Janice is saying. His silence explains how he feels. "I get it." Janice smiles. "You do?" "Yes, Can I ask you a question?" "Sure, shoot." "What do you do?" "What do you mean?" Janice asks. Mark turns to Janice. "You're asking me all these questions, I just thought you might be a reporter or something?" "I'm a journalist." "Oh, that explains it."

"So, Janice what would you say to someone who lost a job they loved, worked there for over twelve years and suddenly, that job was gone and there was nothing they could do about it? I'm asking you this because, that happened to me and when I looked for peace, it was nowhere to be found. I did find despair and you know what despair told me?"

"What?" Janice asks. "Do what you have to do to survive. So, I started my own job doing my own thing the way I wanted to do it making my own money the way I wanted to make it," Mark says nodding his head in pride. "Good for you Mark," Janice responds. "Just make sure you don't become bitter about your past," Janice replies. Mark becomes angry. "Why not, I was done wrong Janice! The company did me wrong not telling me we were in the hole when the head bosses knew all along!"

Janice shakes her head. "You sound bitter Mark." "No, I'm not!" "Yes, you are, listen to your voice, it is aggressive, like a lion arguing with other male lions about who's going to eat the deer first, calm down." Mark breathes heavily as he turns his head away from Janice. "I hear what you're saying Mark, just don't do what they did that got them in the situation in the first place."

Mark responds... "Capitalism has no boundaries Janice." "What?" Janice asks. "I said, Capitalism has no boundaries." "What do you mean?" "I mean, there are no limits to getting all the money in this world." "Okay, so your saying, you can make as much money you want to make what's the big deal Mark?" "I'm saying, I can do whatever I want." "Wait a minute Mark, are you saying you would steal from your clients?"

Mark's eyes stare at Janice through the darkness of the airplane then turns his head away. "Mark, how can you live with yourself knowing your screwing people over with their life savings?" Mark turns his head facing Janice. "We did it at DinoCore. Look, I don't make them invest with me. I offer them options to how they can make money off the money they have that they want to invest, that's all." "That's all, what, that's not enough? You know they're not going to get a return on what they invest Mark."

Mark's upper body twists facing Janice. "Listen young lady, it's a dog eat dog world out there, and I'd rather be the dog than the one that's getting eaten." Janice shakes her head disagreeing. "That's a great analogy Mark. I'll remember that when I pick some old man's pocket while walking down the street."

"That's not the same thing," Mark replies. "Oh yes, it is, the only difference is, he doesn't know me, or when I'm going to do it. Your clients know you and they trust you, they just don't know your screwing them out of their money until it's too late." "You know what, you don't know what you're talking about."

Mark stares at Janice.

"Are you with the SCC?"

"Who?"

"The SCC."

"Who are they?"

"They work for the stock exchange, monitoring companies to make sure they are on the up and up. Are you one of them?"

"No, I'm not, sorry to disappoint you."

"Then why you are asking me personal questions?"

"Because, I like to talk Mark, I'm just trying to make conversation with you. Is that bad?"

"No."

"Okay then. Trust me Mark, we can be friends."

"I have enough friends Janice."

"So, you say, but are they really your friends or just acquaintances?"

"I don't know and don't care, as long as they make me money."

"Is that all you care about Mark?"

"No, it's all I need."

"You need that peace we were talking about."

"I have peace when I'm making money."

"The right way or the wrong way?" Janice asks

"Does it matter, as long as I have it right?" Mark asks.

Janice laughs, "You sound like the devil."

"What?"

"The devil when he tells Jesus, I'll give you all the entire world if you do these things."

Mark laughs.

"Hey, that's not a bad deal."

Janice turns looking at Mark.

"You think?"

"Well yeah, I get to be the richest man in the world."

"Oh, yeah that's great when you're spending eternity in hell.

"At least I accomplished something, right?"

"Yes, you accomplished selling out your soul which was never meant for him to have."

"Then whose is it anyway?" Mark asks.

Janice turns to Mark, stares at him, "God's."

A month later, Christy leaves the hospital and entering a rehab facility. She is still on a walker as the rehabilitation facility workers help her regain her normal functions with her legs. During a rehab session, she smiles and laughs at times as the workers encourage her. After an extensive workout, Christy breathes heavily resting on the side railing. She is quickly given a chair by one of the orderlies named Alice. Christy graciously sits down.

"Thank you, Alice. Whew…that was a work out for sure."

"How do you feel Christy?" Alice asks.

"I feel winded you know? I never thought walking could be so hard."

"That's because you haven't used your legs in months Christy. The severity of your car wreck didn't make it any easier."

"Yes, don't remind me," Christy says.

The orderly pauses for a second.

"I heard you almost died or something?" Alice asks.

"Almost? I did die, not once but twice from what the doctors said," Christy replies.

"Wow Christy that's amazing you're even hear!"

"Tell me about it. People say I am a walking miracle." Christy thinks about what she just said. "Well, I don't know about the walking part, but I'm still a miracle."

"If that's what they said, you sure are one."

"Thank you, Alice," Christy responds.

"So, if you don't mind me asking, what happened when you died?"

Christy thinks for a moment. Alice decides to let it go.

"If you don't want to talk about it, I understand. Some of our patients that were in bad accidents are so stressed out when they get here, many times their trying to recant what happened to them while at the same time trying to get back to who they once were? We try telling them it all takes time to rehabilitate yourself and talking about what happened seems to help them understand that time is on their side."

"I've talked about it at the hospital, and I feel like it has helped me tremendously, but I'm still dealing with a lot of unanswered questions about what happened to me during my out of body experience."

Alice nods her head in agreement.

"Oh yeah, I totally understand. I don't know how you take it all in, you know, the whole process of everything?" Alice asks.

"Yes, I know. The police showed me the pictures of my car, and I just cried."

"Because of the horror of the accident?" Alice asks.

"No, my car, I loved that car," Christy responds with conviction.

Alice laughs aloud.

"I'm serious Alice," Christy responds laughing.

"It was a 2014 convertible BMW, dark blue with a royal blue top. I picked it out and everything. I would let the top down, and my hair would just fly all over the place, and I loved it."

"I hear you. I bet it was a nice car. I wish I could afford something like that."

"Don't bother. You know, after thinking about it, any convertible would've been fine with me. It's the name of the car you are really paying for."

"What do you do for work?" Alice asks.

"You mean what did I do?" Christy responds.

"Well yeah, I mean, I know you're not working right now because of your accident, but when you go back to work, what do you do?"

"Well, I was an investment broker for a marketing firm until they closed the doors going out of business."

"Oh, sorry to hear that Christy," Alice replies.

"I'm not sorry. That job was driving me insane anyway and maybe there will be some good out of it," Christy says.

"Let's hope so Christy. Who knows, maybe you can turn your story into a book or something?"

Christy thinks about it. The thought excites her. "Hey, maybe you're right. A movie would be better."

"I would love to see that if it does, what do you think your story would say?" Alice asks.

"I think a story would say how to live and how not to live."

"That sounds interesting Christy," Alice says.

"You think so?" Christy asks.

"Oh, most definitely, but what would be the reason for people how not to live looking at your life?" Alice asks.

Christy pauses for a moment sitting in the chair.

"I would have to say the title should be "Live for Life," and the subtitle should say "Enjoying the people around you. Don't use them to get what you want."

"Hmm Christy, that sounds very interesting. Make sure you have some drama in your story."

"Drama?" Christy asks.

"Yeah, like something that caused your accident would be one, then there has to be something you want after your accident that moves you forward towards your goal," Alice says.

"What do you think that should be?" Christy asks.

Alice's brain thinks for a moment.

"What do you want right now?"

"I want to walk again, and then I want to find my purpose in life," Christy says.

Alice thinks about it.

"That's fine, but in a book or movie, that would be a little boring Christy to be honest."

"Oh, really?"

"Yeah. I want to know more about the accident. You said you died twice so tell me what happened when you died, that's something that would grab your audience's attention," Alice says.

Christy is silent for a moment.

"Well, I do have something to tell about that experience, but that might scare some people."

"What do you mean?"

"What I experienced, was like a horror movie Alice, but in real life."

"Who hasn't seen a horror movie Christy?"

"No Alice, my out of body experience would scare you to death, not life."

"I'm not getting you."

"Alice, I watched myself leave my body."

Christy pauses to make sure she is saying it right.

"I felt myself leaving my body after the accident. I was standing right there looking at them perform CPR on me."

"Oh, wow Christy, that' it," Alice says.

"What's it?" Christy asks.

"What you just told me. Tell that experience! That's the key to grabbing your audience's attention. You explain everything you experienced in vivid detail."

Christy shakes her head no. Alice notices it.

"What?"

"No Alice, they won't believe me."

"Yes, they will."

"No, they won't. You think they will, but they won't."

"How do you know?" Christy asks.

"Because that's something you see in a horror movie, I don't recall too many people on talk show's talking about hell, maybe heaven, but definitely not hell."

"Why not Christy?"

"Because no one wants to go there, that's why! Think about it, if I asked you, hey Alice, I have two choices for you when you die, Heaven, or Hell, I'm going to make the choice for you, I'm picking Hell for you. You would slap me silly, wouldn't you?"

Alice laughs as she nods her head in agreement.

"Yeah, I would."

Christy stares at her.

"See what I mean?"

"Okay, then Christy, this is what you should do. Explain your story in a way that convinces them that Hell is a place they do not want to go," Alice says.

Christy thinks about it.

"That would work Alice, you sound like a preacher or something."

"I don't know about that, I just know what you experienced was not by accident. Make every moment count because you survived. Your life isn't about you anymore, it's about others around you that you can help make their life better."

Christy laughs.

"Okay, if they make this into a movie, I will be sure to put you in it Alice."

"Good because you know I can act, right?"

"Really?"

"Yes!"

Christy acts like she's confused.

"What do you mean, crazy? You know how to act crazy?"

Alice gives Christy a sarcastic look.

"Oh, so you got jokes huh?"

Christy laughs.

"Okay come on, let's have a go at this walking again, and then you will be finished for the day."

"Sounds good to me" Christy responds.

Christy stands as Alice helps her walk along the treadmill path.

CHAPTER THIRTEEN

"Connecting Flights"

Meanwhile in Istanbul, Marks plane lands for the connecting flight to Bangkok. Mark stretches his arms and legs as the plane taxis on the runway. Janice finishes reading a book she had for the flight. "What are you reading?" Mark asks. "Oh, it's a book about this guy who was promised the world only later to lose his soul. "Who is the guy?" "Some businessman." Mark is curious. "What would make him want to do that?" "What else, greed." The plane approaches its jetway as Janice and other passengers stand retrieving their carry-on luggage from the top compartments. Janice glances down at Mark. "It sounds like you Mark.

Mark takes a deep breath as he shakes it off as he stands to his feet. The flight attendant approaches the P.A. system to speak. "We have arrived in Istanbul. The time is approximately 8:00 p.m. Please make sure you have all your personal belongings with you upon exiting the plane. Some of you will be connecting to other flights. Please read all signs available, they will guide you to your connecting flight. We hope you enjoyed your flight with us. We were happy to serve you on this flight, and we hope you will fly with us again. Thank you for flying Turkish Airlines.

All passengers exit the plane. As they exit, the Pilot and Co-Pilot thank them for flying with Turkish Airlines. On the jetway, Mark and Janice walk side by side as she extends her hand to him.

"Well Mark, it was nice meeting you," Alice replies.

Mark shakes her hand.

"Likewise."

"Do you have family here?" Mark asks.

"No, I'm meeting some friends who moved here after college. They have jobs here now," Alice says.

"Oh, I see," Mark replies.

"Who knows Mark, we might see each other again flying back."

"Maybe," Mark answers.

The two exit the jetway into the seating area.

"So, I'm so hungry," Mark says.

"Do you want to grab something to eat, my treat. My ride isn't due for another forty-five minutes."

"You're buying?"

"Yes, are you surprised or something?"

"No, not at all. It's rewarding when a lady buys since us guys always fit the bill."

Janice laughs.

"That is so true Mark."

"And since you talked my ears off all the way here, this is the least you could do," Mark answers.

Janice laughs again as she slaps Mark across the shoulder.

"I didn't talk all the way here silly, we slept majority of the way."

"I know, just joking."

"A funny one at that," Janice says.

Mark glances around at the eateries to see what food establishment interests him. The golden arch is the only one that catches his eye.

"How about McDonalds?"

"Sounds good to me," Janice replies.

They walk to McDonalds as Mark glances at his watch.

"In a hurry Mark?"

Mark enters McDonalds with Janice following him.

"No, just seeing what time it was. I have forty-five minutes until my next flight."

Mark and Janice stand in line. Mark turns around realizing they are next in line.

"Janice, go ahead and tell them what you want."

Janice steps up to the counter.

"Hi, I'll have a Quarter Pounder with cheese, extra pickles, fries, and a coke."

The cashier rings up Janice's order as Mark steps forward to give his order.

"I'll take a number 1 without pickles."

"What type of drink?" The Cashier asks.

"Sprite."

"Will that complete your order?"

"Yes," Mark replies.

"Your total comes to $20.75. Will that be here or to go?"

"That will be here,"

Mark replies as he turns to Janice who agreed to the meal. Janice hands the cashier a fifty-dollar bill. The cashier receives the money as she rings register causing it to open. She grabs Janice's change and hands it back to her along with a receipt with the number of their order.

"That will be right up," The cashier responds.

"Thank you," Janice says.

Mark and Janice stand off to the side as other customers standing in line move forward to be serviced.

"Wow, this place is pretty busy," Janice replies.

"Yes, it is, but think about it, how many McDonalds would you ever see here?"

"Very true Mark."

A young lady appears behind the counter with a tray of food on it.

"Number 23," she says.

Mark responds, "That's us."

Mark receives the tray of food as Janice follows him to a seated area. They sit with their luggage next to them as Mark hands Janice her food.

"We need some ketchup," Mark replies.

He exits the table and proceeds to the front counter looking around for napkins, and condiments. Mark turns around seeing the section for napkins and other supplies. He grabs a few napkins, and a handful of ketchup packets. Mark returns to their table handing several ketchup packets to Janice.

"Thank you, Mark, your such a gentleman."

"I try to be."

Janice takes a bite into her sandwich.

"Hmmm, good," she replies as she chews and digests a piece of her sandwich. Mark does the same. The two satisfy their hunger as they eat.

"So, Mark, tell me this, you never answered me whether that was your car shot up or not. I didn't tell you I saw a guy that looked like you leaving that car."

"Did you?" Mark asks.

"Yes, I did. Was it you?"

Mark is silent as he chews his food. He nods his head yes as Janice's mouth opens wide.

"It was you?"

"Yes."

"I knew it was, so, what happened?"

"Some guys just started shooting at me."

Janice stops eating.

"For no reason they targeted you?"

"Yeah."

"Was it for your car or something?"

"I think I recognize the shooter, I'm not sure though."

"Who was it?"

"My bosses nephew. Again, I'm not sure," Mark replies.

"Why didn't you stay and wait for the police?" Janice asks.

Mark sets down his sandwich on the wrapper it came in.

"Because I didn't want to wait for them to finish the job."

Janice ponders Mark's comment.

"That's a good point."

"They'll contact me, I can be sure of that" Mark says as he continues eating his food.

"I know what you're thinking Janice, I'm not a criminal."

"I didn't say you were Mark."

"But you thought it," Mark replies.

Janice feels guilty as she responds.

"Well yeah, Mark after what you told me about what you've done and what you now do, otherwise, why would your bosses nephew want to kill you?"

"Because of what I know about the company."

"What do you know?" Janice asks.

"I can't say," Mark replies.

"I knew it was you when I put the two together, it wasn't hard to figure out. Whatever you know, must be some heavy information."

Mark agrees, "Yes, it is."

"So, when the police contact you, you're going to give them all the details?"

"No, I have to be in Bangkok for my business, or I could lose all of my clients. I must be at this meeting. They can keep the car for all I care, I'll just get another one."

"Wow, big spender," Janice says.

"So, Janice, you know so much about me, tell me about yourself."

"Well, I'm a graduate student. I'm from Stone Mountain, Georgia. I love to read books, not much more to tell."

"Or is it, you don't want to tell me?" Mark asks.

"No, I just haven't lived long enough for there to be much to tell."

Mark nods his head.

"Your right, but stick around, this world will not disappoint you."

The two finish their food, then leave McDonalds. Mark escorts Janice half way to the exit. He extends his hand towards her.

"It was a pleasure to meet you Janice, thank you for the meal."

She shakes his hand as well.

"Likewise. Thank you for eating with me, my pleasure. You take care of yourself and stay out of trouble."

"I will," Mark replies.

The two go their separate ways.

In Atlanta after five months of rehabilitation, Christy is discharged from the rehabilitation center. She walks again on her own but with a slight limp. She says goodbye to the staff that helped her get back on her feet hugging each one of them individually. Tears flow from everyone's faces as Christy's mom picks her up at the main entrance. As Christy leaves waving goodbye to the staff members, they return the favor waving back. Inside Christy's mom's car, the two begin talking. "So, honey, how do you feel?" "I feel great mom, I mean, I'm walking again but with a limp. The doctors say, it's possible it could go away after a while depending on my body's healing process. I have all my faculties, so I can't complain," Christy says." "Your blessed," Ms. Billings says. "I'm blessed for sure," Christy comments. "I'm so glad you will be staying with me honey." "Thanks for taking me in, since I have nowhere else to go Mom. All of my funds are depleted now." "At least you are alive Christy. You can get all that stuff back." Ms. Billings realizes something. "Oh, I forgot to tell you, some guy called the house asking about you." "Who was it?"

"He didn't say, he just hung up when I wouldn't tell him any information about what hospital you or where you were staying."

"Well, was it my old job you think?"

"No because if it was, they would have identified themselves. The guy sounded really young and he asked really strange questions like, were you going to live, or did you lose any limbs, or did you have security around you, stuff like that."

Christy thinks for a moment.

"Yes Mom, that's odd. That wouldn't be Mr. Boykins," Christy responds.

"Do you think you know who it might be?" Ms. Billings asks.

"No, I don't have a clue. I thought it might be Mark."

"Mark?"

"You know Mark Collins from my high school?" Ms. Billings thinks to herself.

"Mark Collins?"

"Oh, yes, I remember Mark. That was not him, I remember Marks voice."

Christy sighs.

"Oh mom, how could you possibly remember Mark's voice, you haven't talked to him in years."

Her mom turns her head towards Christy as she drives.

"I remember Mark Christy, I'm not that old. His voice sounds like Barny Rubble from The Flintstones when he talks. That's why I know it was not him."

Christy laughs aloud.

"Mom really, Barney Rubble?"

"Yes, Barney Rubble why, is that funny or something?"

"Yes, that's a cartoon character Mom. That's the last thing somebody wants to be remembered of."

They laugh in unison.

"I'm going to tell him what you said," Christy says.

Her mom continues driving as she glances at Christy periodically.

"Oh, honey, please don't," Ms. Billings says.

"I have to, I want to see his reaction when I say it."

"Oh, Christy, I'm telling you don't."

Moments later, they arrive home.

"I had all your things placed in a storage facility, I will give you the key when we get in the house," her mom states.

They exit the car and enter the house. Opening the front door of the house, the family dog "Faith" welcomes Christy jumping all over Christy's legs. Christy's mom gives the dog a command. "Faith sit down!" Faith steps back and sits down looking up at Christy's mom waiting for another command. Christy becomes angry as she places her things on the table. "

"Do you know, my job didn't send me a card or flowers while in the hospital?"

"I wouldn't worry about that Christy."

"They owe me back pay too."

"Well, how are they going to do that Christy, when they are out of business?" Ms. Billings asks.

"I don't care, they owe me."

"I have to get a lawyer just in case they don't pay me," She says.

"How much do they owe you?" Ms. Billings asks.

"My bonus and two weeks' worth of pay. They probably thought if I died, they wouldn't have to pay."

"Well, you've been through a lot Christy. Did they show you the pictures of the accident?"

"Well yes," Christy responds.

Christy imagines the pictures of the accident. Christy's mom interjects. "I have some money in a separate savings account to help you get back on your feet if you need it." Christy quickly rejects the offer. "Oh, no mom…I can't…" "Christy, honey, you will need it to help with your hospital bills. You know insurance companies these days don't cover everything." Her mom pauses for a second. "Honey, you've suffered a severe traumatic brain injury. It's going to be a long while before things get normal again." Christy turns her head away from her mom as she glances out the window of the house. "Mom, please don't remind me."

Christy sits down on the plush couch with her mom following behind her. "Christy are you okay?" "Yeah, I just got a little tired that's all." "Well, rest up while I will fix you something to eat." "Okay great," Christy says as Faith walks over to her licking her hand. She rubs Faith's head as she leans back in the couch to relax. An hour later at dinner time, Christy finishes some of her dinner that her mother prepared for her. "You're not hungry?" Ms. Billings asks. "No, sorry Mom." "It's okay. How are you feeling, okay now?" "I'm still tired." "Anything I can do?" "Just being here for me is everything mom, I really appreciate it a lot. I guess I didn't expect to feel the way I feel right now. I thought things would go back immediately to what they were." "Like I said honey, it's going to take time. You don't want to rush your recuperation."

Later that night, Christy enters her old room she once slept in as a child and young teen. She stares at the pictures on the wall still present. They room looks the same as if she never left to start her own life. She smiles as she walks over towards her old bed. She plops down on it wondering what once was and what will now be. Christy prepares for bed. At approximately 2 A.M. Christy tosses and turns in her bed sweating profusely as she replays the accident and out of body experience in her mind. Christy visualizes herself driving down the freeway next to the semi-truck as her car loses control swerving into the path of the semi-tractor trailers wheels. Christy screams as she envisions the trailers tires coming towards her. She snaps out of her nightmare waking up screaming. Her mother rushes into her room with her dog Faith following. Ms. Billings turns on the light only to see Christy sitting upright in the bed with sweat all over her face. Christy stares at her mom and begins to cry. Her mother rushes over to her hugging her daughter tightly.

    The next morning, Christy awakens only getting two hours of sleep. She is drained as her mother enters her room. "Christy are you awake?" "Yes, mom." "How do you feel?" "Tired as usual. I didn't sleep much at all." "Let me fix you some tea and some breakfast, then you need to take your pills and try to go back to sleep." "Okay, mom, thanks." "Breakfast will be ready in a minute." "Okay," Christy says. Christy sighs plopping her head back on her pillow. Faith walks over to her bed looking up at her whimpering. She rubs Faith's head as Faith in return, licks her hand then scampers away. Christy stares up at the ceiling as she closes her eyes slowly to go back to sleep. In her dreams, she sees what looks like her best friend Jessica off in a distance. She approaches her calling out her name, "Jessica!" Jessica does not respond turning her back towards Christy. Christy approaches Jessica placing her hand on her shoulder. "Jessica? Hey, are you okay?" Christy's hand turns Jessica's body around slowly as Jessica appears in skeletal form.

Christy screams quickly snapping out of her dream opening her eyes as she sits straight up in bed breathing hard. She glances around the room, then at her alarm clock realizing her short nap lasted only fifteen minutes. She climbs out of bed, but her legs are asleep causing her to fall hard to the floor. The dog Faith barks as she runs into the room pacing back and forth concerned about Christy. Christy yells for her mom, but her mom does not come as Faith rushes over to Christy licking her face while barking. Christy, frustrated, shoos Faith away from her as she yells for her mom again, but still no response. Christy becomes even more frustrated as her eyes begin to fill with tears.

    Christy grabs onto the chair in front of her managing to pull herself up slowly piece by piece of her body until finally she's sitting in the chair. She drags her legs in front of her. And begins massaging them to wake them up. Suddenly her feet and toes are moving along with her legs regaining feeling. Her mother finally enters the room with a tray of food. Christy in a disgusted tone, responds. "Where were you! Didn't you hear me calling you?" Christy's mom responds. "Why, what's wrong?" Christy yells… "I needed help, that's what was wrong!" The dog Faith and Christy's mother look at Christy bewildered. Faith whimpers and runs out of the room while Christy's mom places the tray of food down on the bed. "What happened Christy?" Her mother asks walking towards her. "Here, let me help you back in bed." Christy slaps her mom's hand away. "No thank you, I can do it myself!" Her mother quietly steps back, turns around, then leaves the room.

Later that day, Christy's mother drives her to the storage unit where all her things reside. Christy exits the car opening the storage door seeing all her valuables stacked inside. She walks over to the couch covered in plastic rubbing it remembering what her life once was before the accident. The visual appearance of all her things, stuns Christy as her eyes blink fast to control her tears from falling. Unable to hold it in, she loses control of her emotions. Her mother grabs her hugging her tight as she cries in her arms.

Later, Christy and her mother arrive home. Christy enters through the front door exhausted as Faith approaches her for attention. She plops down on the couch rubbing Faith's head. "Boy, I'm beat mom," Christy says. "Christy, you should go to the doctor tomorrow and tell them about this. You're tired all the time. We just went to the storage, then back home and your already tired." "No, I think I'm just doing too much mom." "Doing too much how?"

"I'm walking to fast I think," Christy replies. "I doubt that Christy." "Well its' probably because I got so emotional looking at all of my stuff in storage and realizing I don't have my home anymore, that's why." Her mom sits down in the chair across from her. "So, are you going to go to the doctor tomorrow?" "What for, all they're going to tell me is to get some rest which is so hard for me to do." "And that is every good reason for you to tell them you're not sleeping Christy." Christy thinks about it. "Well okay, if you think I should." Christy's mom stands and kisses Christy on the forehead

as she walks away to her room with Faith following behind.

CHAPTER FOURTEEN

"The Doctor's Office"

The next day, Christy takes a trip to the doctor' office. Walking in, she feels frustrated and tired as she signs her name on a sheet of paper attached to a clipboard. The front desk assistant checks her in. "You can have a seat and the doctor will be right with you shortly," she says. "Thank you," Christy responds as she sits down next to her mother. Her mother speaks to her in a low tone. Christy looks at her mom responding in a low tone. "My life is a mess right now mom," Christy says. "Everything will work out Christy. God will make good out of this you watch," Her mother responds. Christy stretched her hands out wide. "How?" "I don't know how Christy, I just know he will...he always does," Ms. Billings says. Christy shakes her head in disbelief. "You know mom, I thought I was going to change my world. I don't believe in that now," Christy says. "Don't give up on God Christy," Her mom says. "I didn't say I did," Christy responds. "Yes, you did...you just said it with your words Christy. Watch your words, they have power good or bad."

Christy's name is called by one of the nurses. She stands up proceeding to the door where the nurse awaits her. Christy's limp causes her to take more time than the nurse would expect. "Sorry I'm so slow," Christy says. "Oh, that's okay, take your time." In the back area, the nurse checks Christy's blood pressure, her temperature and then her weight on the scale. Then she escorts Christy to the room where the doctor will see her. They both sit down as the nurse asks Christy why she came. "So, Ms. Billings, what brings you in today?" "Well, I recently had a bad car accident and after my recovery, I've been feeling tired all the time." "Oh, I'm sorry to hear that." "The nurse glances at Christy's medical chart as it pops up on the computer." you, because I almost died." "Oh wow." "But I'm here because I've been having trouble sleeping at night too," Christy says.

The nurse types some information on the computer. "I see you've suffered a traumatic brain injury from your accident." Christy agrees. "Yes, I did." "Christy, I'm looking at your medication prescribed. So, that' not working well for you?" "It does sometimes." "Maybe we need to give you a hire dosage. I will let the doctor know." "Okay." The nurse jots down some information on the notepad. "Okay, she will be in to see you shortly." "Okay, thank you so much." "No problem Christy." The nurse leaves the room as Christy sits on a gurney alone in total silence. She glances around the room hearing faint voices from outside in the hallway. Suddenly the door opens to her room, as her doctor, Dr. Vance appears. "Hi, Christy." "Hi, Dr. Vance." "How are you?" "Not so good." Doctor Vance sits down on a stool in front of a computer screen and keyboard. "Okay, what's the problem?" "I'm have trouble sleeping which I think is contributing to me feeling tired all the time."

Dr. Vance listens intently nodding her head. "I heard it was really bad. I'm glad to see you are okay. Doctor Vance glances at the notes the nurse left for her to read about Christy's condition. "I see you had a brain injury from the accident. The medicine the hospital prescribe is not working for you?" "Sometimes it does and sometimes it doesn't." "How about we increase the dosage?" "Okay, but, I don't want to feel like a zombie you know?" Christy asks. "I understand." Doctor Vance pauses. "We can give it a try, and if it's too much, we can try something else. Your brain must rejuvenate itself Christy. It's like a muscle that's injured, and it takes time for it to get its strength back. It will take more time than usual. Everything will work out Christy." Christy agrees. "Yes." Dr. Vance begins typing into the computer as Christy looks on. "What else are you taking Christy?" "Over the counter?" Christy asks. "Yes," Doctor Vance says. "I'm taking Motrin, Advil, and sleeping pills."

 Dr. Vance continues reading her information on the computer screen. "Are you experiencing any mood swings, depression, or anxiety?" "I do have mood swings, no depression, anxiety yes," Christy responds. "What about any dizziness, or loss of balance?" "No, not yet at least, knock on wood. The doctors at the hospital said I should expect it but nothing yet." Christy pauses for a moment. "Oh, but I did have loss of feeling in my legs sometimes which causes me to lose my balance and fall." "Was this recent?" asks Dr. Vance. "Yes." "Okay, um, have you had any loss of consciousness?" "No loss of consciousness," Christy says. "Okay, Christy, let me check you over," Doctor Vance says standing in front of Christy.

"Okay," Christy says. Dr. Vance checks Christy's heartbeat with a stethoscope pulling up her shirt. She checks behind her ears with an Otoscope.

"Your ears look good, and you have a regular heartbeat Dr. Vance says as she feels behind Christy's ears and neck. "Does this hurt?" Doctor Vance asks. Christy responds in a soft tone, "No." Dr. Vance feels around Christy's head. When she moves over to her right side which is the side she has the limp on, Christy responds in agony. "Ow, that hurts." "You have some soft tissue still healing on this side," Doctor Vance states. "I can only sleep on my left side right now," Christy explains. "Let me check your motor skills," Dr. Vance says as she walks over to the drawer retrieving a small reflex hammer with a rubber face. She taps Christy's left knee gently with the hammer as Christy's knee lifts forward. Then she repeats the same method on her right knee. Christy's right leg slightly moves.

Dr. Vance finalizes her minor checkup with Christy. "Okay, so, you have slight reaction of reflex in your right leg, and that is the cause for your limp. It also explains the loss of motor skills coming from your right leg transmitted from your brain to your spine which causes the delayed reaction to your leg. This will happen from time to time. But I would advise you to walk more to keep the blood flowing in both legs. Taking long walks in the park or around the block several times will do this. The more you use your legs the more you will keep the blood flowing, which will get your right leg strong again. The more you use your brain to think about walking, the more you will walk. Do you use a Cain?" "I have a walker and a wheelchair from the hospital." "I'm going to give you one here at no charge. This will help you when you lose your balance on occasion." "Okay, thank you Dr. Vance, I appreciate it." "No problem Christy, we want you to get you back to the normalcy of life again." "God knows I need that for sure," Christy says.

The doctor sits back down and begins typing on the computer. "I'm going to write prescriptions increasing your dosages. You let me know if they are working or not. Here's my email address." Doctor Vance says handing Christy a slip of paper. "Take one once or twice a day. Hopefully, this will help your body get back on schedule with sleeping too." "Okay, thanks," Christy responds. "Your pharmacy is still the same?" Christy thinks for a moment. "Oh no, I moved in with my mom. She stays on Moore street. I believe there is a CVS Pharmacy on Delany road near her." "Let me see," Doctor Vance says checking on the computer as her eyes scan the computer screen. "Oh, yes there is a CVS there. I will issue your prescription to that location." "Okay, I appreciate it Dr. Vance." "No problem Christy." Dr. Vance pauses for a second. "Okay, I want you to do a follow-up, let's say a month from now, just to see where you are. If you need to see me at any time, you can message me on "Your Chart" and I will respond immediately. If there is an emergency, you go to the hospital immediately," Dr. Vance says. "Yes, I understand," Christy responds. Dr. Vance stands shaking Christy's hand. "It's great to see you Christy. You take care of yourself, I'll see you soon,"

Dr. Vance says. "Thank you doctor Vance for seeing me," Christy says. "You bet Christy."

Moments later, Christy appears from the waiting room. Her mom is reading a magazine until she glances up seeing her daughter standing waiting. "Oh, you're done," Her mom says as she stands setting the magazine down on the table. The two of them walk out of the waiting room. "So, what did they say?" "Dr. Vance increased my dosage giving me new prescriptions and she did a mini exam to check all of my faculties to see if they were working properly. She also gave me a Cain for my limp and to help me keep my balance." "Oh wow, that was nice of her to do that. Cain's are not free you know?" "I know now mom." "Well, come on, let's get something to eat. We can drop off your prescription and by the time we finish eating, it should be ready." "Okay, I am hungry," Christy says. They leave the clinic heading towards home.

A month later, Christy adjusts to her new life helping her mother around the house and volunteering at her local recreation center two days out of the week. She also found a part time job at a local Walmart store nearby. Today is her second day on the job. As Christy stocks products on the shelf, a young man approaches her.

"Christy?" The young man asks.

Christy turns around to see who he is, but she does not recognize him. The young man smiles.

"Christy Billings?"

"Yes?"

"Hi, you look familiar to me."

Christy thinks for a moment.

"I do?"

"Yeah."

"I'm sorry, I don't recognize who you are," Christy says.

The young man extends his hand.

"Oh, I'm Nathaniel Boykins."

Christy's mind tries to connect the name with the face.

"I'm sorry, I still don't…"

"That's okay, we've probably passed each other in the hallways several times."

"I'm Mr. Boykins nephew, you know, your former boss at DinoCore?"

"Yes, I remember now. Mr. Boykins yeah, I just don't remember you. I just recovered from a serious car accident, so my memory is kind of vague at times."

"How are you doing now?" Nathaniel asks.

"I'm fine, how are you?"

"Great, just great." Nathaniel stares at Christy. "Wow, it's been a long time. It's so good to see you. I heard you were in a bad car accident, so, you're doing all right? Sorry I couldn't come a see you. I didn't have any information of where you were."

"That's okay, I'm making it day by day. It's a process. Thanks for asking though."

"It's my pleasure. You were a spit fire for the company, that's what my uncle used to say."

Christy blushes. "Oh, I'm flattered."

Christy, nervous about her appearance, takes her right hand fixing her hair as Nathaniel gives her a compliment.

"You're looking good."

"Thank you." Christy pauses for a moment. "So, what have you been up too?"

"I'm working with another Marketing firm now. It's fun and challenging."

"Oh, that's great" Christy responds.

"Yeah, I'm like the Chief Marketing Officer there."

Christy is surprised.

"Wow, really? That's great, so how is your uncle?"

Nathaniel becomes somber.

"He passed away two months ago."

The news shocks Christy.

"I'm so sorry to hear that."

"Thank you. Everything that happened with the company destroyed his health, and the IRS came after him and took everything."

"That was sad about the company, very sad. I'm praying for everyone that worked there. I hope they can find good jobs after all of this."

"I agree." Nathaniel pauses for a moment.

"You know Mark Collins, right?"

"Yes, I do, we worked together."

"Well I've been trying to reach him do you have his contact number or know where he is?"

"No, I haven't heard from Mark in a while. I heard he came by the hospital to see me, but I was heavily sedated. He left me flowers though."

"That was very nice of him, Nathaniel says."

"What did you want to talk to Mark about?" Christy asks.

The question throws Nathaniel off.

"Just business stuff."

"Oh, hey, now that you mentioned DinoCore, do you know how I can find out how to get my bonus or severance pay, because I never received them."

Nathaniel lowers his head before he speaks. "Yeah, the IRS really messed the company over. They tied everything up in legalities. My Uncle could not get out from under it. They seized all his assets, froze the company accounts the day before he planned to write the checks to everyone for the bonuses. He loved all of you guys, and it broke his heart that he couldn't keep his word in the end." Christy thinks for a moment. "Why did the company shut down again?" Nathaniel pauses for a moment. "You don't remember?" "No, I'm sorry," Christy says. "The company went bankrupt Christy, and the SCC wanted to press charges on my Uncle for unlawful trades, but he beat it by paying top lawyers to defend him. Later he found out he owed all these taxes with the company he thought he paid, but never did when he found out his financial adviser he gave his financial advisor power of attorney but, he squandered the money we found out he was dealing with a Mexican drug cartel." "Oh, my gosh, that's crazy. Whatever happened to him, did he go to jail?" Christy asks. "No, the Cartel took care of him. They found his body in his burned-out Mercedes's somewhere in Mexico."

Christy is speechless but manages to speak a word. "That is awful." "Yeah, I heard about the drug cartel thing. Mark told me." Nathaniel sighs. "Oh really?" Christy thinks about what she said realizing the wrong words were spoken. "I mean, I don't know much more about that." "So, what are you doing here?" "I just got something part time for now." "Oh, I see, well, I would like to treat you to lunch one day when I'm off again, if that is okay with you? Where are you staying?" "Oh really, um, that would be nice. I'm staying with my mom." "Yeah, If I can get your number I can find out your day off and then we can do lunch," Nathaniel says. Christy agrees. "Okay, let me give you my number." Nathaniel pulls out his cell phone. "Okay, shoot." "It's 555-389-0851." "Got it." Nathaniel places his cell phone away. "Well hey, let me get my hug." Nathaniel leans in to hug Christy. She subconsciously agrees to the hug as they embrace for a second. "It's good to see you again Christy, bye." "Bye Nathaniel," Christy says as he walks away.

Meanwhile in Bangkok, Mark is running his new business. He is on the phone with a client while his partner Steve stands at his door. "Okay, Bill don't worry, you're going to make a lot of money. Okay, great talking to you, bye." Mark hangs up the phone. "That was the rich tycoon you spoke about?" "Yeah, that was him. This guy is sitting on a ton of money already Steve. He's a billionaire. What's with that?" "That's what having a lot of money will do to you I guess, but this is what we want right?" Steve replies as he notices Mark's concerns. "What's wrong?" "I don't know." "You don't know about what?" Steve asks. "All of this," Mark says with a conviction as he allows his index figure to massage the temple of his brain. "Man come on, don't do this, we are locked and loaded here. "Marquee

Enterprises Consulting Firm MECF. This is you man, this is what we do."

Mark quickly rises from his chair hearing the words from Steve cut into his soul like a knife. "But like this Steve?" Steve quickly glances around, then steps all the way into Mark's office closing the door behind him. "Whoa, keep a lid on that Mark. This is our secret remember? We rob rich people, don't let the cat out of the bag. What's wrong with you?" Mark takes his right hand feeling through his hair as Steve presents his evidence. "You have twenty employees working for you now, they are depending on you for their income. If one employee finds out this is all a fraud, we are screwed. Do you know what the Bangkok government does to criminals who steal other people's money?" "No what?" Steve turns around walking away. "I don't know, but I know it's bad." "The response makes Mark laugh. "You know Steve, you should be a comedian?"

Steve turns around to confront Mark. "All I know is, I am in this with you all the way. Remember our motto "Take no prisoners" Why?" Because it's too much baggage," Mark says. "Right," Steve agrees. "Now get your head back in the game so we can make a ton of money." "And then what?" Mark asks. "What do you mean?" "I mean after we make all of the money we can make, then what?" Steve shakes his head. "Man, then we make some more, that's what we do. Who cares if we don't do it by the book, the rest of the world doesn't." "Yeah but, we are not the rest of the world." Mark points to the phone where he had a conversation with the biggest client on his list. "I met him. The guy would give you the shirt off his back if he had too. Money is nothing to him, but loyalty is everything."

The comment does not amuse Steve. "Mark, that speech would be great if I was applying to be a Priest, but dude, I am a crook, and so are you." Steve pauses to allow the words to sink into Mark's ears. "This company is a crooked company, need I go on?" Mark waves Steve away with his hand. "Do you think we would have the clients we have now if we told them, invest a thousand shares and I guarantee you, your return will be zero? No, we bait them and hook them, that's what we do," Steve says. "Oh Steve, would you just cut it out? I get it okay, I'm in, I'm okay, I just had a moment." Steve's satisfied. "Good, now I can enjoy my lunch." Steve heads towards the door. "Chow babe." He opens the door walking out as Mark stares at him while his conscience and his flesh war with each other like two male lions fighting over dinner for their families.

At the end of the day, Mark retreats to his new home, a two-bedroom condominium in Chiang Mai, Pho Chai at The Star Hill. It's a fully furnished establishment surrounded by a mall and a University. The cost for Mark, was a little over five hundred thousand. He enters his place loosening his tie and dropping his briefcase on the kitchen chair as he enters his living room. Looking down outside his window, he sees people swimming at night in the elegant pool with an overhang style edge. The light of the pool casts the shadows of the bodies in the pool along with the night light overcast beauty of the city.

Mark feels safe away from the violence that once confronted him on the streets of Atlanta when his expensive car was shot up.

The telephone rings as Mark answers it. "Hello?" "Mr. Collins?" The male voice on the other end asks. "Yes, this is Mark." "Hi, this is Aaron from E-Nuff Insurance company." "Hi," Mark responds. "I'm just calling to inform you; your 2014 Maserati Grand Turismo was declared totaled. I understand you live in a different country now?" "Yes, I faxed you guys all of the information you needed about my whereabouts. My business is here in Bangkok now." "Okay, we will send you a check for the value of your car. Have the police concluded their investigation as to who might have caused the damage to your car?" The agent asks. "No, there's still an ongoing investigation." "Oh, I understand. Well, it's been two months and we haven't heard back from the police department so, were going to go ahead and write it off as totaled. Sorry for the inconvenience Mr. Collins."

The news elates Mark. "Thank you." "Do you plan to buy another one like this, or one similar?" "No, I'm going to get something less expensive since I'm out here. The less attention, the better." "I understand. The car you had was a cool car, one of my favorites. Hope I can afford one like that one day." "I'm hoping for you pal." "Thank you," The agent says. "Thank you for calling me, it was great working with you guys." "Okay, Mr. Collins, take care." "You too, bye," Mark concludes. "Bye," The agent says. Mark ends the call, walking out of his living room as he grabs the remote control turning on the T.V. as the local Bangkok news broadcasts. Mark has his television set to the English language translation as he sits down to relax in front of his big flat screen console.

That next morning, Mark stands in a meeting with his employees while Steve stands off in the back of the room. "Is everyone here? Good. Okay, let's get started. This company's primary goal is to make money for our clients and to make money for ourselves. Now, I don't know about you but, I love making money. I feel good when I'm making money, don't you?" All his employees in the room agree nodding their heads. "Exactly, see what I'm saying, everyone in this room agrees with me. Now what does that say? That says we all have the same goal, right?" Mark waits for a response as his employees stare at each other realizing they need to nod their heads which they do. Mark continues speaking. Mark pauses for a second. "You have to show me action. Actions speak louder than words. Why you ask? Because actions show you mean what you say and in this business baby money makes the world go around so that means every client you have must buy and keep buying, period. If they're not buying, then you're not selling, and that means you don't belong with this company."

Mark paces around the long table where his employees are seated consisting of fifteen men, and five women. "These two methods work hand and hand like a marriage. If you are not taking her hand to propose, guess what? You aren't getting married, it's just that simple. Take your clients by the hand and propose to them showing them they can be richer that they already are. Tell them, I have an offer you can't refuse. That quote is from the movie The Godfather for some of the non-movie goers who didn't know. Court your clients with their likes and dislikes. In this business, it's a marriage people, simple as that." Mark pauses again. "Now let's say, your client loses money and they want out? What do you do? What did I say this business was about?" Mark raises his hand up to his ear waiting for a response from his employees. "A marriage," His workers respond in unison. "Exactly, and in any marriage, when there is a problem, you do what….? You talk about it. You don't just walk away and hope things will iron themselves out because it won't."

Mark walks back to the front of the room. "I want you to talk to your client. Convince them that every set back is a set up for something better. Be believable when you say it. In a marriage, if the wife doesn't believe things will get better, then prepare for the funeral because that marriage is dead." Mark sits down in his chair. "I want to see record sales from you guys and girls this quarter. No if's and's or but's. I believe in you, and I want you to believe in me. You are married to this company right here right now. You give 110% or I will show you 0% of pay on your paycheck along with the door." Mark claps his hands. "Let's get to it people." All his employees stand to their feet heading back to their stations ready for battle while Steve stays in the room.

    Mark fumbles through his note pad. "That was impressive my friend. You had me convinced," Steve says smiling. "I'm glad to see you are out of your daze. I was concerned for a minute." "Oh, really, how so?" Mark asks. "Well, if your speech sucked, then our sales would suck." Mark smiles. "I didn't go anywhere man, I'm still here." "I hope so because we have a lot riding on this and Mark, believe me when I say a lot." "I hear you Steve, don't worry," Mark says. "So, what about that girl Christy, is she coming soon or what?" Steve asks. "I don't know. I will have to see how she's doing." "You should call her and see what's up?" "I will, what's the rush Steve?" "Oh, no rush, you were the one talking about how she's this spitfire of a sales pitch. I just thought, since she was your side kick, imagine what she can do over here." Mark leans back in his chair. "I'll give her a call Steve." Steve raises his hand, "Okay, cool man. I guess I'd better get in here and show the troops how it's done." "Yeah, I think you'd better," Mark says. Steve laughs as he stretches his body as if he's preparing himself for a good workout. "Before I go, how's your new place," Steve asks. The comment brings a smile to Mark's face. "I love it man. The view is out of this world. What about your place?" "The same, costly though. We have to check each other's place out," Steve says. "Tell me about it," Mark replies. "Mark, the girls at my apartment, wow." "Control yourself Steve,"

Mark says. Steve makes his way to the door opening it looking back at Mark. "I always do." Steve closes the door behind him.

A week later, Christy receives a phone call from Nathaniel. She agrees to lunch with him. An hour later, he picks her up at her mother's home. She greets him at her front door. "Hey." "Hi Christy." Christy's mother with her hand extended, approaches him. "Hi, Nathaniel, is it?" "Yes Ma'am." "I'm Christy's mom, nice to meet you." "Likewise, Ms. Billings, it's my pleasure." "Christy told me, you two worked together?" "Yes, we did. I came late to the company before it closed. My uncle owned the company." "Oh, I see," Ms. Billings says. Christy's mother pauses as she fishes for more questions. "So, what is your uncle doing now, that the company is closed?" "Oh, he passed away." Christy's mother places her hand over her mouth. "Oh, I'm sorry to hear that, I did not know." "That's okay, we are doing okay as a family working through the loss." "That's good to hear," Ms. Billings responds.

    Christy breaks the ice with a different response. "Thanks for coming Nathaniel, we'd better go." "Oh, no problem Christy." Nathaniel pauses for a moment. "So, what's your favorite place to eat?" Christy thinks for a moment. "I like Applebee's." "Okay, Applebee's it is." Nathaniel reaches for the door for Christy to walk through. Nathaniel turns around waving goodbye to Christy's mom. "Nice meeting you Ms. Billings, I'll have her back safe in a couple of hours." "Please do Nathaniel and thank you for taking the time with her." "You bet." Nathaniel escorts Christy to his car. He opens the passenger door for her as she enters. He closes the door and walks around to the driver side to get in. The engine turns over as Nathaniel's two door Mercedes backs out of Christy's driveway heading down the street. "This is a nice car Nathaniel, I'm not a Mercedes fan though. "Oh no, why?" Nathaniel asks with a shocking tone. "I'm a BMW girl. BMW's have the horsepower." "Yeah but, they don't have the class like Mercedes." Christy laughs. "Get out of here, are you kidding me? You're a guy and you're saying this?" "Yeah, because I'm right." "You do know, guys are supposed to love BMW's because it's a guy's car. Mercedes is more for girl's." "So, you're an expert on cars, really Christy?" Nathaniel laughs. "If this is true, then why would you buy a BMW?"

Christy laughs. "Because it has more power, I just told you." Nathaniel laughs along with her. "I'll give you a pass on that one Christy. The car is silent for a moment as Nathaniel drives down the road. "Thanks for going to lunch with me," Nathaniel says. "Oh, no problem. I needed to get out of the house," Christy responds. "So, how do you feel?" Nathaniel asks. "I feel pretty good, I usually get tired after a couple of hours, but I haven't lately with the new dosage of medicine I'm taking. I feel better now." "Well, the doctors are doctors, and they should know what they are doing when you need help," Nathaniel responds. "Now that I remember you, I remember you having a twin brother, how is he doing?" Christy asks.

Nathaniel is thrown off by the question. "He's okay, we don't talk much anymore since my uncle passed. He blames me for stressing our uncle out with the things about the company."

The news shocks Christy. "Oh, wow Nathaniel, sorry to hear that. It's not your fault the company went bankrupt. Things were not right when you two showed up on the tail end. I just wished I had known more about what was going on." Nathaniel becomes suspicious. "More like what?" He asks. "Well, from what Mark told me a lot of things could've been prevented," Christy says. "Specifics?" Nathaniel asks. "Like the books being cooked to make it seem like we were in the black when really we were in the red. Like the secret meeting about what was really going on with the company." Christy turns to Nathaniel. "Were you at any of the emergency meetings?" Nathaniel quickly denies it. "Me? No way. My uncle would never allow my brother and I never to know any disclosers about the company." "I thought so," Christy responds. "So, you know a lot of stuff that was going on behind the scenes? Can you feel me in, because my uncle loved that company with his whole heart, and I believe people didn't care what happened to him and they let the company tanked?" "I only know what Mark told me and what I just told you. If anyone knows everything, it would be Mark. He was at several of those secret meetings."

    Nathaniel's throat develops a lump as he swallows. "Wow, so you two know a lot of what really happened." "Pretty much, but like I said, Mark knows way more than I do." The two finally arrive at Applebee's. Nathaniel parks next to the front door. "Were here, I will walk you to the front door." "Okay, I can walk you know?" "I know, but why walk to the front door when I can walk you to the front door?" Christy laughs aloud as Nathaniel smiles. They both exit the car as Nathaniel escorts her to the front door and opening it for her. The two are seated as they order their food. A half hour passes by as they talk while eating their entrees'. "So, how do you like your new job?" Christy asks. Nathaniel smiles thinking about being a hit man. "I just love it you know? I feel like I get to do what I love and what I am gifted to do," He says. "Yeah That sounds great! Now after my accident, I feel like we all have a purpose in life, but many of us don't know what that purpose is, and we go around aimlessly living a mundane life." Nathaniel listens intently. "I agree Christy. I can honestly tell you, I'm living mine now."

Christy nods her head in agreement. "I couldn't agree more with you Nathaniel. Go for it." The two are silent for a moment. "See, I had the big house, the fancy car, money in the bank, a hot boyfriend, or should I say boyfriend's plural." Christy laughs at herself. "That's another story, all I thought about was me. I can say life moved so fast for me it never allowed me to listen to God. Do you understand what I'm saying?" "I do," Nathaniel responds. "I just ignored my calling in life," Christy says. "What do you think that calling was?" Nathaniel asks. "Telling the world that God loves them regardless of who you are and what you have or don't have," Christy says smiling. "If God can change me from the way I was towards people, I know he can change anybody." Nathaniel takes a sip of his Coke. "So, you have you heard from Mark yet?" Christy takes a bite into the last portion of her Turkey Sandwich. "No, still haven't heard from him. I know he said he was starting his own company, he's probably doing that now?" "Oh yeah, where?" "Bangkok." "Oh, cool." "He'll probably call me and tell me about how everything is going." "Well, let me know, but don't tell him I'm asking about him, I want it to be a surprise," Nathaniel says. "Sure thing, I won't tell," Christy responds. "That's good to know," Nathaniel responds smiling.

CHAPTER FIFTEEN

"Lunch with Friends"

It's the weekend, and, Christy and her mom are at the mall getting some fresh air. As Christy window shops, a finger taps her on the shoulder. She turns around and to her surprise, it's Angela. "Hey Christy!" "Oh, hi!" "What a surprise to see you here," Angie says. "Same here," Christy responds. "I see your up and about looking good." "Yes, I am, but I still have this small limp. I'm managing though. What brings you here to the mall?" Christy asks as Angela lifts her shopping bag. "I've been here a good hour and a half. Christy notices Angie's shopping bag is full. "Oh, silly me. I see your shopping bag is full." "It sure is," Angie responds. "Are you here by yourself?" "Oh, no, I'm here with my mom. She's still in Marshalls," Christy says as Angie glances over at the Marshalls store entrance. "Oh, okay. Well, are you hungry right now? It would be my treat," Angie says.

Christy glances at her watch. "Yeah, I'm hungry. Let me see if my mom wanted something I can bring back for her." "Okay, sure," Angela responds as Christy calls her Mom on her cell phone. "Hello, mom? Hey, I just ran into a friend, she wants to treat me to lunch. Are you hungry, or did you want me to bring you back anything?" Christy's eyes sway to the left as she listens to her mother's response over the phone. Angela stands waiting gracefully with a smile. "Okay, you sure you don't want anything?" Christy pauses for a response. "Okay, I'll call you back in thirty minutes, take your time shopping. Okay bye." Christy ends the call.

She glances at Angela and says, "Okay, let's go eat." "Great, I know a great place in the mall, follow me," Angela responds. The two of them, walk side by side continuing their conversation. Minutes later, they arrive at a small Café. Inside, both ladies grab two stools sitting by a tall round table. Christy slides her small frame onto the chair while Angela does the same. Her tall frame makes it much easier. "I wish I was as tall as you Angie." "Oh, give me a break, being tall is a hassle sometimes. Guys want short girls; short guys want tall girls and that means one plus one does not equal two." Christy laughs aloud. "Be thankful the way you are, that's what I always say." Christy glances over the menu. "Wow, the menu looks good." "I told you," Angela responds.

Later, they order their food. Christy orders an Angus Beef burger with lettuce, tomatoes, onions, cheese, ketchup, mustard, and a small amount of mayo on the edge of the meat. Her sides consist of steak fries and a Coke. Angela orders Chicken Fingers with a side of honey mustard sauce and a side of regular fries with a coke. Both ladies chow down their food like two rabbits getting first dibs at the bowl of food. "Thanks Angie, I really appreciate this." "No problem, I'm glad we connected. God had a plan for me today," Angie says. "Why do you say that?" Christy asks. I was about to go the other way to shop in another store. By then I saw you. We would have missed each other," Angie says. "Oh, this food is so good Angie. I've never had a hamburger taste this good," Christy answers. "Isn't it filling? I've been coming here for the past five years now," Angie says. "Really?" Christy asks. Angie nods her head yes.

"But enough about me, this moment is all about you,"

Angie responds as she wipes her mouth and hands with her napkin. Christy finishes chewing her food.

"Tell me how you're feeling, and how you felt about DinoCore closing its doors?"

"I'm coming along as you can see," Christy says.

"Yeah? You know that adds to your character?"

Christy smiles.

"Stop it."

"No, really. Look at it this way, a guy won't notice you, and you get free handicap parking."

Christy laughs and almost chokes as she sips on her Coke thinking about Angie's comment.

"Thanks a lot Angie."

"You're welcome," Angie smiles saying.

Christy gathers herself as she finds the words to express about DinoCore.

"When DinoCore closed its doors, it pushed me into a corner I never thought I would be in. It was a bad thing that happened to me and to everyone there, but I realized how less of control we really have over our lives. I cried for hours about it in the hospital and after my recovery. Months later, I didn't know what to do about my bad experience and I'm seeking God for answers about the next chapter of my life. I guess the accident put me through a test that was intended for me all along."

Angela quickly interrupts Christy.

> "Oh, no Christy, that wasn't God," Angela says.

Christy thinks to herself.

> "I don't understand."

> "Christy, when bad things happen to us, that's not God at all. That's the other guy."

> "What other guy?" Christy asks.

> "The devil."

> "I thought he was make believe?"

> "Oh, okay. How do you know he's real?"

Angie pauses for a moment.

> "Look around you, all of the bad things that are happening. God does not create bad things. Everything he does is for our good."

> "Why do bad things happen to good people then?"

> "Because of sin on the earth through the fall of man through Adam and Eve. Christy were never

going to be perfect because of sin on the earth. We can strive for it, but we will always come up short because we are humans that have a free will that can get it right sometimes and get it wrong too. I'm a Christian and I love God more than you can imagine but I'm not perfect," Angie says.

Angie laughs.

"What's so funny?" Christy asks.

"Well, yesterday I cussed out this old man for cutting me off in traffic. I was wrong, but I did this to this old man. I only do it when I'm really, really agitated."

Christy laughs.

"It just comes out, but God is working on me with this. Stop laughing please?" Angie asks laughing.

"So, I pulled up next to him to tell him how bad his driving was. He didn't even know I was there. So, we are at the light and I'm honking my horn at him, I mean leaning on it."

Christy laughs uncontrollably.

"Angela, no you didn't!"

"Yeah I did. So, I started cussing at him so loud to get his attention. People were walking by on the street turning to see what was going on. The old man finally looked over at me." Angie pauses for a moment as Christy waits with anticipation.

"And then what?"

"With no expression, he turned his head back and floored the gas pedal on his car. He was drove that big Cadillac like I've never seen before. It was big and old. The car's back wheels started spinning with smoke coming from behind it. That car shot off like a rocket."

Angie pauses for a moment.

"Smoke was all in my face. It got in my mouth and I was coughing and spitting everywhere. Then the cars behind me were blowing their horns at me."

Christy laughs bewildered at Angie.

"Why were they blowing their horns at you?"

Angie throws her hands up.

"Because the light was green!"

Christy bursts with laughter holding her hand over her mouth.

Angela sips on her Coke.

"They didn't care about the smoke and the fact I couldn't see that the light was green! That old man timed his take off. I believe he's done it before. I don't know, maybe he was some street racer when he was young, I don't know."

Christy is crying with laughter. "I'm looking crazy and I got the little fish thingy on the back of my car with the words Jesus in the middle of it you know?"

Angela pauses for a second.

"So, do you want to know the moral of the story?"

"Yes please," Christy replies with excitement.

"Never disrespect your elders. I swear…"

Angie catches herself.

"Well I shouldn't swear…sorry…but if I was racing that old man, I know I would've loss, I can swear on that. He would've taught me a thing or two about racing that day for sure. I bet he had some high powered custom motor under that hood too."

Christy laughs again.

"This is too much Angie, stop it!"

"I'm glad you find it funny because I sure didn't when it happened."

Christy gathers herself as Angie smiles.

"You know Christy, I never saw you laugh, not once ever when we worked together?"

Christy thinks to herself.

"Wow Angie, you know what, I think your right."

"Why is that?" Angie asks.

Christy thinks for a moment.

> "You know, I think it's because I was never really happy on the inside and no one ever made me laugh like you just did."

Christy pauses for a moment.

> "You know when you love your job so much that it consumes you to the point you have no other identity with family and friends, I guess you become a prisoner to it because it takes everything from your personality and who you really are."

> "Wow Christy, that's pretty deep. I never saw it like that. You put things in perspective for me, yes for sure. When I got you fired, I never once thought about how it would impacted my life, my emotions, and my self-worth."

Angela pauses for a moment as her eyes begin to welt up with emotion as she stares out the window as people walk by in the Mall.

> "I am truly sorry for what I did to you Angela, truly sorry. What I did was wrong, and I shouldn't have done that," Christy says.

Angela smiles grabbing Christy's hand softly holding it.

> "I forgive you Christy. Look at where I am now. I would never have imagined us sitting down together having lunch. Maybe punching you in the face, and pulling your hair out, but not this," Angela says.

Christy laughs shaking her head as Angela sighs.

"Life is funny. You never know how it will turn out. I think that's why we must trust God that he will work things out no matter what."

Christy agrees.

"True, very true."

"To trust someone, you have to know them. Some people trust the devil more than God because they believe his lies, and his fears every day. I always say, everything good is God. Everything bad is the devil. That's life."

The next day, Christy finishes her part-time shift as her cell phone rings. Christy answers,

"Hello?"

"Hey," the voice says.

"Who is this?" Christy asks.

"Christy? It's me Mark."

"Mark?" Christy asks.

"Hey, yeah, what's up?"

"Mark, hey, how are you?"

"Oh, I'm good. Things are going well. I called to ask you how you were and how your recovery was going?"

"Thanks for asking. I'm coming along quite well actually. I get therapy when I'm not working."

"Working? Where do you work now?"

Christy is hesitant to respond.

"Oh, I got a small job to get me back in the swing of things."

"I see. Are you still in that beautiful house on the hills?"

"Oh, no, I had to let that go. My medical bills were too much to handle."

Mark agrees. "That's understandable."

"Mark, where are you?" Christy asks.

"I'm in Bangkok running my own business now," Mark answers.

"Really, wow, you said you were going to do that," Christy responds.

"Yep, I'm doing it," Mark says.

"That's great!"

"Christy, I was calling to see when you wanted to get back to doing what you do, you know, what you were the bomb at?"

"What, you still want me to come work for you?"

"Yeah, does that sound bad?" "Oh, no, that would be great, it's just, you're in Bangkok though."

"Look, I'm setting up some offices in the states. One of them will be in Atlanta in the downtown area, so you won't have to come out here to Bangkok."

"Well, that makes my decision a lot easier, but I'm still in recovery mode and..."

Mark interrupts her.

"Oh, there's no rush. It's going to take me a minute to set up shop out there, so you have time."

Christy likes what she hears.

"Okay then, let's keep in touch, and I'll let you know where I'm at mentally and physically and you can give me a date when you will be in business here."

"That sounds great Christy."

Christy immediately remembers something.

"Oh, Mark?"

"Yeah?"

"Do you remember..."

Christy stops herself remembering what Nathaniel told her that he wanted to surprise Mark and for Christy not to tell him or mention his name to him.

"Oh, I just had a brain freeze, never mind," Christy says.

"Oh, that's okay, it happens to all of us," Mark says.

"So, when do you plan to be in Atlanta?"

"Probably in a couple of weeks."

"Let me know when you get into town."

"I definitely will Christy, take care of yourself and get well soon."

"I will, thanks for the call and checking up on me."

"Most definitely," Mark replies.

The two end their conversation.

Christy clocks out of her job. She walks outside where her mother is waiting. She enters the car. "Hey, mom," She says. "I noticed you weren't limping a lot," Her mother says. "Really?" "Yes, you didn't notice it?" "No, not really, I'm so use to it now. How did I look?" Christy's mom drives out of the parking lot. "You looked like your old self, confident and secure." "That's great to hear, because I really needed that." "That's what mothers are for right?" The car is quiet for a moment, then her mom speaks. "Oh, I forgot to tell you the young lady you told me about, Angela, called the house. I don't know if she called you on your cell, but she wanted to know if you wanted to go to church with her Sunday." Christy thinks about it. "I've never been inside a church before, I don't know." "You've been in church before Christy when you were a kid." "Okay Mom listen to what you just said, I was a kid. I'm in my twenties now, that's a long time." "Christy, you act like you're going to sing at the President's Inauguration. You're just going to church to visit, not join the darn thing."

Christy let's out a huge sigh. "I don't even know what to wear." Her mother shouts, "Christy!" "What?" "You wear clothes, geez." "I know that. What style of clothes?" "She said anything." "Okay, that's reasonable, but what if they ask you to stand up or something?" "Why would they do that?" "I don't know, maybe because you're a visitor." "Oh, well I don't believe they would do that, I mean what if it's a big church and you have hundreds of people that are visiting, that would take the whole service for everybody to give their name wouldn't it?" Christy and her mom glance at each other simultaneously. "Yeah," they say together in unison. Christy thinks for a moment. "You should come too mom!" Christy says with excitement.

    Her mom shakes her head. "No, I have my own church to go to. I don't like big churches." "You don't like big churches? Well, there were crowds of people at the mall the other day and that's a big place. You looked fine to me, you even had a smile on your face as you went from rack to rack to rack with the crowds of people in their shopping." Her mom slowly turns her head looking at her daughter as she drives. Her mother has a look of annoyance written all over her face. "Leave my shopping alone, that's my time of peace." "Well, I think you should go." Her mom thinks for a moment. "I'll tell you what, you go first, then I'll go second." "Why?" "Because if you can take it, then I know I can take it." "So, you want to use me as a Guinea pig?" Her mom laughs saying, "You bet." "Okay mom, you're on."

Christy understands. "I get it. If I have him, I'll make it despite the storms around me. If I don't have him, I may still make it, but it will be harder to figure things out when the storms around me are too much for me to bear on my own?" "You got it Christy. The one thing you must know is, the devil is your enemy. And when you're in battle with an enemy, you must know what he is capable of. You can't fight an enemy you can't see, and the greatest thing the devil ever did was convince the world he doesn't exist. You see all this evil all over the world, don't you?" "Yes." "But you see different people doing it right?" "Yes." "And you see good all over the world also with different people doing it as well. In both good and bad, people are making choices to yield to God or to the devil. That's life Christy, that's life."

That Sunday, Angela picks Christy up for church. Christy enters her car wearing a white and black sundress. "Hey!" "Hey girlfriend, looking good!" "Thanks, you look great too." "Yeah, thanks." "So, how are you feeling?" "I feel good, thanks for asking. I really appreciate you picking me up." "Oh, no problem." The girls drive off headed to Angie's church. After thirty minutes later, they arrive walking inside through the lobby and into the sanctuary to find a seat. Once seated, a skit performed by the church begins. The skit presents a young lady named Jessica who dreams of success and will do anything to get it. During the skit, Jessica finally achieves her dreams. One day she awakens looking at herself in the mirror and doesn't like what she sees, so she smashes the mirror. It shatters in pieces into her sink and onto the bathroom floor as Jessica glances at the pieces seeing half of her face in a reflection.

She talks to God. "I thought I would be happy, I have everything I ever wanted God, why am I so depressed? Why do I feel this way? Why can't I be happy on the inside?" God speaks to her in a still small voice. "Because what you were after was shallow. It has no substance, no life." Jessica looks around the room. "I don't understand?" God speaks again. "What will you do if you lose your job, your house, and your car? If these things are your source of happiness, how do you expect to be happy without them?" Jessica speaks to God again. "But I thought these are the things we live for. What is life if we are not pursuing something?" God speaks again. "I want you to have these things, but I don't want these things to define who you are." "God, who am I then without these things?" "You are my creation and I love you so much. I gave life to you, but you haven't given me your life. I want you to have an intimate relationship with me. I want to be in every part of your life, not just the church part. I want you to be content with who you are and not what you have."

God continues speaking. "Being shallow is hollow. That is where things are predictable. I am in the deep end of the pool where life is unpredictable at times, many times the waves are calm, sometimes there are great storms raging by the enemy, Satan, but if you are where I am, you are safe with me no matter what happens. Let me teach you how to swim." "But what if I drown?" asks Jessica. "Even if you drown because you've missed it or made a mistake in life that you cannot come back from, you will be with me forever because you put your trust in me enough with your life to swim in the deep waters where I am. I will be your lifeguard and we will spend eternity forever. Don't be afraid." Jessica questions God. "So, you want me to let go of my life, all my fears, all my worries, all my wants, my thoughts, my possessions, my family, everything I value and treasure to you?" "Yes." "But what will I have to control?" "The freedom to choose in the life that I've given you…the will to choose between right or wrong. You will always have that power. That is the greatest gift other than my son that I've given to the world."

Jessica thinks for a moment. "Okay, I can do that. So, what do I do now?" "Rest in my presence by spending time with me every day. Talk to me, tell me what's on your mind." "But you already know, you are God, you know everything." "Yes, I know everything about you, but I want you to tell me what's going on in your life." Jessica agrees. "Okay, but I think I should clean up this glass first before we get started, this is a mess." God laughs. "Jessica, you're just like Martha in the Old Testament, leave the glass, that glass isn't going anywhere." The skit ends as the church stage darkens. The staff of the church begin removing the stage props as the Pastor approaches the stage speaking. "Awesome skit huh?" The congregation claps. "Jessica realized having the things she wanted in life, didn't give her the values she thought she needed. She was unhappy with her life. Why?" The pastor pauses for a moment. "I'll tell you why…just like Jessica, we too put our value in the things we have and the things we are pursuing, but all along, those things will never satisfy us the way a relationship with God can."

"We live in a world of wants and more wants. And when we get those wants, we realize we want something more. Have you ever bought a new car and after a while that car didn't feel new anymore?" New things are just that…new. But over time they wear, and they get old. God is telling us, come sit with me my son, my daughter, and talk to me. I already know everything that is going on in your life, but I want to hear it from you. Tell me how you really feel about your life and what's going on in it. Talk to me." The pastor walks across the stage to the other side of the congregation. The congregation is silent. "How long will we continue to give God the leftovers of our lives? He deserves everything we have, the best of us. He wants to sit down and eat a well-cooked full course meal with you and in the process, talk with you about everything that is going on in your life." An hour later, the service ends and Angie and Christy stand in the lobby talking. "So, what do you think about the service?" Angie asks.

Christy becomes excited. "I enjoyed it, thanks for inviting me." "Thank you for coming with me," Angie says. Moments later, Angie's five friends see her approaching her with hugs as Angie introduces Christy to them. "Hey everybody, this is my friend Christy." All the ladies greet Christy with hugs as well. "Hi Christy, nice to meet you." "Likewise," Christy says. Angie introduces all the girls. "This is Rachel, Tia, Molly, and Amy." Christy waves at each one of them. "Hi," She says. "Nice to meet you Christy," The ladies respond in unison. Rachel chimes in. "So how did you two meet each other?" "Angie glances at Christy waiting for a response. "Oh, we used to work together," Christy says. "Oh, at Google?" Molly asks. "No, at Dinocore," Christy says.

Immediately all the ladies remember Angie talking about a person named Christy with whom she had problems with at work. The girls emotions transition to a somber mood as their facial expressions change. "Oh, I see," The ladies respond in unison. Angie immediately changes the subject. "So, what's up girls? Want to go get something to eat?" The girls stare at each other waiting to see who will be the first to make up an excuse not to. Tia makes her move. "Oh, I can't, I have to pick up my son from his dad's. I told him mommy will be picking you up today!" All the girls laugh together. Molly has plans too. "Yeah, I got a paper to finish before class tomorrow." That leaves Rachel and Amy to give their excuses. "I can't, I have other plans," Pam and Rachel respond together. "Me too," replies Amy. "Well, ladies, I'm going to run upstairs to see if I can catch Rick before he leaves. He's serving today in the film department. Got to run," Pam says as she scurries off. All the girls say their goodbyes to each other as Angie glances at them individually. "Okay, yawl, I guess we will have to do lunch next time." The girls agree. "Yeah, sure, that would be great. Okay, see you," they say as Angie and Christy wave goodbye to them. "Nice to meet you Christy," the ladies respond.

Out in the parking lot, Christy makes a comment. "Wow, your friends sure didn't like me once they knew who I was." Angie laughs, "Yeah, you noticed huh?" The two enter Angie's car. "So, what did you tell them about me Angie?" Angie backs her car out of the parking spot. "I told them what was going on at work between you and me back then and they all prayed for me, stuff like that." "Okay, like specifics?" "What? You want every detail of our conversation or something?" "That would help," Christy says. Angie laughs again. "Christy come on. It wasn't like I described you as some evil wicked witch of the west." "Well, they looked like they wanted to pull my hair and claw my eyes out," Christy says. Angie sighs. "They are church girls, they wouldn't do that." "You think?" Christy asks. Angela gives in. "Okay, I told them how mean you were to me and how I had to fight the hateful thoughts and feelings I had toward you." Christy feels hurtful as she glances out of the passenger window trying to hold back her tears. Angie tries to console her. "I'm sorry Christy. I'm still human even though I'm a Christian."

Angie takes her right hand rubbing Christy's shoulder and back area as she drives. "I'm truly sorry. If it will help, I will talk to them to smooth things over." Christy's old ways start to rise in her. "Don't bother." Angie pauses for a moment. "Excuse me?" "You invited me, so I would see how much I'm hated by your friends!" Angie turns to Christy. "I would never do that to you Christy!" Angie's eyes water as she blinks rapidly to control her emotions. "Gosh Christy, I would never do you like that. I'm not that kind of person, I said I'm sorry. I will talk to them, they are cool girls to be around, really. I made a mistake telling them everything that went on." Christy agrees. "Yeah, I agree with that." Christy pauses for a moment. "I never knew I was that mean to you. I just reacted to who I was and not who I wanted to be."

Angela chimes in with a response. "You know Christy, I truly thought you were like a female hitman." Christy caught in the moment of her emotions bursts with laughter. "What?" "Yeah, I used to think you killed people on the side or something because you were so cold and callous." "Oh my gosh Angie stop, please." Christy continues laughing as Angie continues talking. "I'm serious. I thought I was on your hit list because you detested me so much." Christy dabs her eyes with a napkin. "I thought one night you were going to follow me home, sneak into my apartment, kill me, and tell everybody at work I had quit or something." Christy laughs uncontrollably. "Angie, you're too much. I never thought you were this funny." "Guess what?" Angie asks. "What?" Christy asks. "Me neither!" Angie responds.

CHAPTER SIXTEEN

"Nathaniel Meets the Cartel"

In El Paso, Texas, a passenger plane arrives at the airport. In the gateway of the airport, as the passengers file off the plane, a familiar face appears, Nathaniel Boykins walking with a carry-on bag over his shoulder. As he enters the jetway in the lobby of the seating area past awaiting passengers for the next flight, he walks with confidence wearing his dark sunglasses making it hard to see through his eyes into his soul as he makes his way to the escalator. As the escalator travels down to the lower level where the retrieval of luggage bags resides, as he travels down the escalator he checks his messages on his phone. At the bottom, two Hispanic men at the bottom of the escalator wearing dress shirts and slacks with casual shoes approach Nathaniel giving him the nod. All three men walk towards the exit past people grabbing their luggage eager to get out of the airport and go home, or visit relatives, or start their vacation. Outside awaits a black Chevy Suburban with tinted windows all around and a driver behind the wheel waiting for all three men. They enter the vehicle and drive away.

After a twenty-five-minute drive, the black Suburban arrives at its destination. In front of the vehicle sits a huge mansion with brown brick and plenty of landscaping consisting of shrubbery, maple woodchips, and white rocks. Two front doors appear the perfect size for two Grizzly Bears to walk through standing side by side. Inside each door are carved stain glass see through murals in color allowing you to see the fully lit chandeliers hanging inside. As Nathanial exits the vehicle, the trickling sound of water grabs his attention. He turns his head towards the sound seeing a gigantic statue of a horse standing over a waterfall. The two men escort Nathaniel inside the home as the Suburban drives away. Inside the home are tan marble floors with an accent of brown glistening inside them. Above are three huge chandeliers lined in a row illuminated as the sparkling glass makes the lighting brighter than what it appears. As Nathaniel follows the two men down the hallway, they approach two-framed doors guarded by two men with shoulder holstered weapons. One of the men at the door knocks for Nathaniel and the two men. After half a second, the door opens. Behind it are two more armed guards with HK416 semi-automatic weapons guarding a distinguished man named "Felipe' "The Shadow" Morales" sitting behind a huge maple wood desk with a matching entertainment shelf behind him.

The bearded man glances at Nathaniel in the doorway shielded by his armed guards. Nathaniel is patted down for weapons as he waits for his cue to enter. The distinguished man lifts his hand ordering Nathaniel to enter. The armed guards step aside while Nathaniel passes by them as the two men that brought Nathaniel disappear. Nathaniel enters the room as the bearded man orders him to have a seat with his hand extended towards the chair in front of him. Nathaniel graciously sits down removing his sunglasses as the man finishes his phone call without saying a single word. His eyes stare at Nathaniel as he palms both of his hands together into a balled fist. "So, gracious to see you Nathaniel." "Thank you for having me Senores' Felipe'." "Have you found my money yet?" Nathaniel is silent before he calmly speaks. "No, I haven't." "Ah, I see. So, you travel all this way to tell me this yes?" "No Senores' Felipe', I'm here to inform you that I have a huge lead on Mark Collins." "Is that so?" "Yes, he's started a business in Bangkok, and I believe your money is with him."

Felipe' nods his head as his eyes search for more answers. "What about this Christy Billings, does she know where my money is?" Felipe' asks. "She's the one that presented this information to me. Do you want me to take her out as well?" Felipe' nods his head yes. "When you get my money back. I want no loose ends." "Okay, I will need some more cash to do this. You can pay me the rest on the back end once it's done." "More money?" Felipe' asks with conviction. Nathaniel is hesitant to respond but does. "Yes. I can guarantee I can get this done, but Bangkok is far away from the states where I normally do my work." "I see," Felipe' responds. "How much?" "Five thousand," Nathaniel responds. "So, that is five thousand now, and five thousand later?" "Yes, that is correct." Felipe' pauses for a second then motions one of his men over next to him. The man leans in to hear what his boss has to say as Felipe' whispers words. The man nods his head, then briskly walks away.

Felipe' stares at Nathaniel who looks around the room at the impressive art work on the walls. "I love this room. Did you decorate this yourself?" The remark causes Felipe' to laugh. "No, no, my wife and daughter did all of this." "Hmm. I would have to say they did a great job for your man cave." Felipe' smiles. "Very comedic you are. Tell me, are you doing this alone, or with your brother?" My brother, no, I have no idea where he is." "Let me ask you Nathaniel, is he going to be a problem for what he knows?" "No sir, he will not be a problem." "And how do you know this?" Felipe' asks. "Because he is my twin brother. Our loyalty together goes beyond these walls. They began at birth and will end at death." The words seem to satisfy Felipe's ears as he points his index finger at Nathaniel. "Very well spoken."

 The door to Felipe's office opens as the Consigliere' enters with a small duffle bag. He hands the duffle bag to Nathaniel who gladly receives it. Nathaniel unzips the bag checking its contents. Happy at what he sees, he zips the bag up. The Consigliere' sits in a chair diagonal from Nathaniel. "Is that enough" asks Felipe'. "Yes, it is," Nathaniel says. "It should be, that's twenty-five thousand," Felipe' responds as he leans forward in his chair. "So, you will retrieve my money, dispose of Mark Collins, and his assistant Christy Billings. I am paying you over what you asked because the extra will be given to my men to do the job for the three of you if the job is not done. That would be Mark, Christy, and you, understand?" "Yes, Senores' Felipe', I will get the job done." "I would hope so. I invested a lot of my money with DinoCore. I was promised by your uncle with this last investment, that my money would be laundered back to me with interest. Now millions of my money is out there somewhere in someone's hands. That's what I get for trying to do things the honest way."

Felipe' pauses for a second. "Now I am sorry you had to do what you had to do to your Uncle, but he was not an honest man, you do know that right?" "Yes, I do." "He doesn't keep his word, or should I say, he didn't keep his word. In this line of business, your word is everything. What you did for me to your Uncle, was a sign of true loyalty." "Well, if I didn't, I would be lying next to my Uncle, right?" Felipe' stares at Nathaniel. "That is true, but that would have been your fault, not mine. Everything in life can run smooth if people would just keep their word. This is knowledge from me to you for free, remember this." Nathaniel nods his head yes. "Are we done here?" Felipe' asks. Nathaniel laughs. "I should be asking you sir?" Nathaniel's smile quickly diminishes when Felipe' nor his Consigliere' does not laugh.

Nathaniel quickly retracts his words. "Okay, wrong choice of words." "You are a comedian no?" Felipe' asks. "No, I just like to break the ice," Nathaniel responds as he puts on his sunglasses. "Ice? What ice?" asks Felipe'. Nathaniel stands confused as he throws up both of his hands while smiling. "Hey, thanks for the meeting, let me go and take care of this business for you. I will call you with the updates." Nathaniel quickly sees himself out of Felipe's office as Felipe' sits bewildered glancing at his Consigliere' who shrugs his shoulders in response.

That Saturday back in Atlanta, Georgia, Christy volunteers with Angie on a mission's trip at a soup kitchen in the downtown area. They both serve food to various homeless people. While serving them, they greet them with a smile. Moments later, Christy and Angie are seated with a man and woman. The man and woman tell them a story about their lives. "I used to be a stock broker," The Man says convincingly. Christy seems very interested. "A stockbroker, really?" "I sure was young lady," He says. The man takes a sip of his soup. "One time, I made a million-dollar deal in a week." "Wow that's really interesting." "Yeah, tell me about it." "So, what happened after the deal?" "Oh, I lost it the next day the stock market dropped at 700 points." Christy has a lump in her throat as she swallows thinking about the severity of that loss. "That sounds so awful. In one day, you lost it all?" Christy asks.

The man nods his head in agreement as he pauses for a moment. "You know, the worst thing in life is having so much money you could buy anyone or anything, then in twenty-four hours losing it all and you can't buy nothing." "Well, money isn't everything, right?" Angie asks the man. The man glances back at her as the soup on his spoon balances itself waiting to enter his mouth. "Try telling that to the clients' money you lost." Christy is curious. "So how did you tell them what happened?" "I didn't. I let someone else do that. I disappeared and that's why I'm here. I lost everything I had including my self-respect. I'm sure they read about it in the paper like everyone else." The homeless woman adds to what the man just said. "I had my own business. I used to own several salons around the metro area." The woman pauses for a moment.

"I lost them all when I didn't pay my taxes on all of my properties. After I saw what the government could do, I just didn't care anymore." "But, didn't you know you had to pay your taxes every year on your businesses?" "Yes, but my book keeper said the books were in order. Later I found out that they weren't, and that she hid accounts from me. She stole thousands of dollars from me I later found out." The woman pauses for a second. "I believed her when I looked her in the eyes. She was a certified accountant, and the numbers seemed on point, but she knew how to fudge the numbers to make it look good." "That's horrible" says Christy. "So, did you sue her for that?" "She fled the country, and I couldn't find her. After paying several private investigators and going to court to face the IRS, I ran out of money so here I am. I don't trust know one no more."

"This is so sad," says Angie. "So, what advice would you give to people you see every day?" Christy asks. The man turns to Christy. "I would tell them to be thankful for everyday you're breathing' because in a flash it could all be gone." He pauses thinking for a second. "Isn't it in the Bible somewhere it says, our life is a vapor." Angie responds. "Yes, it says that." The man raises his hand. "You could be here today and gone tomorrow just like that." He snaps his finger quickly causing Angie and Christy to jerk their heads simultaneously. The woman agrees. "I would tell them, just be thankful and don't ever judge a book by its cover.

You know, when you look at the cover of a book, you don't know what's going on inside it. You must read it to get what's inside and know what that front cover is about. I mean, you look at him and me, and you would've never known what we've been through or where we came from. We are all a step away from losing it all. You can't trust the world you live in all the time. It has a system of its own, and that's greed. Everybody's greedy wanting more until there's nothing left for the rest of us to live on."

Christy is curious. "So, what are we to do then? I mean, money makes the world go around right?" The woman stares at Christy. "Does money make the world go around or is it leading the world to an end? How much does this country owe what, over a trillion dollars? How will that ever get paid? Think about that, and get back to me cause' honey, I'm not going anywhere." Hours later, Christy and Angie leave the soup kitchen. In Angie's car, they discuss their encounter. "That was really interesting huh?" Angie asks. "Yeah, it was more depressing than anything I could imagine," Christy replies.

Angie glances over at Christy.

"What's wrong?"

"Oh nothing, I was just thinking about what she said."

"Yeah, I'm going to be pray that they get back on their feet real soon," Angie responds.

"Can you believe that Angie, I mean, they had everything and it's all gone in a blink of an eye."

"Yeah, it's very sad."

"How could that happen Angie? I mean, this is America you know, where you get the American dream?"

"It's life Christy, that's the only thing I can think of. They were just dealt a severe blow."

"I know Angie, but nobody ever expects anything like that right?"

"Christy, all you can do is live your life the best way you know how, and only God can show us all that. Every day a choice we make can either be bad or good. We all get up to go to work, pay bills and take at least a vacation or two a year, then do it all over again."

"That's the way I used to live. But there has to be more to life than that right Angie?" Christy asks.

"Well yeah, Christy, I mean, living your dream, your destiny, what you are really good at that impacts others' lives in a positive way. That's the only way to a better life that I can think of, but you must find out what that dream is, and to do it. The only answer to finding that is knowing why you're here on this earth and what to do while you are here."

"Isn't that the American dream though?" Christy asks.

    Angie thinks about the question.

"What is the American dream to you Christy?"

Christy thinks for a moment.

"Owning your own home, having a family, nice cars in the driveway, the house with a pinked fence," She says.

"Isn't that what you had?" Angie asks.

"Well, yeah," Christy responds confused.

"Were you happy with that?" Christy thinks again.

"Well honestly no, come to think of it."

"Why do you say that?" asks Angie.

"I guess because at the time, I never had any peace about having that on the inside. I was always agitated about something like having to pay the huge house payment, or paying for the expensive car," Christy says.

> "You had no peace at all, but you had the big house, the nice car, and you were one of the top executives at DinoCore and you still weren't happy?"
>
> "No, I wasn't, I would have to say."
>
> "Wow Christy. You know, at that time in my life I got fired, and I was still happy on the inside, not the outside."

Christy remembers that moment as she lowers her head.

> "Thanks for reminding me Angie."
>
> "I'm just saying, I wasn't trying to convict you or anything. I was thinking about how we all think

it's supposed to be, but it never turns out that way."

Inside the car, the mood is silent as Angie turns to Christy.

"So how do you feel now where you are at in your life?" Angie asks.

"It's funny because, I have a sense of enlightenment happy after everything that happened to me," Christy responds.

"Really?" Angie asks.

"Well I wouldn't say I'm doing flips about it, but I know I have a different perspective on life right now. I believe God is working everything out for me."

Angie smiles as she continues driving Christy home.

CHAPTER SEVENTEEN

"Volunteering"

The next day, Christy watches T.V. in her mother's living room when suddenly there is a knock at the front door. Christy continues watching T.V. thinking her mother will answer the door, but she doesn't. Christy now annoyed, finally gets up to answer it. When she opens the door, Nathaniel stands greeting her. "Hi, Christy." Christy is shocked to see Nathaniel. "Hey, Nathaniel, what's up?" "Hey Christy, I just stopped by to see how you were doing." "Oh, you drove all the way out here just to see me?" Christy asks as Nathaniel smiles. "Yes and no. I was in the area doing some business, and I thought about you and wondered how you were doing." "Well, that's sweet of you Nathaniel, I'm doing well." "May I come in?" Christy rolls her eyes. "Oh, yeah sure, where are my manners, please do." Nathaniel steps inside.

Christy closes the door behind him. Max comes from the back room approaching Nathaniel as he remains standing. Max smells Nathaniel's feet and legs. Nathaniel kneels to pet him. "Hey boy, how are you doing huh?" Max begins panting hard, then twists and shakes his body as if to relieve himself from any unwanted critters on his body. Christy leads Nathaniel to the couch to sit down. "So, you're doing well I see," Nathaniel says. "Yes, I am.

My limp seems to be going away. The doctor said it might." "Yeah, I noticed that," Nathaniel says. "So, how are you?" Christy asks. "I'm good. Business is good," Nathaniel responds. "That's good to hear. I'm starting to miss the grind of making deals with clients and getting them to invest huge amounts of money," Christy says. "Yeah? So, what's stopping you?" "My memory. My brain is still healing," Christy says nodding her head.

"Well, you're coming along, just give it a little more time," Nathaniel says as Christy glances at the T.V. screen agreeing with him as she turns her head towards him with a nod. "Time is all I have, right?" Christy asks. "You bet," Nathaniel responds. The room is silent as Max lays on the living room floor in front of them grooming himself. "Hey Christy, have you heard anything from Mark?" Christy thinks as her eyes gaze up into the ceiling. "Yes!" "You have?" Nathaniel asks convincingly. "Yeah, he called me." "Really, when?" "Last week. Yeah, he called to see how I was doing." "How is he?" "He's doing great, he's got his business up and running in Bangkok." "Really?" "Yeah." "That's funny because the reason I asked was, I'm heading in that direction to do some business for a little while. Do you have his address?" I had some stuff of his I wanted to surprise him with."

Christy turns away from the T.V. to respond. "No, but I can get it for you." "Christy, I would love you to death if you did." "Sure, no problem. Boy, you must really have something Mark must need." Nathaniel with a smirk on his face chuckles. "You have no idea. Some business associates of mine in El Paso, Texas want to give him something to help his business flourish." "I'll call him tonight, then call you and give you the information you need. Is that okay?" Christy asks. "Cool, but please don't tell him it's me, I want it to be a surprise," Nathaniel says. Christy's old habits kick in. "What's in it for me?" Christy asks. Nathaniel is thrown back by the question. "Excuse me?" Christy laughs. "You heard me, what's in it for me?" Nathaniel thinks about how to answer the question. "I don't know, what did you have in mind?" "You're the gentleman, you tell me?" Nathaniel's brain deciphers the female code for dating. "How about a dinner and a movie?" Christy with a smile on her face, stares Nathaniel in his eyes. "Now you're talking."

Nathaniel nods his head. "Okay then, its' a date." "When are you headed Marks way?" "Next weekend." "Perfect timing. I'll call him tonight and get the address for you." Christy pauses for a second. "Mark asked me when I would be ready to get back to work?" "What did you tell him?" "I told him, it would be awhile. He said he planned to expand his business here in Atlanta." "Oh really?" "Yeah." "When does he plan on doing that?" "I'm thinking next month. I should be ready to go back to work doing what I used to do before my accident." Nathaniel becomes interested. "Wow, I didn't know he would be coming back here to the states if ever." "Why is that?" Nathaniel realizes his mistake in his response. "Oh, well, usually when a company leaves and starts a business overseas, they plan on staying there if not forever because it's cheaper there to do business than here." "Maybe you could wait until he comes back here and surprise him then?"

"Oh no, I can't wait that long." "Well, it was just a suggestion," Christy says. "I thank you Christy sincerely. He's going to love this surprise, it will kill him," Nathaniel says laughing in an evil tone. "Well, I'd better go." Nathaniel leans to pet Max, but instead of a warm return, Max barks at him. Nathaniel jumps back. Christy quickly scolds Max. "Max, stop that! You know better than to do that to our guest." Nathaniel massages his hand which was almost bitten by Max. "It's okay, I think I disturbed his grooming process." "No, Max is just being a nuisance, that's all," Christy says.

Nathaniel walks toward the front door with Christy following him. She opens the front door for him as Nathaniel gives her a hug. Max barks in the background. "Quit Max!" "Thanks Christy, call me tonight and give me that information okay?" "I sure will. Thanks for stopping by Nathaniel." "No problem Christy, by." "Bye." Nathaniel leaves out the door as Christy watches him for a moment, then closes the door. She turns her attention to Max. "Max, you're going to get it! Now what if you would have bitten his hand off huh, he would have sued!" Max whimpers for affection. "Nope, not buying it Max, go to your room now!"

Around 10 p.m. Christy calls Mark. "Hello?" "Hey Mark, it's Christy." "Oh, hey Christy, what's up?" "Not much. I Just called to see how everything was going?" "Good, you ready to get back to work?" The phone is silent for a moment. "Ugh, no not just yet. I need a little more time. But hey, can I send you my resume?" Christy asks. "You don't need to do that Christy, I already know your credentials," Mark says. "It's just procedure, you know for you records," Christy adds. "Christy, come on, you're a solid candidate, you know that. I would hire you even if you weren't qualified. Were good friends and we go way back." "I know that Mark, I just want to do things by the book." Mark sighs over the phone. "Well, if you insist." "Great, what's your address, and I'll put it in the mail." The phone is silent. "Christy, I'm in Bangkok, you do know technology now, you could email it to me, right? By the time I'll get it, it could be Christmas, and that's an understatement. Just email it to me."

"Yeah, I forgot about that, silly me. My brain is still recuperating." "It's okay, I understand." "Hey," Christy says with excitement. "What's up?" Mark asks. "I still need your address, I want to send you this thank you card in the mail anyway." "Oh, well, yeah, no problem." Mark gives Christy his address as she writes it down on a sticky note. "Okay, thanks, I'll call you back soon when I'm ready to get back into the swing of things," Christy says. "Okay, sounds good. Tell your mom I said hi." "I sure will." "Later Christy, thanks for calling," Mark says. "Okay, bye," Christy says. "Bye." The two end the call on both ends of their phone.

Surprisingly, Nathaniel calls Christy. Christy answers her cell phone.

"Hey Mark, what, you forgot to tell me something?" Christy asks.

"Mark? No, this is Nathaniel."

"Oh, hey Nathaniel."

"Hey, I thought you were going to call me back?" Nathaniel asks.

"Yeah, I was, I just got off the phone with Mark."

"Really?"

"Yeah," Christy says.

"You didn't tell him…" Christy quickly interrupts Nathaniel.

"No silly, it's a surprise, right?"

Nathaniel laughs.

"Of course," Nathaniel says.

"Okay, do you have a pen and paper?"

"Yeah, hold on," Nathaniel says.

Christy hears the shoveling of paper through her phone as Nathaniel gathers a piece of paper and something to write with.

"Okay, shoot," he says.

Christy slowly gives Nathaniel Mark's address.

"Okay, got it. Hey, thanks a lot Christy, you won't regret it," Nathaniel says.

"Don't forget you are taking me out."

"How could I forget that Christy, you're a gem."

"And don't you dare tell Mark I gave you his address," Christy says.

"I won't, believe me."

"Okay."

"Hey, I got an early meeting in the morning, that's why I called you. I wanted to get to bed early tonight, but thanks for the info," Nathaniel says.

"No problem," Christy responds.

"I'll give you a call tomorrow or something," Nathaniel says.

"Okay, cool, bye," Christy responds.

"Bye Christy."

The call ends as Christy lays on her bed rubbing Max lying next to her while thinking about Nathaniel."

CHAPTER EIGHTEEN

"Destination Bangkok"

Three days later, a plane arrives in Bangkok. At the exit gate, passengers of Asian descent file out one by one. Among them is Nathaniel dressed in a suit holding his duffle bag. Nathaniel makes his way through the airport onto the main street. Outside, he glances around for a taxi. A taxi approaches him pulling close to the curb. "You need ride?" Nathaniel stares at the man, then responds, "Yes." Nathaniel enters the cab and hands the man a piece of paper with an address on it. The man stares at the sheet of paper. "I need to go here; can you take me?" Nathaniel asks. The taxi driver nods his head yes. "Come, we go." The cabbie replies. "I put luggage in trunk, yes?" Nathaniel quickly resists. "No, no, I got it."

The cab drives away. While in route, Nathaniel enjoys the scenery into the downtown area. With the windows down, the humidity of the tropical climate of the night air fills the cab. The streets are packed with people riding mopeds as their means of transportation. Various vendors are lined up along the streets selling their products. Some people buy, while many don't. "You're from the states, yes?" The taxi driver asks. "Yes, I am" Nathaniel responds in a calm voice. "You like it there?" "I love it." "I went to the United States, I have family there." "Oh yeah, where at?" "Georgia, and San Francisco," The cabbie replies. "Is that, right?" "Yes."

"Where in the states are you from?" The taxi driver asks. "Arkansas," Nathaniel responds. "Ah, I see. Never heard of it." "Don't worry, you're not missing anything. Wow, really?" "Yes, he is a taxi driver there like me here." "What a coincidence." "I've been to Georgia. It is a very big place. The United States too, very big." "Yes, it is." "What do you do?" Taxi driver asks. "What's that?" Nathaniel asks. "Job? What job do you do?" "I'm a business consultant." "Ah, I see. Good money, yes?" "Yeah, I make good money." The taxi driver glances back each time Nathaniel responds. "You like being a taxi driver?" Nathaniel asks. "It pays well, but not what my brother makes in States." "Why don't you move there then?" "My wife and kids are here, this is home. Would love to go, but it would be hard on them, they don't speak any English."

The taxi arrives at its destination. "We are here," The driver says. Nathaniel glances at the high tower apartments around him. "You stay here?" The taxi driver asks. "A friend does," Nathaniel responds. "Very expensive place. I want to live here but can't afford it." "Is that right," Nathaniel asks. "Yes," taxi driver says. Nathaniel glances at the meter. "How much do I owe you?" "Fifteen dollar," The taxi driver responds. "What's your name?" "Lee." "My name is Rick." Nathaniel hands Lee a twenty-dollar bill. "Keep the change Lee. Thanks for the ride," Nathaniel says. "You are welcome Rick, nice to meet you, enjoy your stay." "I will,"

Nathaniel says grabbing his bag as he opens the back door exiting the cab. He closes the door and glances up at the towering apartments again consisting of three buildings. Nathaniel approaches the apartment where he believes Mark Collins lives. Lee drives away as Nathaniel proceeds down the walkway towards the front entrance of the apartment. As Nathaniel enters, a flat screen T.V. plays a night talk show host in Bangkok.

At the front desk, a man typing on a computer keyboard, notices Nathaniel entering the front door. The host nods his head at Nathaniel. "Hi," Nathaniel says. "Hi, I am interested in renting one of your apartments. Do you have any vacancies?" The young man is confused at the question. Nathaniel rewords the question. "Empty rooms?" The host understands. "Oh, yes, we have several empty rooms. You want to buy?" The host asks. "Rent, yes." "Just you or roommate?" "Just me," Nathaniel says. "One or two beds?" "One bed." The young man glances at his computer screen for availability. "We have three one beds. Our guide shows you tomorrow. Good time for you?" The host asks. "No, I need one tonight," Nathaniel says. "Ugh, tonight no good," The host says.

Nathaniel stares at him with no response making the host very uncomfortable. The young man runs his finger over the computer screen. "Guide is not here." "I need one now," Nathaniel demands. "Ugh, now? Ugh, okay, yes. Name?" "Peter," Nathaniel says. "Last name?" "Carter, Nathaniel responds." The host types Nathaniel's fake name into the computer. "Ok, all set. Here are your keys. Your apartment is on 14th floor room 14B." Nathaniel extends his hand. The young man shakes it." "Very well, bye." "Bye" Nathaniel responds.

    Moments later, Nathaniel enters his room opening his duffle bag. Inside the bag two outfits, with under clothes, socks, and hygiene products. Nathaniel walks over to the window staring out of it. The moment captures his attention until his cell phone rings. "Hello?" Nathaniel says. He pauses for a second. "Yes, I'm here. He's here, I have all his information with me. I text you my current location a minute ago." Nathaniel is silent as he listens to the voice on the other end of the phone. "Good, I will meet him there. Make sure he has everything I need." Nathaniel ends the call as a knock at the front door sounds. He answers the door. Opening the door, he sees a young lady smiling with joy the way she was trained when showing and signing new tenants to a room. "Hi, I have lease to sign for you." "Okay, I thought there wasn't a tour guide in tonight." "I'm here." Nathaniel welcomes her into the kitchen area to sign the lease agreement. As the both stand in the kitchen, Nathaniel reads over the contract then signs. He hands the contract to the young lady who is still smiling as she was instructed to do.

    She gladly receives the signed contract nodding her head as a thank you for Nathaniel's service. "Your welcome packet is here to read. Anything you need, contact office and we help you. Bye enjoy stay." "Thank you," Nathaniel responds. The young lady leaves closing the front door behind her. Later that night, Nathaniel leaves his apartment waiting for a taxi. Finally, one arrives as Nathaniel hops in with the taxi driving away. The taxi takes him across town, then drops him off. Nathaniel walks over to a man sitting in a black sedan with tinted windows. Nathaniel enters the back seat. "Glad you could join us Mr. Boykins." "Likewise," Nathaniel says. "Enjoying your stay in Bangkok?" "I haven't been here long enough to know," Nathaniel responds. "You will like," The driver says. "Do you have what I need? Nathaniel asks. "Most certainly," The driver responds. A man in the back seat sitting next to Nathaniel hands him a small bag. Inside is a handgun with a silencer attached. Nathaniel opens it looking inside. "Like what you see?" The driver asks. "Most definitely," Nathaniel responds as He hands the man an envelope in return. The man opens it seeing five thousand dollars wrapped in one hundred-dollar bills. "Like what you see?" Nathaniel asks the man seated next to him. "Most definitely," the man responds. "Good." "I have a question for you Mr. Boykins?" The driver asks. "What's that?" Nathaniel asks. "Why would a man want to kill his friend?" Nathaniel smiles opening the back door. "He's not my friend," Nathaniel says as he exits the vehicle while closing the door and walking away.

Meanwhile back in the states, hours pass at the morning shift of Christy's job. Christy finally leaves the store. As she enters the parking lot walking towards her mother's car, she collapses to the ground. Her eyes begin to flutter as she sees her mom running up to her aid yelling her name. "Christy! Christy! Baby are you okay?" An hour later, Christy is laying on a hospital bed having tests done. She is plugged up to a machine with tubes running out of her arm. Her mother enters Christy's room. A nurse stands by Christy's side holding a chart in her hand while she jots down notes of information from various machines in front of her. Her mom stands on the other side of the bed away from the nurse to hold her daughters hand. Christy is bewildered. "Mom, what happened to me?" "Christy, you fainted honey." "I fainted?" "Yes, you were walking towards the car, then your eyes fluttered, and you fell to the ground." Her mother pauses for a second. "You don't remember anything?" Christy thinks for a moment, then responds. "No, I don't."

"What's wrong with me mom, I thought I was getting better?" "Well, that's what the nurses and doctors are going to find out. We will have to wait for the tests to get done." Christy's eyes begin to water as her mother rubs her arms. "It's going to be okay honey. Don't worry, you're safe here in the hospital." "Christy glances at her mom. "I don't understand, why this?" "I don't know honey." Tears stream down Christy's face. "Will I ever be how I used to be?" "Yes baby, I believe you will. We have to trust God to heal you, that's all." The nurse applies an IV tube into Christy's arm as Christy flinches a little. Suddenly, in walks Angie. "Hey girlfriend!" Angie smiles as Christy smiles back at her. "Hey Angie!" Christy realizes her hair is disheveled as she tries to fix it with a smile. "Ugh it's a bit late for that Christy, I already see your hair is all over the place babe, just go with it girl. Accept it." Christy tries not to laugh but does so anyway.

Angela greets Christy's mom. "Hi, Ms. Billings!" "Hi Angela, thank you for coming." "Thank you for calling me. I just got off work." The nurse leaves the room for a moment. Angie and Christy hug each other. "I'm glad you're talking and looking around after the way your mom described what happened to you. It didn't sound good at all," Angie says. Christy's mom pats her daughter on the shoulder. "I'm going to grab something to eat downstairs in the cafeteria. Did you want anything?" "No, thanks mom. I'll leave you two to talk. Do you want something Angie?" "Oh, no, I'm good thanks." "I'll be back in a minute," Christy's mom says. "Okay mom," Christy responds with a raspy voice. Angie looks up at the T.V. for a second. "So, what are you watching?" "Christy looks up at the T.V. as well. "Oh, I have no idea what I've watched on T.V. since my accident. I don't even have a T.V. in my old bedroom at my mother's house," Christy says.

      Angie responds. "Well, you're not missing much. There's a reason they call T.V. the boob tube." Christy is curious. "No why?" "Because some things you end up watching can make a boob out of you," Angie says as Christy chuckling trying to hold it in as her laughter fills the room. Christy responds. "That's a lot of boobs then." Angie agrees. "Tell me about it Christy." Christy laughs again. Her obnoxious laugh causes some of the nurses in the hallway to see who it is laughing. "I am so glad you came by Angie. You're a true friend. I really needed this." "Christy, don't thank me, thank God your still alive after what you've been through. Can I pray with you?" Christy glances around the room. "Yeah, sure." Angie holds her hand as the two of them close their eyes and begins to pray together. "Father, we thank you for the opportunity to come together to pray for our sister in Christ Jesus, Christy Billings. We pray for her complete healing from the crown of her head to the souls of her feet. We thank you for your healing power right now in Jesus name. As you said in your word, believers will lay hands on the sick and will recover. Right now, we believe and receive your healing power in her body in Jesus name, amen." The prayer ends as Angie and Christy open their eyes simultaneously.

Christy proceeds to wipe her eyes as she smiles with joy. "Thank you," she says. The room is silent for a moment, then Christy asks a question. "Can I tell you something Angela?" "That experience that I had, when my spirit left my body, and I went to that place you said was called Hades. I thought I was going back there when I blacked out. I still have nightmares about that experienced and I think, what if I had died and not been brought back to life? I would still be there Angie and that scares me." "Try not to think about that Christy, you're not that same person anymore. Remember you accepted Christ as you're a savior that Sunday at my church. You're a new creature in Christ now." "But how can I forget that Angie?

That's not something you never forget. It's not like some horror movie that you can turn off when you get scared because you don't want to watch it anymore. I think about my friend Jessica. She's never coming out of there, ever Angie." A worried look on Christy's face brings back that horrifying moment.

"Christy, that place, was not made for any of us. Heaven is where we all should be when we leave our physical bodies. The only thing that stands in the way of us going there is our free will to choose not to by denying God in our hearts. The key that unlocks the door for us to live forever, is salvation in Christ Jesus. You must tell the world your story the way that people will understand why we need to be saved. Deep down, we all know God is real. But many of us don't know why we must be saved, and why we need God. Your story will tell them that. Tell your story Christy. You can do it." "I see," Christy says.

CHAPTER NINETEEN

"Taking Out Mark"

On a Friday morning as Mark prepares to leave for work entering the elevator, he presses the "L" button for Lobby. The door closes, as the elevator travels down from the 20th floor. Mark stares at the numbers as they illuminate from high to low. The numbered button stops at floor 15. The door opens as Nathaniel enters the elevator wearing dark sunglasses and a fake beard, standing before Mark. He speaks to Mark. "Hey, how's it going?" "Pretty good, it's Friday," Mark replies. "Yes, it is," Nathaniel says pressing the "L" button for the Lobby as the door closes. "Friday says party time for me after a long work week," Mark replies not recognizing Nathaniel at all. "Same here," Nathaniel says turning his head slightly to face Mark. "You live here?" Mark asks. "Yeah, just moved into the building actually." "Really? What do you do if I might ask?" "I'm a broker." "Really?" "Yes." "In what?" "Real Estate." "Good business," Mark says.

 "The reason I asked because, I do investments for clients, and there is a huge market here." Mark hands Nathaniel his card. Nathaniel receives the card looking at it. "Give me a call if you want to invest. I can guarantee you a manageable return of profit." "Oh, really. So, you have your company here?" "Yes," Mark says. "A lot of companies from the are doing business overseas now,"

Nathaniel says. "Yeah," Mark says. "So, you're from the states I take it?" Nathaniel asks. "Yes," Mark says. "Where about?" Nathaniel asks. "Atlanta," Mark says. "Oh." "Where are you from?" Mark asks. "I'm from Mississippi, outside of Jackson," Nathaniel replies. "Oh, okay," Mark says. "I'll give you a call when I'm ready to do something," Nathaniel turns to Mark responding. "That would be great. You won't be disappointed," Mark says as the elevator arrives at the Lobby. The elevator door opens. Mark and Nathaniel walk out together as the two shake hands parting ways. "Nice meeting you," Mark says. "Likewise," Nathaniel replies.

Mark heads towards the garage area to retrieve his car. Nathaniel hangs around in the front lobby glancing at his phone but watching where Mark is headed. Nathaniel slowly follows him. Mark enters through a glass door as the door closes behind him. Nathaniel stays back watching where Mark is parked. He stands off to the side watching him hit the alarm to his sports car, a white 2016 Audi R8. Mark enters his car, starts up the engine and drives away as Nathaniel watches, studying Marks parking number on the wall reading number 22. Nathaniel walks away.

  Meanwhile, at Mark's office, Mark is busy signing twenty new clients investing their money with his company. His partner Steve enters his office looking relaxed without his suit coat, wearing tan slacks, brown dress shoes, and a pin striped dress shirt with a red tie. "Man, we are rolling!" Steve says. "Don't you knock?" Mark asks. "No, why should I?" "Because it's rude when you don't." "Oh, give me a break," Steve says laughing. "No, what's rude is if we didn't sign these new clients off the hook. You know how much money they make?" "How much?" Mark asks. "I don't know, but it's a lot like close to a billion for each." "Whew!" Mark reacts taking a deep breath as he smiles from ear to ear. "But there's a problem," Steve says. Marks mouth opens wide. "What?" "We need your girl to handle these boat load of extra clients. I had to put them into a third account. There wasn't any more room. Mark raises his hands. "So?" Mark asks. "So?" Steve asks as he walks over to Mark sitting in his Mahogany chair in front of his desk. "That means I have to do extra work because there isn't anybody else to handle these extra clients bro. If we had your girl who you say is top dog handle these clients, were good."

Mark leans back in his chair thinking about what Steve implied. Steve stares at him waiting for a response. "Are you hearing me bro?" Steve asks. "I did," Mark says. "I mean, if not her, then somebody with the skills to do this. We are expanding, and I mean big. We don't want our clients leaving us because we don't have enough workforce to pay attention to our clients returns on their investments." "You are right. I'll give her a call and try to push her to come aboard. I just don't want her messing things up being that she's still recuperating from the accident. You do know she had a brain injury? I need to head back to Atlanta to set up shop like we planned." "Okay, cool, the sooner the better," Steve says standing to his feet. "Alright, I'm out, back to doing what I do best, making money." "Do your thing," Mark says. "You know I will, and you should too," Steve says. "Hey, you know I will, I'm the owner of this company joker," Mark says as Steve laughs. "Don't I know it," Steve closes the door behind him.

Later, Mark is on the phone and calling Christy. He listens as the phone continues to ring. Finally, she answers. "Hello?" "Hey Christy, this is Mark, how are you doing." Christy is at home lying in bed anxious about getting back to work doing what she loves, she gives Mark a good report. "Oh, I'm doing good, stronger each day." "That's great Christy. So, when can you come work for me, I'm about to set up shop in Atlanta soon because my business is really taking off and we are on overload with new clients," Mark says. "When are you coming here Mark?" "I'm planning to come to Atlanta by the end of the week to set up an office there, I was wondering if you would be able to head that office?" "Oh, yeah, for sure. Just give me a call before the day you are coming in, and I will be ready." "You sure?" "I will be ready for sure." "That's great Christy. I have some things to sort out with my company. I have to make things right with my soul," Mark says. "Mark, wait a minute, what's wrong?" Christy asks. "Nothing I can't handle, don't worry about me Christy. Anyway, how is your Mom?" "She's fine." "Tell her I said hi." "Okay, I will."

Before Mark hangs up the phone, Christy responds.

"Hey Mark?"

"Yeah?"

"Did someone come to see you?"

"See me? Like who?"

The phone is silent for a moment.

"Well, it's supposed to be a surprise, but since you didn't say anything, I had to assume he hadn't showed up to your place yet."

"Who are you talking about Christy?"

"Nathaniel."

"Nathaniel?"

"Yeah, you know Nathaniel from DinoCore? Mr. Boykins nephew?"

Instantly, Mark has flashbacks from the night of the shooting at his car. He remembers seeing the face of Nathaniel in the passenger seat.

"Yeah, I remember him, you gave him my address?" Mark asks.

"Yeah, he asked me for it saying he would be out there for business, and he had something very important to give to you. He said it was a surprise and you really needed it."

Mark swallows with a lump in his throat.

"Hello Mark? Are you still there?" Christy asks.

"Yes, I'm here. When did he tell you, he was coming?"

"I talked to him three or four days ago, so he should be out there already. Maybe he got tied up with business or something, you know how it is. I hope you're not mad at me for giving him your address."

"No, no, I'm not mad Christy, thank you for telling me because he probably would have missed me leaving back to Atlanta to jump start an office there."

"Again, I'm sorry Mark, he made it sound so important. He kept saying you really needed whatever he had, but he would never tell me what it was. He made it seem like a life or death situation," Christy says.

"Yeah, I bet he did. Well, maybe he can still catch me before I leave. You have his cell number?" Mark responds asking.

"Oh, yeah, for sure, hold on," Christy says.

Mark waits as he hears papers shuffling over the phone.

"Here it is."

"Okay, shoot."

"It's 555-387-6120," Christy says.

"Got it. Thanks Christy," Mark replies.

"Oh, Mark, don't call him I told you, otherwise he will be mad at me."

"Okay, I won't Christy. I'll just wait to see if he pops up."

"Okay, thanks Mark," Christy says.

"Take care of yourself, and I will call you when I'm on my way there."

"Cool, sounds good."

"Okay, bye Christy."

"Bye Mark."

The conversation ends as Mark thinks about the night Nathaniel almost killed him.

After work, Mark stops by a local Sports Bar to unwind. Upon exiting his vehicle, Mark adjusts the gun he just purchased behind his waistband under his suit as he enters the bar. Inside, he sees Steve and some friends. "There he is," all four men chant together. Mark stretches his arms out wide as he takes a seat at the small square table. Steve stares at Mark. "Yeah?" Mark asks. The three other guys seated at the table need no introduction. Frank is a senior broker from a nearby firm.

Ted is a bank executive, and Tim, a financial consultant. All of them together spell one word... money. Mark leans in to tell the three guys a secret. "Guys, we made so much money this week alone, I can't tell you. But I can tell you, our company will be one of the top companies in the country." "Really?" Ted asks. Mark nods his head yes as he sips on his beer. "I'm telling you," Mark says taking his index finger and pointing it down on the table. "Right here, right now, CS Associates is on its way to the top," Mark says. Frank interrupts. "Stand in line my friend, stand in line. You know you hot shots always come into town and think you're going to run everything. We've set up shop here for ten years now, we own the market." Mark laughs. "You guys have been around, yes, but it's a new day Frank." "What is it that you know that we don't already know Mark?"

Mark thinks for a moment. "I'm not going to tell you because that would be bad for my business!" Everyone at the table laugh aloud. "Mark, come on. Save yourself some time and come over to Strauss Bell and Casey. We're already doing what your trying to do," Frank says. Mark shakes his head no. "Been there and done that." "Oh, I forgot, DinoCore," Frank says pausing for a moment. "I could have told you DinoCore were a smoke screen. Any fire department could see that smoke coming a mile away. You were standing in a burning building not even knowing it was burning pal," Frank says as Steve interrupts him. "No, that's not true. They cooked the books so well, the CEO forgot how he did it." Frank shakes his head no. "Okay, so what? I was there until it burned to the ground. But look at me now?" Mark says as he leans back. Suddenly, his gun falls to the floor. Steve along with the other three men back up to look. "Is that a gun Mark?" Ted asks. Steve points to Mark. "Mark, what's with the gun?"

Mark picks the gun up from the floor. "Protection my friend." "From who?" Frank asks. "Anybody," Mark says rubbing his fingers through his hair as he thinks about his remark. The table remains silent. An hour passes by as it gets late. Mark glances down at his watch. "Time for bed guys." "It's still early," says Tim. "Tim, you should know, sleep is your best friend. If you don't sleep, you will miss something," Ted says with conviction. Mark places his hand on Tim's shoulder. "No, my friend, if you stay up all day, you will miss everything because you won't be able to pay attention," Mark says grabbing his car keys. "I'm out guys." The other four agree. "Yeah, it's about that time I guess." All five men leave tips on the table and head out the door to their cars. "Friday?" Some of them chant. "Friday, it is," Mark says along with Tim and Frank. Seconds later, Tim, Ted, and Frank drive away in separate cars as Steve and Mark stay in the parking lot to talk. "You okay man?" Steve asks. "No," Mark responds. "What's up?" "Someone tried to kill me before I came over here." Steve is shocked. "Dude, why didn't you tell me?"

"Because knew you would freak out and think it had something to do with our business here." "Does it?" Steve asks. "In a way, yeah," Mark responds. "Well then that's why I'm freaking out now Mark! Come on!"

Mark turns away, leaning up against his car. "Mark, talk to me bro. What's going on? Why would somebody take a shot at you?" Steve asks as Mark pauses for a moment. "Because I took some drug cartel's money." Steve swallows with a lump in his throat. "You did what?" "You heard me," Mark says. "Why on earth would you do that Mark?" "Because I thought no one would know." "But they do know," Steve says. "Yeah now," Mark agrees saying. "You took the money for us to start this company, didn't you?" "Yes, DinoCore was a front for the Juarez Cartel ran by Felipe Morales called the shadow. He wanted to launder their money through a legitimate claim. I stole half their money from one account, Mr. Boykins took the other half." "And where is this Mr. Boykins?" Steve asks. "He's dead," Mark says. "Do they know you're over here?" "No, well, I don't know. That's why I have this gun for protection," Mark says. Steve demands an answer. "Come on Mark." "Okay, the girl I told you about, the one I wanted to come into the business?"

Steve's eyes sway from side to side.

"Yeah, the one that was in the accident, Christy."

"Yes, that one."

"Okay?"

"She told a guy that used to work with us where I was by accident."

"So?"

Mark looking down at the ground as he speaks, raises his head, and stares at Steve.

"That guy is the one who shot at me back in Atlanta."

"Who is he?"

"Mr. Boykins nephew."

"I don't understand. He's the nephew of the man that is dead that owned the company."

"Why would he shoot at you?"

"I don't know. Only thing I can think of is, he thinks I had something to do with his Uncles death, or…."

"Or what?" Steve asks.

"Or, he works for the Cartel," Mark responds.

"Jesus Mark," Steve says.

"Don't do that."

"Do what?"

"Use God's name in vain."

Steve is surprised. "You are telling me not the use God's name in vain, but you took some drug cartel's money, are you kidding me Mark?" "I know I messed up Steve," Mark says. "No, you sinned Mark, that's what you did!" "Don't act like you are so spiritual." "I never said I was," Steve replies convincingly." "We both know what we're doing with this company Steve," Mark implies as the two of them lean up against Marks car. "I know that but, we're living a dream right now. We are making so much money!" "Are we? We're stealing other people's money just like I stole from the Cartel, that's what we're doing Steve," Mark says. "Well, if it's not us, it would be somebody else." "Does that make it right?" Mark asks. "I here you Mark, okay, we were wrong. What do you want us to do, call up our investors and say, hey, I'm sorry, I need to come clean? I'm really stealing your money for my own personal wealth and gain?" Steve says.

"Do I need protection Mark?" "No, I can handle this guy Nathaniel, he's just a kid." "A kid? How old?" "In his late twenties." "He's not a kid Mark!" "He's a kid to me Steven!" "So, what do we do now?" Steve asks turning to Mark. "We can find the Cartel and give them our investors' money and try to recoup the rest in trades," Mark says. Steven laughs. "Good luck with that idea. Do you know what the Cartel will do to us just for aggravation? They will skin us alive, then say thank you as their burying us." Mark turns and enters his car starting the engine. "Mark, I say we forget about all of this and get back to work. The problem will go away, trust me. Mark!" Steven says. Mark closes his door and drives away.

About twenty minutes later, Mark arrives at his home pulling into the garage of his apartment. The door elevates into the ceiling of the garage as Mark stares at the gate swing upward. He drives under it parking in his designated spot. He turns off the engine and the headlights when suddenly a man wearing a hat sunk down on his head, suddenly appears at Mark's driver side door. Mark turns looking at him realizing it must be Nathaniel. Nathaniel raises his right hand with a gun pointed at Mark. "Nathaniel!" Mark yells out as the gun fires three consecutive shots at Mark. Mark slumps over in his driver's seat as Nathaniel runs away through the parking garage out into the street. Mark lays motionless in his car.

A month later, Christy's health improves as she joins Angie's church. Later that day at home, she contemplates calling Mark telling him she is ready for work.

Her mind can't stand the urge of not being on top anymore. Marks offer sounds so good as Christy's mind and body battle with her spirit as the thought of money, prestige, and independence cross her mind like a movie screen. In her heart, she hears a still small voice in her heart telling her "things are not what they seem. This is not my best for you. Don't take this job." It's not what it appears to be. Trust me."

Christy talks to herself… "God, I don't understand. This is my chance to get back what I lost." The still small voice in her heart responds, "What you lost was the same thing that made you unhappy. I can give you back what you lost if you trust me and my way for you." Christy's mind gives her fits as her telephone rings. She answers it. "Hello?" "Yeah, hi, may I speak to Christy Billings?" "This is she? Who's this?" "Hi, this is Steve, I work with Mark, were partners. I don't know if he told you about me, but he told me to give you a call. I'm here in Atlanta right now setting an office up. Mark said you would be ready to take the job here in Atlanta?"

Christy is elated with happiness. "Yeah for sure!" In her mind, she thinks this must be a sign to take the job. Whatever she felt in her heart, she feels was a mistake. Christy smiles, but inside she doesn't feel right. She ignores the feeling. "I'm ready Steve, when do you want me to start?" "How about tomorrow morning?" "I'm there." "Okay, here is the address." Christy scrambles around in her room looking for a pen to write down the address. She becomes frustrated but somehow finds a pen. She jots down the address Steve gives her over the phone.

The next morning, Christy awakens. She meets Steve at the office in downtown Atlanta. Christy's emotions are screaming at her, as Steve preps her for her job assignment. Christy ignores her feelings as Steve continues talking. "I heard what happened to you. You look good, I don't see a mark on you." "Thank you, Steve. That was a kind remark. Hey, where is Mark, I thought he would be the one coming out here?" "He got caught up in Bangkok and couldn't make it. He said he would call you and explain about it. I'm so glad you're working for us, you won't be sorry for coming on board with us, I promise you. You are going to be back on top where you belong Christy," Steve says.

"I figured you would say that." "You have what it takes Christy, Mark told me everything about you. I bugged him to get you in. I know you were recovering, but I didn't want him hiring anyone else." "Wow Steve, your making me feel like a movie star," Christy says. "And that's why I chose you Christy," Steve says. I'm going to give you the keys to the kingdom of success the right way, not like the cheap way DinoCore did. We are going to rock," Steve says. "Okay Steve, I believe you. So, when do you think Mark will be coming back to the states again?" "Oh, he's been sick back in Bangkok. But he will be here as soon as he can." "Oh, I thought you just said he was caught up in business and couldn't make it?"

Steve pauses realizing his mistake. "Oh, yeah, but, he was sick first before he got caught up in business. Don't worry, he'll be here, we're partners." wow, sorry to hear that. Is he going to be okay, how sick was he?" "Oh, you know Mark, he's a trooper, it just caught him off guard. He got back on his feet really quick, that's why he couldn't make it, to get caught up with work." "If you say so," Christy says.

Later around noon, Christy leaves the office to meet with Angie for lunch. Angie is a little late arriving. As she enters the restaurant, she finds Christy sitting alone at a booth by the window. She walks over to her. "Hey you!" "Hey!" Christy says. "Sorry I'm late," Angie says. "Oh, that's okay," Christy responds as Angie sits down. "So, what's the big news you had to tell me?" "Well, I quit my job at Walmart because I just got a new job." "Hooray for you Christy! I am so happy for you. So, what new job did you get?" "Well, you remember Mark from our old job?" Angie's brain tries to remember the face with the name. "No, I don't think I remember him." Christy helps her remember. "Mark was the one that approved of me firing you." Angie is taken back to that moment as her mind flashes back to that moment. "Oh, yeah, that Mark," Angie says. Christy continues telling her good news. "Well, anyway, he called me." "Oh, he did, did he?" "Yeah, he's got his own company now and it's doing well, so good that he wants me to come aboard to work for him." The waiter brings water and napkins to the table. "Hello," says the young man. "I am Mark, I will be your server today."

Angie instantly snaps at him. "I don't need napkins Mark, thank you," she says. The waiter is startled by Angie's outburst towards him. "I am so sick of that name Christy." Mark the waiter is appalled. Angie snaps her head looking up at Mark the waiter. "Excuse me Mr. Mark. We are not ready to order right now, so would you please give us a minute and buzz off. I will call for you after my heated discussion with my friend here is over, thank you very much!" Mark backs away from the table, turning around and walking away. Angie's demeanor shocks Christy. "Angie!"

Angie turns facing Christy with an angry tone. "What?" "What has gotten into you?" Angie snaps her neck as she responds. "Funny you should ask that, I was about to ask you that same question." Christy is bewildered. "What?" Angie retorts. "What do you mean what? You of all people should know, after the way you treated me along with the help of Mr. Mark, you would even think of hanging around this guy when he knew I did nothing wrong to get fired in the first place. He was just backing you up and feeding your egotistical hormones." "Angie...what...your sounding like something I would say back when I was..." "Back when you were a witch?" "Angie, my goodness. Why are you so mad at me? I thought you would be happy for me getting back to doing what I loved," Christy says.

Angie pauses for a second. "Yeah with who Mark, the spark." "Angie, Mark is a good guy," Christy says. "You expect me to believe that Christy? Did he just join the "Vienna Boys Choir"?

"What do you want me to do, buy the album? He hasn't changed. He knew I was right in his office that day, but he fired me anyway." "How do you know he hasn't changed Angie?" Christy asks. "I just know!" Angie says with an angry tone. "Christy, I thought you've changed. I thought you were becoming the person you were meant to be, kind, generous, loving, and caring." "Angie, I am. I have changed," Christy pleads. "No, you haven't! You're going back to the same mess that turned you into what you were before we were friends!" Angie says. Christy's eyes widen. "Were friends?" Angie turns her head away. "Angie?" Angie continues looking out the window of the restaurant. "Please Angie, don't do this. You're the only true friend I have. You've showed me so many things about God, and life." Christy pauses for a second. "I need your friendship to carry me through this, please?" Angie turns to Christy. "Then as a friend, I am telling you, this job is not for you."

      Christy's neck snaps back. "How would you know that this job is not for me? Have you been spying on Mark? Angie stares at Christy. "Angie answer me!" "Yes, I have. I looked Mark up to see what he was doing. I heard of his so-called company." "What did you hear?" Christy asks. "It's a fraud Christy." "A fraud, like what?" Christy asks. "He's not running a legitimate business," Angie says. "How, what, who told you this?" "I have my sources," Angie says. Christy gets mad. "You know what Angie, I think you're just jealous of me being back on top. You have your nice job as a manager in marketing, and you don't want me to have mine. You would love for me to stay at Walmart and suffer, wouldn't you?"

Angie is surprised. "What?" Christy continues her rant. "Yeah, and you know what else I think, I think you've been jealous of me all along." "Oh my…." Angie says before she's interrupted by Christy. "That's why you gave me such a hard time at DinoCore, and that's why I fired you!" Angie's mouth opens wide. "What, Mark fired me with your help! You fired me because I was a Christian!" Angie says. "And I'm so glad I did!" Christy says as she stands to her feet from the booth. "I am back, and you better watch out!" Christy grabs the glass of water and tosses it into Angie's face. Angie's body jumps from the cold waters presence as it splashes all over her as she sits with her mouth open in a state of shock.

Angie raises both of her hands with her arms stretched out wide. "No, you didn't," she says with conviction. Christy storms off towards the door of the restaurant as Angie sits still in shock alone with dripping water from her face. "Oh, you better get back here Christy, I am going to tear you a new one!" The exit door flies open with Christy storming past it.

Eight hours later, Christy's on the phone talking to investors. "Thank you for choosing us as your number one investment broker. Okay, bye." Christy hangs up the phone feeling elated as she talks to herself. "What a day, I just closed a major client and bought myself a luxury apartment downtown, life is great!" Christy's secretary Patricia, an African American female 5'7 brown skinned with hazel eyes and long jet-black hair, in her early twenties, enters her office. "How did it go?" "Oh, great, I closed him." "Yeah?" "Oh, yeah," Christy says. "You are good. How long have you been doing this, I was told you were a pro?" "Ten years in this business." "You must love what you do?" Patricia asks. "Yeah, it's great to close someone, and make an impact in the market. What about you Patricia" Christy asks. "I was a foreign exchange student over in Japan, I did some modeling their too. I'm fascinate by the Asian culture, plus my dad was stationed there for a minute in the Army when my brother and I were kids. But, I'm originally from California, Oakland area. I'm in Atlanta working on my music career." "Wow Patricia, you have a very interesting life."

Patricia pauses for a minute as she glances around Christy's office standing in her red dress. So, do you." "It wasn't so exciting six months ago," Christy says. "Why, what happened?" "I was in a bad car accident and almost died." "Wow." "Before that, I used to work for a marketing firm named DinoCore." "Oh yeah, I heard about that company, it like shut down or something because of corporate fraud?" Patricia asks. "Yes, something like that," Christy says. Patricia is curious. "So, like, were you involved in that?" "No, I was not when all of that happened." "That was awful, all of those people losing their jobs." "Tell me about it," Christy says.

Two weeks later, things are moving fast at the office for Christy. She's signed five more clients to invest in the company. Full of smiles, Christy shouts with joy as Patricia turns around in her chair giving her the thumbs up. Later at lunch, Christy sits at a small table by herself in her business suit at a local deli shop. As she sips on her cup of tea, she glances at a log sheet of the profit the company made for the quarter. She notices the based Company name in Bangkok is different from the name Limitless Christy runs in Atlanta. She glances at the column showing the returns expected for the year, Christy notices they don't add up. She sets down her coffee as her hands scramble through her carry-on briefcase for the sheet showing her client's pre- quarterly earnings statements. Christy quickly grabs her calculator and typing in the numbers adding, subtracting, then dividing by twelve for the year. She is astonished at her findings.

  She gathers all her papers shoving them into her briefcase while rushing out of the deli shop. Bystanders look wondering what has troubled her to leave out the shop so fast. Inside her new convertible BMW exactly like the one she had her accident in, she presses speed dial on her cell phone to her office. Patricia answers the phone. "Limitless Investments, may I help you?" Christy's voice answers with great worry. "Cancel all of my appointments for the day Patricia. I'm giving you the rest of the day off!" "Mrs. Billings, what's wrong?" "Nothing, I have an important meeting at the office." "But, I don't understand, is everything okay, you don't sound good?" "Just do it Patricia please, and call Steve and tell him to come to the office immediately!" Patricia, appearing nervous, responds. "Okay, I will get right on it." "Thank you." Christy ends the call. Meanwhile, twenty minutes later, Christy sits in her office waiting for Steve. Suddenly, Steve walks in while talking on his cell phone. "Okay Jim, that sounds good, I will get back with you." Steve enters

Christy's office. approaches Patricia at the front desk. "Hey where is Patricia?" "I gave her the day off," Christy says. "You what? Why?"

Christy tosses a folder in front of him. Steve glances at the folder, then at Christy." "What is this?" Steve asks. Christy points at the folder. "Look for yourself." "Christy, it would have been better if you called me and told me what the problem was, because I don't see a problem here." Christy huffs and puffs. "Steve are you kidding me, you don't see the problem?" Steve closes the folder and shoves it back at Christy. "No, I don't." "You know exactly what is going on Steve.

What, you didn't think I would ever find out?" Steve stands glancing at Christy. "Find out what Christy?" "The scam Steve, and where is Mark!" "What scam Christy? These are some serious accusations you are claiming here, I mean, I brought you in to get you back on your feet and your accusing me of what?" "You brought me in? No, Mark brought me in, he started this company. I asked you a question, where is he?"

"Answer the question Steven, where is Mark? He has not called me, text me, nothing!" "I told you, he's sick. As soon as he gets well, he will be here." "You know, he never told me he had a partner." "No?" "No," Christy says. "I don't see why not, we are partners." Steve pauses for a second. "Listen Christy, I understand that you are upset. I need you to keep a lid on this, can you do that?" Christy is appalled. "Keep quiet? No, this is criminal Steve, just like DinoCore. I'm not going to be a part of this! I thought Mark was joking about some of the things he mentioned to me, but after DinoCore, I knew he wasn't serious about it. Did you know what he was doing?" Steve turns his back at Christy, then turns around leaning forward on her desk with both hands. "Lower your voice Christy, and yes, I knew what Mark was doing. He is the CEO and I'm his senior partner, but I didn't know about his dealings with the drug Cartel. Don't tell anyone about any of this, it would be bad for you, me and Mark." "What? Are you threatening me Steve?"

The room becomes silent. "Yes Christy, I am. Listen, you've been through a lot, and I would hate to see you lose your life over something like this." "What did you just say?" "Come on Christy, you heard me. Mark told me how your boss Mr. Boykins wanted to fire you because of your hot-headed mess firing that young lady, but Mark talked him out of it. That lawsuit can still be in place, but it would be against you alone since DinoCore is no more.

Do you want to risk that? I'm sure with the doctors' fees you owe, you don't have the money for a good lawyer, and the apartment you just leased along with that BMW can go away like the wind. I hold the key to your success, remember that. So, yes you owe us. You owe me the partner in charge of this company, to keep your mouth shut for whatever you know or may know. You see nothing, and you know nothing, okay? Just be happy you are getting paid right now. You're on top where you want to be, and if you want to stay on top, zip your lips."

Christy remains silent, as she and Steve have a stare down. Steve leaves the office and building leaving

Christy alone to think. Christy lowers her head as tears fall from her eyes.

CHAPTER TWENTY

"Clearing A Conscience"

That night, Christy stays late at the office searching through a flash drive she took from Marks office when they worked at DinoCore. On the flash drive are her computer of all the clients that were invested within DinoCore before it went out of business. Names, dates, and amounts are on the flash drive. One of the names on the list, she remembers Mark mentioning he stole money from is Felipe' Morales. The amount Felipe' Morales invested shows $3,000,000.00. Christy decides to search the name Felipe' Morales on her computer, but nothing comes up. Christy thinks to herself. Then she decides to type in a search for Mexican Cartels. On the computer several Cartel groups appear with names of leaders. Christy has flashbacks of the conversation she and Mark had in his office about this man. Mark's voice echoes in her eardrums. "I stole money from a man named Felipe' "The Shadow" Morales." Immediately Christy's eyes lock onto the "Juarez Cartel" name. Next to it, she sees the name "The Shadow" next to it.

      Christy is taken back by the information she reads next to the name. Pictures of bodies lying in the street, burned out vehicles, and bullets in walls on the street capture her eyes. As Christy pulls up the first window listing money transactions. One account is a mystery to her. Christy sees the name associated with that account. The name says Sterling Boykins CEO of DinoCore. A phone number appears next to the name "The Shadow." Reluctantly, Christy dials that number as her heart beats rapidly. Surprisingly it rings several times before someone answers it with a Spanish accent. "Hello?" Christy remains silent as the voice responds again. "Hello? Who is this? Hello?" Christy quickly hangs up the phone. Sitting alone in her office, a great amount of fear consumes her body. In her office, only the sound of traffic outside passing by can be heard.

    Christy quickly logs off her computer when her office phone rings. She answers it. "Hello?" On the other end of the line is complete silence. Christy hears someone breathing on the other end of the line. She hangs up the phone, turns off all the lights to her office and grabs her purse running out the building to her car. Rain pours as Christy stands at her BMW breathing heavily as she fumbles with her car keys trying to hit the alarm. She finds the alarm button pressing it disarming the alarm and entering her car. Inside her car, her eyes quickly look up in the rear-view mirror. Suddenly, there is a knock on her window. Christy is startled as she turns her head seeing a homeless man standing by her window. "You got change lady?" Christy responds in fear. "No, go away please!" The homeless man stares at her, turns around and leaves. Christy still nervous, turns on the ignition starting her car and putting it in drive. She backs out of the parking spot and speeds out into traffic with cars blowing their horns at her.

The next morning, two men wearing dark sunglasses, enters a café Christy frequents before going to work. They watch Christy as she sips on her tea at a table. One man dressed in tan slacks, and a tan sport coat with a baby blue polo shirt underneath. His partner standing off to the side wearing a white shirt, dark blue sport coat, and black pants. Christy frequently looks up noticing the two men staring at her. She becomes nervous. One of the men pay for his donuts and coffee at the register. His partner continues watching Christy as she turns her head away from him, so she doesn't appear she is watching him as well. The man at the counter receives the change from the man, "Thank you." Both men leave the Café causing Christy to feel relieved. Minutes later, she leaves the Café to her BMW.

As she approaches it, both men from the Café confront her. "Ms. Billings?" Christy startled, quickly turns around. "Yes." The first man to speak is agent Mason. "Hi, I am agent Mason, this is agent Mosely. We are with the FBI. We would like to ask you some questions?" Christy is flabbergasted. "About what?" "About your association with Mark Collins and Limitless Investments. We understand you work at their office downtown." "Well, I'm on my way back to work, can you ask me some questions another time?" "No ma'am, and I wouldn't worry about going back to your office." "Why?" "Because your office has been seized by the Federal Government. We have agents they're now going through all of the files." Christy responds clueless. "Seized?" "Yes," Mason responds. "Your boss Mark Collins has been indicted on five counts of fraud, money laundering, embezzlement, and tax evasion. The U.S. Marshals are looking for him right now as we speak. It won't be long before we find him. Do you know where he is?"

Christy lies. "No, he's very busy running other offices. I can never catch up with him." Both agents glance at each other. Christy stares at them nervously. "This is crazy! Is this some sort of joke or something?" "No ma'am, this is not a joke. If it was, I'd have better things to do for a joke. But for you, I wish it was." "Why?" Christy asks. "Because you will have to look for a new job." Agent Mason pulls out his card handing it to Christy as she becomes angry. "I just got this job! Would you guys please tell me what is going on?" "We just did Ms. Jennings. If you would come with us, we can give you more details." Christy reluctantly follows them to their car. She is escorted to the back seat of the unmarked sedan grey in color. The two agents enter in both the driver and passenger side of the car. Christy asks, "What about my car?"

Mosely responds. "Oh, that's a nice car. It will be safe here, don't worry." "How do you know that?" Mosely responds turning his body around looking at Christy. "I just know rich people like you have rich insurance to afford a car like that so, you can easily get another one if it was stolen right?" Christy is sarcastic. "Ha, ha." The grey sedan backs out of the parking spot and drives away. At the FBI office, both Mason and Mosley pound Christy with questioning to the point Christy cries. "What do you want from me, I just started working there!" "But you knew and worked with Mark

Collins correct?" "Yeah, but..." "And is it true, Mark Collins is partly responsible for a $30,000,000.00 Ponzi Scheme under DinoCore?" Christy both angry, confused, and tired, losses it. "What? No, way, $30,000.000.00? He was never a part of that!" "How do you know Ms. Billings?" asks agent Mosely. "How do I know?" "Yes." "I just know, I worked with Mark for years, and he never did any shady dealings like that. If he did, don't you think he would have let me in on it?" Christy asks.

Both agents look at each other. "You know, we traced money from Mr. Sterling Boykins to the Juarez Cartel through DinoCore, do you know anything about that?" Christy's eyes move from left to right. "Do I need a lawyer?" Both Mason and Mosely look at each other. "You don't need a lawyer unless you have something to hide Ms. Billings. Do you have something to hide?" Christy remains silent as Mason grills her more. "That money from the Cartel was transferred into Marks account then it disappeared. We know Mark stole that money from the Cartel. Did he tell you anything about that?" Christy is silent. "Then there was this lawsuit filed by Angela Harmon for an unlawful firing. You and Mark were named codefendants in that case. What about that?" "Okay, yes, Angela was fired, but you will find documents stating that was because she wasn't doing her job."

"She won that lawsuit Christy," Mason says. "What? I didn't know about that. Let's keep this professional please, call me Ms. Billings." Mosely interrupts. "You didn't know?" "No," Christy says. "The lawsuit was for $200,000 Ms. Billings," Mosely responds. "Well, I'm sorry, I didn't know that." "Just like you didn't know about DinoCore's Ponzi Scheme, just like you didn't know that Mark Collins was a schemer and stole a dangerous Cartel's money? Mark has a buddy named Steven Cordell. Do you know him?" "Yes, he's my boss here in Atlanta," Christy says. "Okay good, now we're getting somewhere because our guys saw him in and out of your office on surveillance video last week and this week. Christy wipes her eyes grabbing a Kleenex to blow her nose. The sound echoes inside of the room. "Can I go now please?" Christy asks. Both agents glance at each other shaking their heads in disbelief.

"Christy, this is a serious situation here. Now, you may not know everything, but you know something. Give us what you know, and we can help you, and protect you. You just closed five sells worth over half a million dollars. Where do you think that money went, to the Goodwill?" Mason says as he pauses for a moment. "It went into Mark Collins pocket Christy," Mason says. Christy's eyes bursts with tears as her mascara streaks from her eyelids like a horror movie scene. "Now, we are going to let you go, but I want you to think really hard tonight about your future. You seem like a smart woman, pretty. I know you don't want to lose all of that in a prison cell for thirty to forty years of your life," Mason says. Those words hit Christy like a ton of brick as the life in her seems to disappear like a vapor. Christy wishes she could die and go to heaven. Moments later, Christy is driven back to her car. She exits the unmarked vehicle entering her car and driving away. Across the street, Steve watches from his vehicle.

An hour later, Christy arrives at Angie's apartment. She knocks on her door. Her mascara now dried up, leaves streaks on her face. No one answers. As Christy turns to walk away, Angie's door finally opens. Christy turns around staring at her for eternity. Angie mouths the words. "Come on in." As Christy enters, she stops at the end of the door where Angie is standing. Angie hugs her tight. Christy almost collapses into her arms. Angie holds her up as best she can.

After several hours Angela consoles Christy. "Everything's going to work out Christy, you have to trust God." "You made a huge mistake but in order to get out of this, you have to let God direct you what to do to get out of this," Angie says. "If I had listened to my heart, and you, along with my mom, I wouldn't be in this mess. Angie, the Mexican Cartel could be looking for me right now. Mark was over me at DinoCore. What if Mark lied and told them I have their money and went on some shopping spree. They know women love to shop!" "Oh, come on Christy, they don't know that," Angie says. "How do I trust God to deal with the Cartel, they are all the way in Mexico? They have the money to touch anyone anywhere," Christy says. "You simply let everything go Christy and you give it to him. All the bad thoughts and fears, then you do what you believe God tells you to do in your heart. That's where the spirit of God resides, in our hearts, our spirit." Christy listens intently. "You know Angie, I thought you would never speak to me again after what I did to you at the restaurant. Why?" Angie smiles. "Because that's not what a Christian does right?" Angie pauses for a second. "Christy, I wasn't an angel for the way I acted when we had lunch that day. I allowed the fleshly side of me take over. I wasn't representing Godly character when I reacted the way I did, and for that, I apologize.

"I'm sorry for throwing that ice water on you," Christy says. "Why Christy, I was steaming mad, I needed to cool off," Angie replies smiling. Christy laughs. "So, what are you going to do?" Angie asks. Christy thinks for a moment. "Well, my heart tells me to tell the FBI everything," She says. "Not if I give them everything I know. I guess that's what they do to get people to talk right? I just wanted to be back on top you know Angie? I finally realized I'm addicted to the love of money and the power that comes with it. I read in the bible that it said the love of money was the root of all evil."

Angie chimes in. "Yeah, and there are thousands of people committing that crime without a dime in their pocket Christy." "You know, I was my happiest when I had my little job at

Walmart, made new friends, joined the church. I mean, I still had my physical challenges from the accident, but I was at peace with everything around me even though it was not much. Don't get me wrong, having nice things and a lot of money is much better, but I think when you are so determined to have that more than God, you become your own god in your own world. Now, I need to find a new job again, probably take this car back and turn it in," Christy says. "It's going to work out Christy. I will help you any way I can. Hey maybe see if I can get you in where I am?" "Yeah, that would be nice, Christy says." Christy stands to her feet grabbing her purse from the floor.

"Well, I'd better go," Christy says. "Okay. Do you need to stay here for a while?" "Let me get home and think for a minute. I think that would be a good idea," Christy says. "Okay, let me know, you are welcome anytime," Angie says. thanks for coming by, I enjoyed your company." "I enjoy your presence Angie." The two hug each other as Christy leaves to her car. Angie watches her drive away waving.

Two days later, Christy arrives with her lawyer at the FBI office. She gives them all the information she knows about Marks involvement with his shady business. She enters a room shaking hands with agent Mason and Mosely. Her lawyer shakes their hands as well. "Thank you for coming Christy. Thank you giving us some information that you know of about Mark Collins," Mason says. "I will do anything to help you guys, but I want to know that I will be given immunity for my part in helping you?" Both agents glance at each other surprised at the question. "Yes, Christy we can do that." "Before I give you this valuable information, I want a written signature granting me that immunity once I give you this. I just want you to know, I had nothing to do with any of this." "You got it," Mason says. Christy pulls out a folder from her full size carry-on purse bag that a woman would normally take on an airplane. The lead agent opens the folder. Inside, are invoices of received payments by clients to Marks company Limitless Investments. On another page, Christy points out the name Felipe' Morales to the agents. "This is the man Mark stole money from that is linked to the Ponzi Scheme. He is the leader of the Juarez Cartel. Mason and Mosely are elated with the information. "Oh wow, we were not aware of this Christy, how did you get this?"

"Well, I stole it from Mark when we worked at DinoCore after he told me the company was about to go under. When he told me why the company was closing, I didn't believe him, and I had to find out the truth for myself. I was going to put the flash drive back before Mark noticed it was gone, then I got into my car accident. So, I looked up this name then searched on the Internet, for Cartel groups in Mexico, and I came up with this." Agent Mosely glances at the folder. "Do you have the flash drive on you?" Mosely asks. "No, it's at my apartment. I needed leverage if you guys weren't going to grant me immunity." Mason and Mosely stare at each other again. "Smart girl," Mason says.

The FBI agent sit back in their seats. "This is what we were looking for all along Mosely. We could never tie all the money together because we were missing one link, and here it is. This account is the major link to all the other accounts. Sterling Boykins and Mark have been laundering drug money off shore to the Cayman Islands then transferring it to another account in Switzerland. The money would then be shipped back to the states washed and cleaned by phony investments and given to various charities and foundations to hide it." Christy is shocked. "Seriously?" "Yes," Mason responds. We have a unit on surveillance as we speak to the holder of one of these charities." Christy shakes her head. "I didn't believe Mark would go this far to do business like this." "This isn't called business Christy, this is called illegal activity. Are you sure you are telling us everything Christy, because if we find out there's more you're not telling us," Mason says as Christy's lawyer steps in. "Hold on a minute, my client just told you all she knows." Mosely motions to Christy's lawyer. "This is just a preliminary question, you don't have to be so informal." "I'm protecting my client's rights," Christy's lawyer states. "And I 'm trying to get an understanding of her involvement with Mark and this company DinoCore, because there are some more things we are finding out about the closing of this company." Christy's lawyer turns to her placing his hand on her arm turning her upper body towards him. "You don't have to answer any more questions Christy." She responds. "I do Gus. I have nothing to hide. I've done nothing wrong." Christy glances at the agents. "Yes, I told you all I know." Agent Mosely rolls his eyes at Christy's lawyer along with a smirk across his face. He turns to Christy, "Has Mark ever asked you to fudge any numbers at DinoCore?"

Christy gives an immediate response. "No never, I don't have the power to do that." "The reason I ask this is because, that award your company received for top marketing sales was bogus. We did an extensive investigation and found out, your company was in the red for four years." Christy is shocked, "No, we worked day and night to get those numbers to where they were." Mosely interrupts her. "You mean where they weren't." The trade commission has the full report. Your ex- CEO Mr. Boykins was arrested when you were in a coma in the hospital. He of course posted bail, then a week later, he was found dead. It made the CNN news, but being you were in a coma, you missed the report.

Agent Mason pauses for a moment. "Christy, what else do you know about the Cartel?" Christy pauses for a moment. "Only that this guy is their leader. I knew something was fishy when Steve came into the office and threatened me." Mosely interrupts. "Threatened you?" "Yes, because I found out the accounts weren't adding up and I confronted him about it. He told me to keep quiet or else," Christy says. Mosely interjects. "This stuff goes on every day in society Christy. Someone's always trying to get ahead of everybody else, trying to get that edge that nobody else has or knows about.

Greed is the god of all gods, and it's nothing but pure evil short of hell itself. No one gets away with anything in this life. Eventually, everybody gets caught. We are here to catch people like this. This is what we do, we eat and sleep this, protecting the injustices created by such people, because if we don't, they will teach their uncles, cousins, aunts, heck, even their momma or daddy how to cut corners and cheat the system." He pauses for a moment. "Mr. Boykins, Mark and Steve are no different." "Well, I hope the information I just gave you will helps," Christy responds.

Mason stands along with Mosely. They shake Christy's and her lawyer's hands. "I thank you all for coming down and talking with us. We may call you to testify Christy." "Testify?" "Yes, because you are the key to this case," Mason says. "Well yes, I guess I can testify." "Good," Mason says as Mosely retrieves a copy of the immunity agreement with Christy. Both agents sign the agreement. Mason hands Christy her copy. We will walk you out and give you that signed letter of granted immunity. We will call you if we need you. I have all of your contact information." "Do you think you need protection Christy? If so, we can have an unmarked car staked out at your place if you want." "No, I think I will be staying at a friend's house for a while." "Okay, let us know if you change your mind," Mason says. "Sure, no problem," Christy responds. Christy and her lawyer leave the office.

In Bangkok, China, Steve enters a hospital walking up several flights of stairs in a hurry avoiding cameras in the building. He enters on the eleventh floor proceeding to room 11A. Steve approaches a curtain peeling it back seeing a nurse assisting Mark. She changes his I.V. bag. After several minutes, the nurse finishes as Steve stands off to the side waiting his turn to Mark. The nurse smiles at Steve as she leaves the room. "What's up buddy?" Steve asks. "I'm getting better every day. Had it not been for that bullet proof vest I bought at that surplus store, I would be a goner right now," Mark replies. "That was good thinking my man. Where do you think this Nathaniel is right now?" "I have no clue, probably back in the states or checking the papers to see if I'm dead," Mark concludes.

"Where have you been?" Mark asks. "Taking care of the company my man. It's a busy job doing it alone, you know that," Steve says. Mark adjusts his pillow as he sits up in his bed. "How did the setup go in Atlanta?" "Oh, it was a hit." "That's good to hear. I'm glad Christy's back to work. We've got to come clean with all the stuff we're doing," Mark says. We need to give the Cartel their money back, start making real investments for our clients and go legit. We know how to do it. I'm done with all the scheming and lying to clients. I lay awake every night, and my conscience has been eating me alive Steve. Doesn't any of the stuff we've done, and were doing right now trouble you?" Steve turns away, then back at Mark. "Why, should it? And I wouldn't advise you to give back The Cartel their money."

The response from Steve takes Mark for a loop. "Why not, we stole their money." "No, you stole their money to start this business. I stole money from the clients we have now. Don't put me with that Cartel stuff," Steve says. "Don't you have a soul and a heart Steve?" "Yes, and my soul and heart is telling me to keep doing what I'm doing, making money." "If they find me, they'll find you too Steve. Why do you think they put a hit out on me?" Mark asks. "Come on Mark, I told you, all we do is make money. Forget that other stuff. We don't make the choices for our clients. They are adults. They should check their own hearts at the door before investing. Steve sits down to reflect what he just said. "That's cold Steve, really cold," Mark replies.

Mark notices Steve's agitation. "Hey, think about what I said. We must do this. No one will know what we've done if we start doing the right thing now by getting all our clients the money they are owed." "They already know," Steve says. Mark looks at Steve. "What? Who, what are you talking about?" Steve with his head down fumbling with his keys, looks up at Mark. The FBI knows what we're doing. "What? Your friend Christy talked to the Feds about us?" "You're lying," Mark says. "I wish I was, but I'm not," Steve replies. The room is silent. "Yep, I wish this was a joke, and the cameras would come rushing in here and we'd all have a good laugh, but as you can see, there isn't a smile on my face. Your friend Christy, who is now our enemy, talked to the Feds Mark!" Mark's face is stoic. "That doesn't trouble you? Well it should because we are done my friend. It's just a matter of time before they find us here in Bangkok."

Mark thinks about everything. "Well, we have to turn ourselves in," He says. Steve is stone faced. "Have you've lost your mind? I'm not going to prison. I wouldn't last an hour in there, and you my friend, being the pretty boy and all, oh they would love you a long time," Steve says. "Stop Steve! Forget about my looks okay? You've been making that joke since we were in College. It's not my fault I look better than you, so enough with the pretty boy jokes," Mark says. Steve loses it. "What are we going to do Mark?" "I just told you. Maybe Christy didn't say anything?" Mark asks as Steve stands to his feet. "Mark, for five hours, I parked down the street from the little Federal Building. I watched her go in. What do you think she was doing in their all that time, teaching the FBI agents Yoga class?" I trust Christy, I know her, she wouldn't do that," Mark says. "You don't know her very well my friend," Steve says. "We go way back, and for her to turn on me like that, no way," Mark says. "Well I think we should get rid of her plain and simple," Steve says convincingly. Mark sits up in his bed wincing from the pain. "What did you just say?" "Mark, we have to do this before she can testify against us in court. I'm not going to jail for 20 or 30 years' man, that wasn't the plan I had for my future!" Steven says. Mark's face has a serious look as he stares at Steve, "I'm not hurting her, and neither are you." Mark pauses. "I'm warning you Steve, leave her alone."

Steve approaches Mark. "I'll do it, you won't have to know when and where I will do it." Mark stares at Steve eye to eye. "So, you are ready to go to prison and then hell for your actions, because that's what will happen to you and me if we do this?" Steve thinks about what Mark said. "Why do you have to bring hell into this Mark? Who said anyone was going to hell for this, that's extreme," Steve says raising his hands. "Where do you think you would go if you did this Steve, heaven? Give me a break! You're talking about taking someone's life and planning it out like you going on some road trip or something, what's the matter with you?" "Look Mark, I know your hurting right now, but by the time you recuperate, you will be in an 8x9 cell with a desk, a bed, toilet and sink. Your view out the window will be a parking lot of cars of people who work at the prison who will get to go home at the end of their shift. That's not my idea of freedom. Let me take care of this and then we can go about our lives as if nothing happened. The choice is yours." Mark turns his head away from Steve. "It's time for you to leave Steven. I'll call you later." Steve pauses for a minute, then rattles the keys in his hands, and walks away. "Call me then," Steve says as Mark mumbles to himself. "I will, collect in hell, all you have to do is accept the charges."

At Nathaniel's Bangkok apartment, he is on the phone with The Cartel. Felipe' Morales is on the other end of the line angry with Nathaniel. "She called me Nathaniel, how did she get my number?" "What, how would I know?" Nathaniel asks. "I traced the call. It's from an office in Atlanta, Limitless Investments. Marks' best friend Steve owns this company. Wherever Steve is, Mark is nearby. I know this Steve knows about my money. Christy works for Steve.

You have to get rid of all three, these are loose ends." "I took care of Mark, he's gone. I'll take care of them both. I'm still in Bangkok, I will be leaving for Atlanta tomorrow." "While your over there twiddling your thumbs Nathaniel, the entire U.S. government and the Mexican authorities will be after me because they will tie this together!" "Felipe', trust me, I will take care of them. I know where Christy lives, she is staying with her mother in the suburbs." "She moved Nathaniel!" Felipe' says. "What, when?" Nathaniel asks. "You are the hitman, you should be taking care of these things!" "Okay, okay, I will. What's her new address?"

Nathaniel waits for Felipe' to give him the address. "At the Towers of West Midtown on 507 Bishop St. NW. Apartments 7th floor apartment 7. I had my men check it out. She's there," Felipe' says. "She just got the place. Well, I'm heading back to the states right away, but she's not going anywhere since she just moved in." "Yeah well, she's probably planning to move since the FBI just shut down the office she works and now she doesn't have any income, so you'd better move fast." "Wait, how do you know all of this?" "It's my job to know everything Nathaniel. You know who I am. My question now is, who are you that you don't know this?" Felipe' asks. The phone is silent. "Okay, I'm catching a flight tonight then heading there." "Take care of this, now Nathaniel!" "I will Felipe' you have my word." Felipe' hangs up the phone. Nathaniel hears a clicking sound disconnecting the call. "Hello? "Okay, bye to you too. Man, these Cartel guys…." The conversation ends. Nathaniel ponders over his thoughts as he begins packing his duffle bag with the few items he brought with him.

Later that night, Steve paces the floor at his apartment in Bangkok. He visualizes going to prison if he doesn't handle the problem before him. The thought troubles his mind. Back at the hospital, Mark thinks about the entire situation as well as his spirit is troubles him about what he's done with his life. To ease his troubles, he turns on the T.V. On the channel is an American Preacher speaking about "Life Changes." Mark sits up in his bed as he reads the subtitles at the bottom of the screen. "You can do the right thing now," The Preacher emphasizes. "Why wait until tomorrow.

Tomorrow is not promised. The Bible says our life is but a vapor. And while you're waiting, the devil is plotting and planning ways to stop you from living a life of joy and peace during your troubles. It is possible to have peace and joy during trials. How, you might ask? By making right choices now and listening to your heart, for in your heart are the issues of life the Bible says."

Mark sits up in his bed thinking hard at what his heart is telling him to do. He reaches grabbing the telephone dialing Steve's phone number. It rings several times until Steve finally pics it up. "Hello?" "Hey man." "Yeah, what's up?" Steve asks. "I'm going to call the FBI and tell them everything," Mark says. The phone is silent. "Steve?" Steve in angry. "You're going to do what?" "We got to do the right thing man, even if it costs us. "Is that right? Well, what about us huh?" "Steve, come on. You know in your heart this is the right thing to do. Don't you want your conscience to be free?" "I want my body to be saved from grievous bodily harm in prison Mark, that's what I want!"

Mark sighs over the phone. "Steve, we can cut a deal with them if we tell everything and give the money that we stole," Mark says. "What, you figured all that out on a calculator or something?" Steve asks. "Steve, come on." "You know what Mark, that's it!" "What's it?" Mark asks. "You turn yourself in without me. I'm going to take care of our problem and you can thank me later." "What? Wait! No Steven!" "I'm leaving tonight heading back to the states, to take care of her and this problem once and for all, then we won't have to worry about this problem ever again," Steve says. "Steve listen!" Steve hangs up his phone ending the call. "Steve!" Marks phone remains silent. "Steve!" Mark slams the hospital phone down on its receiver. Mark flips over the bed covers violently as he slides out of his bed in pain. He slowly walks over to the closet to retrieve his clothes. He slowly slides on each piece of clothing on as he grimaces in pain.

Steve, with his duffle bag in hand, approaches a cab parked outside the lobby of his apartment. He enters the cab. Steve and the cabbie talk for a minute, then the cab drives away. Steve arrives at the airport moments later. He exits the cab throwing his duffle bag over his shoulder. He then pays the cab driver for his service, then enters the airport. Patrons come and go from the less than busy airport being it is late at night to and from their flights. Mark grabs his passport and sports jacket leaving the room making his way down the hallway to the stairway of the hospital. He takes his time down each step to minimize the pain. Meanwhile, Steve's cab reaches the airport. Steve pays the cabbie and enters the airport. He approaches the check-out booth titled Qatar Airways. He checks in. "Hi, I booked an advanced flight. I have an emergency back in the United States. The Agent asks Steve for his I.D. "Identification please?" Steve hands her his driver's license as she types in his information on the computer. At the hospital, Mark finally makes it down the last flight of stairs. Preparation beats all over his forehead from the ordeal.

    Back at the airport, Steve becomes impatient as his eyes scan around paranoid at the various police officers walking around. The ticket agent finishes typing all the information needed for Steve to catch his flight. She hands Steve his ticket showing the cost of the flight he paid for online totaling $2, 1776.00 for a round trip to the U.S. and back to Bangkok with a four-hour layover in London. "Thank you for flying Qatar Airways, have a safe trip," The ticket agent says. Steve walks away as he checks his watch realizing his flight is about to depart. He rushes towards the gate. Glancing at his watch again, Steve quickly places his duffle bag on the conveyer belt while emptying his pockets of coins and placing them with his keys and cell phone in a plastic container as security watches him. Lastly, Steve removes his belt from his waist placing it inside the plastic container and sliding it onto the conveyer belt as it follows through behind his duffle bag. Three security personnel workers stand checking Steve's belongings while scanning what the computer screen sees.

One of the officer's scan Steve's body with a portable electronic metal detector. One watches the monitor screen. The officer waves the device up and down Steve's left side of his body. The device is silent with no detection of weapons on Steve's body. Steve sighs while looking at his watch agitated as the officer takes his merry time. The officer repeats the same procedure now on the right side of Steve's body. The device finds nothing as Steve gathers his things. One of the officers taps him on his shoulder as he points to Steve's feet. "What?" Steve asks irritated as he glances down at his shoes. "Shoes" the officer requests. Steve glances down at his feet. Shaking his head, he proceeds to remove his shoes while walking through the metal detector. The detector beeps which alarms the security detail. Steve is stunned as he turns around looking at all of them.

      Steve realizes he forgot something. "Oh," he says. He reaches into his pocket removing a ring. He shows it to security as it sits in the palm of his hand. They all look at it while the leading officer motions to Steve to place it into another empty bin. Steve turns around walking forward through the metal detector again, and this time, the metal detector is silent. Steve's forehead shows a small amount of perspiration as he quickly gathers all his belongings to make his flight. He quickly walks away hoping he is in the clear as his heart pounds. As he gets further away from the security check point, he calms down as a cool breeze from the jet way cools off his face like sitting on a beach where the air from the waves of the ocean blow on beach goers.

Back near the hospital, Mark flags down a cab. Mark leans into the passenger side of the cab as the driver asks Mark, "Where to?" "The airport," Mark says as he enters the cab. After a fifteen-minute drive, the cab arrives at the airport. The cabbie turns around noticing Mark fell asleep. "Hey buddy, we're here," The cabbie says to wake Mark up. He glances around as his eyes try to focus through his sleepiness. He opens his wallet and hands the cabbie his money, then exits the vehicle. Mark watches the cab drive away. Meanwhile, inside the airport, Steve arrives at the boarding entrance just in time to hand the ticket agent his boarding pass. The agent smiles as she points the way for Steve to board the plane. Steve thanks her and enters the jet way. A calmness consumes him assuring him everything is okay. On the plane, the Pilot and Stewardess greet Steve as he enters along with other passengers finding their way to their seats. Steve finds his seat numbered 4C amongst most oriental passengers along with three other Americans, and two Australians. Steve opens the top luggage compartment storing his duffle bag inside, then closing it as the latch clicks closed. Steve takes a window seat in his row of the Jumbo Seven Forty-Seven airplane.

    Back inside the airport, Mark stands at the front desk of Qatar Airways. "Hi, may I help you?" Mark takes a deep breath. "Hi, I need a flight to Atlanta right away, it's an emergency." "Okay, do you have a reservation?" "No, I don't, this is an emergency." The ticket agent types on her computer checking for flights to the U.S. "I'm sorry, but the last flight to the U.S. is about to depart." "What? When is the next flight leaving for the U.S.?" The agent types on the computer checking. "The next flight leaves eight hours from now." "Okay, I'll take that one." "Okay, will that be one way or returning?" Mark stares the ticket agent in the eyes. "One-way please?" "Any luggage for the plain or carryon?" "Just me," Mark says. The ticket agent smiles as she types in Mark's reservation as she waits for the machine to print it out. Mark becomes restless as his pain intensifies. The ticket agent notices his facial expression. "Sir are you okay?" "Oh yes, I'm fine thank you." The ticket machine prints out Marks boarding pass as Mark hands her his credit card for payment. The ticket agent processes the payment waiting for the card machine to register the words "approved."

It does as she hands Mark a receipt and pen for his signature. "Sign here please," She says. Mark takes the pen and signs. Afterwards, he hands her the receipt and pen. She gives Mark a copy along with his boarding pass. "Thank you," Mark says. "Your welcome, thank you for flying Qatar Airways." Mark nods his head in agreement as he walks away. Meanwhile, on the other end of the airport, Steve's plane slowly backs out from the terminal escorted by the "Pull Tug" flashing its yellow lights. Once the tug positions the plane on the airstrip, it disconnects itself from the Jumbo Jet while giving the pilot the thumbs up. Mark arrives at the terminal watching the plane Steve is on sitting on the runway. He wishes he could run out and stop the plane, so he could get on.

      The Captain of Steve's plane voices over the loud speaker in Thai language as a flight attendant interprets in English. "Good evening passengers. I am Akino Lee your Captain for this flight to London Airport, in seventeen hours so, sit back and relax. Food and refreshments will be distributed during the flight by our Flight attendants. Enjoy the flight and we will be in London before you know it." The speaker phone ends as the plane's engine begins to roar as the Jumbo jet is finally ready to depart. The pilot radios to Air Traffic Control in Thai language. In translation, he says… "Flight 111 ready for takeoff." An air traffic controller responds back in Thai. The translation is as follows… "Flight 111, you are cleared for taxi on runway 34B to runway 36 A."

The pilot responds. "Roger that control." The other two co-pilots in the cockpit navigate controls for the pilot as the Jumbo jet travels from runway 34B to 36A coming to a complete stop. The Air traffic control responds. "Flight 111 you are ready for takeoff," Traffic controller says. "Roger that control, Flight 111 ready for takeoff on runway 36A," the Captain says as the Jumbo jets engines rev for power causing the ground nearby to vibrate.

Air Traffic control responds. "Flight 111 all clear," Traffic Controller says as the plane begins taxiing down the runway as the Captain moves the hand stick forward giving the jumbo jet power. The plane takes off with its wheels picking up speed. Steve looks out of the window at the scenery he is about to leave behind. The jumbo jet picks up more speed as the planes front wheels begin to lift as the pilot inside pulls the hand controls towards him. The front nose of the plane begins to lift as the co-pilot responds. "We are at 30 knots." The pilot responds. "We are climbing," The co-pilot responds. "40 knots," Copilot responds. "Cross winds?" The co-pilot responds, "Winds are northeast of us."

The plane climbs higher as the pilot responds. "Flaps," Co-pilot responds. "Flaps down." "Landing gear up," Co-pilot responds. "Landing gear up," Captain says as the plane peaks to new heights. The pilot pushes forward on the controls in front of him as he powers up on the stick with his right hand. "Still climbing," Co-pilot responds. "Winds at 35," Copilot says. "All clear," says the pilot. The plane levels off as the pilot pulls back on the control stick and powers back on the power stick. The plane finishes its climb as it glides up over the clouds and into the darkness of the night. Steve feels relieved as he turns out the light above him closing his eyes.

CHAPTER TWENTY-ONE

"Wanted by Everyone"

Seventeen hours later, Steve's plane arrives at a London airport. The plane taxis on the runway at a speed of thirty miles an hour. After turning two times down two different runways, it pulls into the designated jet way. Steve becomes impatient as he waits to get off the plane to switch to his connected flight. Finally, he can exit the plane. He glances at his watch realizing he has some free time so, he stops at a Starbucks to get some coffee. After purchasing his coffee, he sits down rehearsing in his mind how he's going to kill Christy Billings.

Meanwhile, millions of miles away in El Paso, Texas, Cartel leader Felipe' Morales instructs his men on their mission in the darkest of night at a private landing field. "I want you to make sure Nathaniel does what he is supposed to do. If he doesn't, you do it, then you take care of him, understand?" His lead man responds in Spanish. "Si' Senor' Morales." The three men walk into the private Lear Jet as the engines engage as Felipe' stands watching as his plane begins taxiing on the private runway. The plane takes off at full speed lifting into the air with its wheels disappearing under the plane. Satisfied, Felipe' walks away to a dark colored SUV awaiting him. He enters, and the SUV drives away.

Back in Bangkok, Mark finally prepares to board his plane as he enters the jetway. Upon boarding, Mark hears the commotion of a man yelling outside in the seating area. Mark stops and turns around to see what is going on. Suddenly, he sees Nathaniel yelling at the ticket agent demanding to get on the plane Mark is on. Mark stands to the side as passengers pass by him to get to the plane for boarding. Nathaniel turns his head looking towards the jetway to the plane. Marks eyes lock onto Nathaniel's. Fear consumes Mark as he backs away from eye contact between them. As Mark turns around to board the plane, he hears the ominous voice of Nathaniel shouting, "Stop the plane, I must get on that plane, I don't care if it's full!" Mark makes it to the plane eager to sit down to rest his wounded body. He has a window seat all to himself. Morning begins in Bangkok as the sunlight beams in through the window shinning on Marks face. After twenty minutes passes, Marks plane makes its departure heading to London. The plane's engines roar as it begins taxiing on the runway. The plane is later cleared for takeoff as it speeds down the runway lifting into the air disappearing later into the clouds.

    At the London airport, later, Steve makes his way to his departed flight from London to the U.S. He stands in line with other passengers boarding. As the line moves forward, Steven hands the ticket agent his boarding pass walking through the jet bridge to the plane. Inside the plane, he is greeted once again by his new pilot and host of flight attendants. He finds his seat and repeats his routing from the last flight stowing away his duffel bag in the top compartment. He glances at his watch eager to get his second flight over with. After several minutes, Steven's flight departs from the terminal and taxis on the runway. Fifteen minutes later, it flies off into the blue skies.

After 12 hours and 22 minutes, Mark's flight arrives at the London airport. It taxis on the runway pulling into terminal C on the Concord. Everyone aboard exits the flight one by one as Mark gets a nudge from a passenger walking by. Mark wakes up stretching his arms and yawning. He stands to his feet as his mind feels fully rested but his body reminds him of his gunshot wound injury as he grabs his left side. He exits the plane walking down through the jet bridge. Mark hears a female voice speaking over the intercom.

"Attention, Tim Porter, please call dispatch."

The voice pauses for a second.

"Tim Porter, please call dispatch immediately."

Mark feels hungry as he searches for a McDonalds to fill his stomach from a long flight because the small meal given by the Airline didn't. His eyes see the yellow arch he recognized before at the same airport. He makes his way through the crowds of people. Mark just remembers he hasn't showered in hours after leaving the hospital. He decides to close his suit jacket to disguise his unwelcomed body scent. Inside the McDonalds two long lines are formed in front of him. He sighs hoping to see a worker approach an empty cash register, but to no avail. Mark's stomach growls as he pounds at it to keep it quiet.

"Be quiet please."

Mark stands in the second line as he listens to the sounds of people behind the counter rushing to make the orders for those who have already paid. The moment defines a sense of urgency to everyone in the establishment as the eyes of hunger in its patrons look on. They look on at the workers as if their eyes demand a sense of urgency to fill their hunger. Chatter from customers entertains those standing in line. The line begins to move as Mark inches closer to his dream of eating a Big Mac with fries and a vanilla milk shake. Marks phone begins to vibrate. He checks his phone realizing he has a text message.

It reads, "Hey you! You miss me?" Mark recognizes the name the message is from. It is Janice, the college student he met on his way to Bangkok.

He responds texting back… "Hi, how are you?"

Janice responds, "Happy that we meet again going back to Atlanta."

Mark texts back… "What are you talking about, where are you?"

Before Mark realizes anything, he is at the front counter ready to give his order. A cashier greets him with a smile.

"Hi, welcome to McDonalds, may I take your order?"

Mark responds, "Hi, I'll have a Big Mac meal with a vanilla shake."

The Cashier presses her fingers on the keys at the register. The young lady glances up at Mark.

"Your total is $12.50," The cashier says.

Mark reaches in his pocket pulling out his wallet. His eyes connect to an American $10.00 bill. It's not enough. "Where is the rest of my money Mark's brain says as panic begins to set in all through his body. A twenty-dollar bill appears on Marks right side handed to the cashier.

"Here, take this," a voice says standing behind Mark.

The cashier receives the money as Mark turns around connecting the voice with the face. It is Janice. The cashier punches in the keys to the register which pops open the cash machine below. As the cash machine below pops open, the change inside rattles. The cashier hands Janice a change of $7.50 as a quarter drops onto the counter.

"Oops, I'm sorry," the cashier says.

"Oh, that's okay," Janice says.

"Fancy meeting you here again," Mark says to Janice.

"I was about to say the same thing to you," She replies.

Mark grabs his receipt and stands off to the side as Janice steps up to give her order.

"I'll have a Quarter Pounder with meal with a Coke."

The cashier rings up the order, "That will be $14.50."

Janice pays for her meal and steps to the side along with Mark.

"Your order will be right up," the cashier says.

Mark covers himself hoping Janice does not talk about how he looks or smells. Suddenly, Marks order of food is up.

"Ketchup?" Mark asks one of the workers. The worker reaches in a box on a shelf under the counter handing Mark several packets of Ketchup.

"Thank you," Mark replies.

Mark starving and can't wait to eat, finds a seat amongst the packed crowd of people already seated. Mark begins eating like a wolf eating a carcass. Janice carrying a red miniature backpack, wearing a grey hoodie over a white t-shirt, black baggy cargo pants, and black leather work boots, walks over and sits down with Mark.

"Wow, Mark, are you hungry or what? You act like you just got out of jail or something."

Mark stops eating feeling embarrassed.

"I just got out of the hospital."

"Hospital?" Janice asks.

"Yes," Mark says.

"What were you in the hospital for?" Janice asks.

"I got shot," Mark says.

"Shot?"

"Yes."

Janice is confused. "Mark, what's going on? You look like a mess, you smell like a mess."

Mark gives a sarcastic smirk on his face.

"Thanks," Mark says.

"I'm just saying, I'm concerned for you, talk to me, I'm a good listener, I won't judge." Janice says.

Mark takes a bite into his sandwich chewing for a minute then wiping his mouth with a napkin. before he responds.

"Some punk kid shot me, whose father I worked for at DinoCore, and I think he did it because he now works for the Cartel. They want me dead because I stole their money."

Janice takes a bite into her hamburger she takes her left hand putting it over her mouth in shock.

"Oh my gosh Mark, the Cartel? Are you insane or something? Those people chop off people's limbs for looking at them the wrong way."

Mark rolls his eyes.

"You watch too many movies."

"Why do you think they put that in movies Mark? Where do you think the movies got it from, my gosh?"

Mark raises both of his hands.

"Okay, I get your point," He says.

Janice swallows her food as she takes a sip of her pop from a straw.

"Mark, why would you do something like that?"

"Greed Janice, just like everyone else," Mark says.

"Well Mark, look at you now, was it worth it?"

Mark pauses.

"No."

"That's an afterthought for sure," Janice says.

Mark is curious about something.

"Where are you from Janice?"

"I'm from Camden Town, Georgia it's near Regents Park. Why do you ask?"

"I don't know, I thought you might be an undercover agent or something," Mark says.

Janice laughs, "Dressed like this?"

Mark glances at her wardrobe. "Yeah."

"Oh, I see. So, if I were, what, were you going to run out of here or something, because I would arrest you right here right now."

"On what?" Mark asks.

"On what you just told me. You just confessed," Janice replies laughing.

"I'm a business man, we don't run from anything, we handle it," Mark says.

"Oh, how cool," Janice replies.

Later, a man in uniform enters the men's restroom with a small bag. He nears the stalls lined up seven in a row. When he approaches the sixth stall, he slides the small bag under the stall. A hand reaches grabbing the bag pulling it away. The man in uniform turns around and leaves. Inside the stall, a clicking sound is heard of metal being engaged. After several seconds, Nathaniel appears from the stall wearing a trench coat. He exits the bathroom out into the public eye of passengers as they walk about, Nathaniel stands with his carryon bag over his shoulder as he glances down at his flight ticket for his connecting flight.

He calculated Mark's arrival at the airport, knowing he is still here. Nathaniel approaches the escalator placing his right foot on the step as it moves upward with the chain of steps. His left foot follows behind his right foot along for the ride up to the top floor of the airport. As he travels up the escalator, he enjoys the view below him. As the escalator arrives at the top of the main floor, Nathaniel steps off as the escalator continues recycling itself for more passengers below. Nathaniel glances at the signs above him looking Marks terminal. In a distance, his eyes lock onto it, but there isn't any sign of Mark waiting to board his flight. To his right in a distance, Nathaniel sees the McDonalds sign and decides to get something to eat.

As Nathaniel enters, he notices McDonalds is full of patrons. Marks back is facing Nathaniel as he turns around seeing Janice who catches his eye. He turns his head away looking at the menu above. Janice shakes her head in disbelief at Mark.

"From what your telling me, you in a whole heap of trouble. What else have you not told me?" Janice asks.

"A friend of mine that works for me is in trouble," Mark says.

"What trouble?" Janice asks.

"My business partner plans to kill her," Mark says.

"Mark!"

"I know it's bad Janice, that's why I have to get back to the States and stop him," Mark says.

"This the guy Steve you mentioned? Where is he now?" Janice asks.

"He's on a plane to the States as we speak," Mark emphasizes.

"Wow, Mark, okay, where is the guy that shot you?"

"How should I know?" Mark asks sarcastically.

"Because if he does not think you are dead, he could still be looking for you," Janice says.

Mark glances around McDonald's paranoid as he looks down at his watch.

"We have to go; our flight is about to leave," Mark says standing to throw away his trash.

"What?" Janice asks pulling out her ticket.

"Oh, wow, it is about to leave!" Flight 833," Janice says as she throws away her trash as well.

As the two leave McDonalds together, Mark turns around instinctively and sees Nathaniel at the front counter of McDonalds preparing to give his order for his food. "Yes, I will have..." Nathaniel turns his head seeing Mark. The two make eye contact as Mark aggressively grabs Janice's arm pulling her towards him. "Come on," Janice is alarmed as she responds, "Hey, my arm!" Mark says as they exit out of McDonalds. Nathaniel stops speaking, and immediately leaves the counter. "Sir, your order?" The cashier says. Nathaniel body produces Epinephrine from his adrenal gland which pumps more blood to his heart as he rushes towards Mark and Janice as they run down the walkway of the airport. Marks heart rate intensifies almost beating out of his chest as his eyes scan all the illuminated signs passing by above him.

Mark sees a sign that reads, "Men's Restroom" pulling Janice inside it with him. "Mark, what's wrong?" Janice asks. "That was Nathaniel!" "The guy that wants to kill you?" "Yes!" Nathaniel exits McDonald's scanning the airport like the "Terminator" for Mark and Janice. As he proceeds through the airport, his eyes read every sign above him. Inside the men's restroom, Mark crouches down examining every stall to see if it is empty. He opens the last stall pulling Janice inside with him. the last stall of the restroom. "Mark, this is the men's bathroom, I'm not supposed to be in here!" Mark stares into Janice's eyes covering her mouth responding, "Today is an exception." Suddenly, the bathroom door opens along with one of the stalls. Mark and Janice hear feet shuffling on the floor as they stand silent like statues. Mark holds up his index finger to his lips as a sign language to Janice to be quiet.

The feet of the person inside the stall stops as silence takes over. After four minutes pass, the toilet flushes in that stall along with feet shuffling exiting the stall. The owner of the sounds is a heavy-set man. He belches as he washes his hands with soap from the electric dispenser. The man checks his hair in the mirror along with fixing his tie. Mark stares at him through the crack of the bathroom stall. Finally, the man leaves as he door closes behind him. Mark and Janice stand together listening to the silence inside the bathroom, but still hearing the commotion of people walking past outside. Mark shields Janice as she crouches down behind him as he turns around and peeks through crack in the stall to see if the coast is clear.

Suddenly, an eye appears staring at Mark. Mark jumps back away from the stall as the door is yanked open with great force as Nathaniel grabs him throwing him out of the stall as the door of the stall slams shut. Mark rolls across the hard bathroom floor. When he stops rolling, a foot from Nathaniel lands on his neck. "Well, well, well, look what I found. Hey buddy! I thought you were dead. What are you doing in here, hiding? You would have been better off hiding in the lady's room. I wouldn't have thought to go in there, if I did, of course their would-be women screaming, attracting security and all that, then, I wouldn't be able to kill you. Well, it doesn't matter now because I'm about to do it anyway, but before I do, I need to ask you one question, where is the money?" Mark in pain holding his side, glances up at Nathaniel. "What money?" Mark asks. "What money? The money you and my uncle stole from the Cartel that ruined DinoCore and my chances of me and my brother owning the company or getting an inheritance to say the least," Nathaniel says.

Mark grimaces as Nathaniel's foot begins to cut off his air supply. "Oh, my bad. You can't talk if you can't breathe. Let me lighten up on the pressure of my Steve Madden shoe against your neck so you can tell me," Nathaniel says. As the pressure of the shoe lightens, Mark is able to breath again. Janice remains in the stall curled up wondering what to do. Nathaniel pulls out a hand gun with a silencer. "I'm waiting," Nathaniel says. Mark begins laughing. The moment throws Nathaniel for a loop. "You'll never be me," Mark says. "Excuse me?" Nathaniel asks. "You envy my lifestyle because you can't have it, and you don't know what to do to get it," Mark says. "That's not the response I'm looking for Mark, so let me coach you to it. I'm going to count to three and when I get to three, the game is over, you got that? One…" Nathaniel pauses for a split second. "Two…" Nathaniel pauses again as he coils the gun by pulling it back. "Three…"

Mark sees Nathaniel's head jolt along with Nathaniel appearing with a shocked look over his face as his body drops to the floor along with his gun discharging. Mark coughs as he rolls over on his stomach to get up. Janice helps him. "Mark are you okay?" Mark now standing tall, glances at the floor seeing Nathaniel and Janice's bag nearby. Mark approaches her bag. "What did you hit him with?" Mark asks. "My books. I guess you could say he got a head full of knowledge," Janice says. Mark turns his head looking at her. "I guess you are right," Mark says. He realizes they have a flight to catch as he turns to Janice. "Let's go."

Janice grabs her bag as the two leave the bathroom heading towards terminal Concord F22. A voice over the P.A. announces their flight. "Flight 833 terminal F22 bound for London is now ready for boarding. "That's us," Mark tells Janice as they approach the terminal F22. Ten minutes later, Mark and Janice are on the plane as it pulls away from the Terminal, and taxis down the runway. Moments later, Flight 833 takes off down the runway and into the air bound for London.

Back in America, Christy prepares for her birthday party. There is a knock at the door of her apartment. Christy approaches the door in her blue dress with bare feet, opening it seeing her girlfriends Cheryl and Leslie standing in front of her. They shout out… "Hey girl, you ready?" "Yes, come in for a second, I need to finish putting on my makeup. You two are always on time," Christy says. Upon entering, Cheryl notices boxes scattered around the apartment. "Are you moving or what?" Cheryl asks. "I have too, I can't afford this place anymore," Christy says. "Oh, well, you can stay with me if you like," Cheryl offers. "My friend Angie said I could stay with her for a while, thanks for the offer though," Christy says. "This place is really nice Christy," Leslie replies.

    In the bathroom, Christy finishes the final touches of her makeup. "Okay, all done. I'll get my shoes on, and we can go." Cheryl and Leslie sit in the living room looking around the place. "This is a nice place," Cheryl responds. The marbled floored kitchen with a checkered glossy black and white counter top captures the eyes of the girls. "Wow, I wish I owned a place like this," Leslie says. "You and me both," Cheryl responds. "You sure you want to let this place go Christy," Leslie says aloud. "Yeah, well, when you lose your high paying job for the second time, you have very few options." Finally, Christy appears from her bedroom ready for a fun night. "Okay, I'm all set to go," Christy says as the three girls head out the front door. Cheryl notices something about Christy as they enter the elevator. "Christy, you seem different." "How?" Christy asks. "I don't know, you just have a glow about you now." "A glow?" Christy asks. "Yeah, I must say, it seems like you've changed or something." "Oh, well, I've been through a lot lately and I have a new outlook on life thanking God for every day I am able to breath, you know?" "I can agree with that," Leslie says. The elevator makes its way to the lobby of the high-rise apartment as the three ladies exit on their way to Cheryl's car.

In the car, the girls continue talking. "The way you are now Christy, I like it," Cheryl says. "What do you mean?" Christy asks. "I mean, your attitude is very different from the way you were before. You were hard to get along with most of the times, very moody." "That's funny, because I would have to agree with you. Now that I look at it, I didn't like myself much either," Christy says as the car fills with laughter from all three girls. "Well, thanks for that honest opinion of yourself Christy," Leslie says. "God's not done with me yet though, I'll be under construction until I leave this earth, that's for sure." "Well, good for you Christy. Let me know when you get there, because I know I need it too," Cheryl agrees. "Me too, we all do," Leslie says.

Behind Cheryl's car is a silver SUV following behind. Inside the vehicle are four Hispanic males who work for Felipe' Morales. "Don't follow so close," A passenger in the SUV says. Back in Cheryl's car, the girls continue talking. "So, what's changed about you Christy?" Cheryl asks. "I'm just deciding to live for God now. I experienced something you can never imagined when I died on the gurney in the ambulance. I will tell you my whole story one day, but life is different for me now. I'm still learning to make right choices that will help others and not just myself, so, I can say, I'm thinking less of me and what I want, and more about how God can use me to bless others," Christy says. "So, what, no more partying, cheating on your boyfriend, cussing people out, cheating on your taxes, stuff like that?" Cheryl asks. "I never cheated on my taxes Cheryl, come on," Christy says laughing. Cheryl laughs, "I know, I'm just joking with you." "Ladies please, whatever I did or didn't do that I should have done in the past, I am sorry for that. I was wrong, please forgive me. But now, I can say that I am at peace for who I am, and day by day, I am learning how much God loves me, so I can share that love to others."

Moments later Cheryl's car arrives at the restaurant. The car parks as the ladies exit the vehicle. Seconds later, the silver SUV pulls into the parking lot off in a distance. One of the Hispanic males, glances around the parking lot looking for someone. "Where is Nathaniel, he's supposed to be here to take her out?" "I don't see him. If he doesn't show, were supposed to do it," The ladies enter the restaurant as a greeter welcomes them. "Hello, how many?" He asks. "We have a reservation for Billings," Cheryl responds. The young man glances on his sheet listed with reservations. "Okay, follow me," He says as the ladies follow him proceeding around a corner as Christy focuses her eyes seeing a group of people present at a long table. She sees her Mother, Aunt, Uncle, Grandmother, and Angie with her friends from church, Amy, Tia, Rachel, Molly, and Pam. They shout in unison, "Surprise!" Christy covers her mouth with both hands excited as Cheryl and Leslie watch Christy stand in awe at the love shown to her. "You guys, no you didn't. I thought I was just hanging out with Cheryl and Leslie tonight?" Christy turns to Cheryl and Leslie hugging them. "Thank you two!" Next, she walks over hugging everyone at the table. "Thank you all for being here, this has really made my day!"

Moments later, two servers approach the table taking each person's order for food while Christy converses with her friends and family at the table. The restaurant is packed with patrons as the bars area has four flat screens T.V.'s showing various sports games playing. The ambience of the restaurant consists of a mixture of live entertainment of music playing throughout the night. As the night continues, everyone at Christy's table finish eating their food. Christy's plate still has a piece of sautéed poached fish Salmon, with a side of Asparagus and Rice Pilaf enough for her to take home. Her drink has a small amount of non-alcoholic Strawberry Dakari left in the glass.

For desert, Christy enjoyed a Marble cake brought out by the restaurant. Next to the cake are two small cupcakes are brought out with two lit candles on one cupcake, and nine lit candles on the other totaling twenty-nine. Christy makes a wish, leaning over them blowing out the candles as everyone cheers for her. To finalize the night, Christy gathers everyone around the table to pray together. They all join hands as Christy leads them in prayer. She thanks God for life and more life abundantly. Afterwards, everyone disperses to their cars outside. The men in the silver SUV wait as they see Christy coming out with her girlfriends smiling and laughing talking about the wonderful time she had.

One of the men glances at his watch. "He's not here. What are we going to do?" "We follow her," another man inside the vehicle says

CHAPTER TWENTY-TWO

"Moment of Truth"

Meanwhile, at the Atlanta airport, Steve's plane lands. Steve exits the jetway into the main seating area and heads towards the escalator to the bottom level of the airport. On a mission, Steve glances at his watch. Outside the airport, he flags down a taxi. Upon entering, he tells the cab driver his destination as the cab drives away. Meanwhile Mark's plane touches down as well from London. Mark and Janice exit the plane heading towards the exit to catch a cab like Steve. In Bangkok, Nathaniel finally boards a plane to Atlanta. He enters his flight with an ice pack on his head. Inside Mark's cab, they rush to save Christy from Steve's wrath. Mark calls Christy's phone but it immediately accesses her email voice recording. "So, what are you going to do when we get to her place Mark?" Janice asks. "Save Christy from Steve," Mark responds. "And how do you plan to do that?" Janice asks. "Contact the police and tell them the address where were going while I keep trying Christy's phone," Mark says.

Janice dials 911 while Mark continues calling Christy's phone as the cab drives towards her place. Across town, Cheryl's car arrives at Christy's. The silver SUV pulls in behind them but parks on the street unnoticed. "Well, thanks ladies, tonight was really a fun night for me," Christy says. "Were glad you enjoyed yourself Christy, so you are sure you don't want to stay at my place until you get situated at where you will be?" "No, I'm going to take up Angie's offer for now. I might end up moving back with my mom. I'm not sure, but I will keep your offer in mind." "Okay," Cheryl says. Christy exits Cheryl's car hugging the girls as she leans in the car from the outside. "See you guys later," Christy says. "Okay," Cheryl says. "You bet," Leslie replies. Christy turns her head noticing the silver SUV parked on the street. She sees the face of a Hispanic male lighting a cigarette. The cigarette illuminates for a quick second revealing the faces of three other men sitting inside the vehicle as all three men stare at Christy simultaneously making her uncomfortable. Christy enters her apartment as Cheryl's car drives away.

Inside the silver SUV the driver smoking his cigarette ponders what to do. "So, do we make our move or what?" "I don't know," one of the men replies. "Let me call this Nathaniel guy." The man dials Nathaniel's number but receives no answer. "He's not answering," the man says. Moments later, Christy arrives up at her apartment. Inside, she plugs in the charger to her phone which does not have any power left. She proceeds to her landline phone that she rarely uses and calls the police. "Hi, I'd like to report a suspicious vehicle parked outside my apartment. There are three men inside, and they look very suspicious." Christy pauses. "Yes, and they were staring at me the entire time I entered my apartment." Christy pauses. "No, I've never seen this vehicle nor them before, that's what makes this very unusual." Christy pauses as she stares out of her apartment window down at the silver SUV. "Okay, the description of the vehicle is a silver SUV. I don't know the make. It's a big and long SUV I know that, and it has dark interior. The driver is smoking a cigarette because I'm looking out my window at the vehicle as we speak," Christy says as she pauses to listen to the 911 operator.

"You are sending a police car? Okay, I live at 510 Bishop North West at the Tower of West Midtown on the 7th floor apartment 7, and my name is Christy Billings." Christy pauses again. "Okay, thank you," she says as she hangs up the phone placing it on the charging console. Christy sits on her couch and waits. Ten minutes later while reading one of her magazines, Christy notices flashing lights outside her window. She peeks through her blinds and notices two police cars surrounding the silver SUV. Outside the SUV are the three men that were inside. They stand in handcuffs as they are questioned. Christy gets a closer glance and sees several handguns being placed on the hood of the silver SUV by the police officers. Thinking about it, Christy wonders what the men were planning to do sitting there with guns on them. After several minutes, there is a knock at Christy's door. "Who is it?" She asks. No response from the person knocking.

Christy believes it might be the police, so without thinking, she opens the door. But to her surprise, it is Steve. "Hey, Christy," He says. Christy is surprised. "Steve?" Christy sticks her head out into the hallway looking around. "How did you get up here?" She asks.

"Yeah, someone was coming out of the lobby, so, I slipped in. Hey, sorry for stopping by so late, but I've been thinking about everything, and I want to apologize for the way I talked to you at the office. I can't do this anymore you know? I need someone to talk to before I talk to Mark and tell him we need to come clean about what were doing. I want to make this right, can we talk?" Christy can't believe what she's hearing. "Oh, yeah, sure, come in." "Great thanks," Steve says as he enters Christy's apartment. Christy forgets to lock the front door. "What made you change your mind Steve? "Oh, yeah, I couldn't sleep thinking about everything. I don't know how Mark is going to take all of this, I guess I will have to do it alone," Steve says as he peeks through Christy's blinds at the police below wrapping up their arrests.

Steve has a seat. "You are not alone Steve," Christy says. "I'm not," Steve asks. "No." Christy pauses. "Do you want some water or something?" "Yes please, waters fine," Steve says. Christy turns and heads towards her kitchen while talking. "I'm so glad you stopped by actually because, the FBI came to talk to me," Christy says. "They did?" Steve asks with a surprised look from Christy's living room. "Yes, and I decided to cooperate with them, so I gave them everything I had to help them with their investigation," Christy says. "You did, did you?" Steve asks as his facial expression changes to a frown. "Yeah. So, I guess you could say this was a divine intervention with you showing up like this." Steve reaches into his pocket pulling out a cordlike object. He stands up and peeks out Christy's window below. The police are gone, which gives Steve the go ahead to do what he is about to do.

Fifteen minutes away, Mark and Janice's cab makes its way towards Christy's apartment. "She's still not answering?" Janice asks Mark. "No, I don't know what's going on, she usually answers immediately because she says each call might be important, I'll try again," Mark says as he dials her number. Janice grabs her phone. "This is agent Montgomery, I need backup to West Midtown Apartments, address 510 Bishop Street, now! Mark turns to Janice with a surprised look. "What, wait a minute, how did you know Christy's address?" Mark asks. "I'm FBI Mark," Janice says. Meanwhile, back at Christy's apartment, Steve proceeds towards Christy's kitchen talking. "So, what did you tell them?" He asks. "I gave them the files of all the clients and a flash drive I had of Marks when we were at DinoCore. On that flash drive was the transaction of the Cartel that Mark stole the money from," Christy says as she fills the glass with water by turning the sink handle labeled "C" as the cold-water gushes from the faucet into the glass. The sound of the water filling the glass is heard as Steve approaches her from the back. "Wow, Christy, you are bravery than I could ever be," Steve says coiling the cord with both hands as he approaches the back of Christy. Suddenly, Christy's phone receives Marks call as it regains 5% of power from charging on zero. Christy's phone rings as Christy lifts her head realizing her ring tone. "Oh, my phone has some juice now," She says as Steve stands directly behind her.

He quickly wraps the cord around her neck. Christy lets out a partial scream. Seconds later, Mark and Janice's cab arrive at Christy's apartment. "Something is wrong, she's not answering her phone, this is unlike her," Mark says hopping out of the cab followed by Janice as she tips the cab driver. The two rush to the main door of the apartment but are unable to access the lobby to the elevator. "How are we going to get in?" Mark asks. Janice glances around for another way inside. Back upstairs in Christy's apartment, Christy, fights for her life as she struggles against Steve desire to take her life. The two tussles inside her kitchen knocking over boxes on her kitchen table. As Christy twists and turns, she elbows Steven in his groin causing him to hunch over. He releases his grip of the cord around Christy's neck as she runs down the hallway past her bathroom towards her bedroom with Steve right behind her. Christy makes it to her bedroom quickly turning around to shut the door, but it is too late as Steve presses up against the door trying to pry it open. It becomes a tugging match between the two, the one with the greatest strength will win.

Downstairs, Mark notices a couple casually walking out of an elevator through the lobby. Mark becomes excited. "Janice, look!" Janice rushes over to where Mark is arriving to see a couple exit through the first door, then the second with Mark waiting for them as a runner would waiting for a baton. The couple open the door as Mark quickly grabs it. "Thank you, man!" The young man along with his female partner, both stare at Mark wondering what his problem is as he holds the door open for Janice and the two quickly enter the lobby of the apartment rushing towards the elevator. Upstairs, Christy screams as she battles with Steve and her bedroom door. Steve has had enough. He leans into the door with all his weight knocking Christy in the air onto her bed. She bounces off the bed onto the floor as Steve runs around the bed towards her. Christy screams again before Mark climbs on top of her with both hands around her neck. Christy fights for dear life clawing and pulling at Steve's shirt ripping several buttons off. She grabs at his face trying to scratch him, but he turns his head causing her hands to slide across his face. Two floors below on the elevator, Mark becomes very impatient as he watches the highlighted numbered buttons inside. "Come on! This is the slowest elevator I ever rode on in my life!" "Were almost there, Mark," Janice says as she pulls out her gun pulling back the chamber.

Inside Christy's apartment, Christy continues to fight for her life this time scratching Steve's face leaving distinct red lines from her fingernails. This enrages him as he growls to shake off the pain. He presses his body closer to Christy's body to prevent her from scratching his face any further. As Christy gasps for air, Steve strengthens his grip hoping to finish the job. He watches Christy's eyes shift trying to figure out what to do as her grip on his wrists begin to lighten. Steve knows Christy is nearing the end as she stares at him. Steve has gone too far to turn back now. Christy's body relaxes as her arms fall to her side. Suddenly, a gun is pressed up against Steven's back. "Get off her, FBI!" Janice takes her index fingers digging into Steven's eyes widen as his hands let go off Christy's throat. Christy's head falls to one side as her body remains motionless. "Okay, relax, relax, don't shoot me," Steve says as he attempts to get up slowly with his hands raised. "Christy!" Mark shouts as he tries to get closer to her. "Is she okay?" Janice asks Mark. Mark hops across Christy's bed to get to her laying on the the other side of the bed on the floor. Mark shakes Christy but she is not moving. "Christy! Christy!"

As Janice prepares to arrest Steven, he quickly turns around knocking the gun from Janice's hand and pushing her against the wall with such force, her body jolts as it slides to the floor. Steve runs out of the room while Mark checks on Christy. Mark calls 911. "911 emergency," the dispatcher says. "I need an ambulance at 510 Bishop Street, the Tower of West Midtown apartments, 7th floor, apartment 7, hurry!" "We already have units on the way there. You need an ambulance too? What is the problem?" The dispatcher asks. "Yes, hurry, my friend is not moving!" "What happened to her?" "She was attacked and she's not moving!" "Is she breathing?" "I...I can't tell, hurry please!" "Can you check for a pulse?" Dispatcher asks. "Janice?" Mark turns his head around and notices Steve is gone. "Where is Steve?" Mark asks as Janice grabs the back of her head. "Hello, are you still there?" the dispatcher asks. "Janice! Check her pulse, I'll get Mark!" "Hello, are you still there?" Dispatcher asks. Mark hops over Christy's bed out the room and down the hallway of Christy's apartment. Janice grabs her head as she stands up yelling at Mark, "Mark wait!" Janice approaches Mark's phone picking it up as she tends to Christy. Steve stands in front of the elevator pressing the

"L" button for Lobby as hard as he can as he watches the lit icon of numbers highlight above his head.

Finally, the elevator door opens and Steve rushes inside it to press the "Door Closed" button. He presses it like he's hitting the button on a game show for the answer. As Mark exits Christy's apartment running towards the elevator, Steve hears feet running at a fast pace. His heart beats faster than his fears as he quickly hits the "L" button again. As the sound of running feet approaches the elevator door, it finally closes as Marks face appears. Mark pounds on the door from the outside with all his rage. The elevator starts to move traveling from floor to floor. Mark determined to stop Steve turns looking for the staircase. He finds it seeing the sign highlighted "STAIRS". He runs towards the door pushing it open as he begins his descent from floor to floor still grabbing his side bearing the pain it brings.

Steve rides the elevator down. He touches his face at the scratches left by Christy. It angers him. "Crazy girl with her cat clawing fingernails!" Steve watches the numbers still highlighted from 5 to 4 to 3. Mark continues his decline on the stairway as sweat beats across his forehead. He doesn't care because he is on a mission. As the elevator nears he lobby floor, Steve breathes a sigh of relief. The numbered lights above finally reach the designated stop for the lobby. Steven waits for the door to open with his head is down as he catches his breath. When the door opens, he exits the elevator only to get a fist across his left cheek. The blow knocks him away from the elevator door as his body crashes to the hard marble floor. A voice behind the vicious blow, responds, "I told you not to hurt her," Mark says standing over Steve like a triumphant warrior as he lays out cold on the floor.

Suddenly, police and emergency units arrive to the scene with sirens wailing. Moments later, several tenants gawk at the scene as paramedics wheel Christy out to the ambulance parked out front as its lights flash illuminating the entire apartment building. Off to the side of the lobby, Steven is handcuffed and escorted outside by police while detectives question Janice. Mark is also handcuffed and escorted away. Steve is placed in the back seat of a patrol car along with Mark. Both police cars take them away. The ambulance speeds off to the hospital as Christy fights for her life once again. On the gurney, Christy dreams of Hades and her best friend Jessica. They stare at each other. "You have so much to give Christy," Jessica says. "Tell the world about this place. Tell them the truth about life and death. Tell them why Jesus died for us, so that we can live for eternity with God." Christy holds Jessica's hand as the both their eyes fill with tears.

"Wait Jessica! I love you, come with me!" Christy pleads. "I can't Christy, I can't! You must go, please, go!" Christy sobs uncontrollably. "But," Christy says as she tries to speak. "I know Christy, I know," Jessica says as she cries too. "I will always love you Jessica! I will never forget you!" Christy says. "I love you too, Christy." Christy releases her hand from Jessica's hand as she slowly backs away from her as the fire around them intensifies. Christy is pulled away from the darkness into the light. As the paramedics perform CPR on Christy in the ambulance, she is revived as her eyes begin to show life again. "We have a pulse!" A paramedic says as Christy begins breathing again. The ambulance continues speeding towards the hospital running red lights as cars pull over to the side of the road out of the ambulance path.

    Meanwhile, at the Atlanta airport, Nathaniel's plane arrives pulling into the gate to park. After twenty-minutes of waiting, passengers become very impatient including Nathaniel as he glances at his watch. "Come on!" A flight attendant walks by him as he taps her arm. "Hey, excuse me? What's the hold up, I have somewhere to be?" "Oh, it will be just another five minutes," She gracefully says walking away. "That's what you said ten minutes ago," Nathaniel voices. About ten minutes later, everyone on board finally exit the plane. Nathaniel is the first one off as he rushes towards the front out of the plane down the jetway through the ticket door. As he enters the seating area, FBI agents Mason and Mosely greet him along with five other agents along with six local Atlanta police officers, and five Airport police officers.

Nathaniel is handcuffed and taken away. "Welcome to Atlanta Mr. Boykins, we've been expecting you," Agent Mason says. "How did you know who I was?" "Your Mexican Cartel friends in the silver SUV gave us a tip. Since they wouldn't give up information about their boss fearing what would happen to them and their families, they gave up you. Want to know why?" Mason asks. "Yeah, why?" Nathaniel asks. "Because they were angry that you didn't show up to do the job you were hired to do making them wait all night." Nathaniel is whisked away with a trail of officers and agents behind him.

Two years later at a Correctional facility in the State of Georgia, Mark Collins inmate 565472 sits on top of his bunk reading two letters he received, one from Janice and the other Christy. He smiles as he eyes scans reading both letters. Reading passes the time for Mark as he does his 10-year bid for the role in his Ponzi Scheme. He was awarded grace by the Judges decision based the circumstances presented and Christy's pleading for a lighter sentence for saving her life and returning the money he stole from his current clients. The government seized the remaining drug Cartel's money Mark held in a private account. "Who is that letter from again?" Marks cellmate asks. "This is from the FBI agent, Janice." "Oh, that woman you thought was a college student?" "Yes," Mark says. His cell mate laughs. "She was an agent the whole time you were telling her everything? I like her man, she's a good one," the cellmate says.

    Hours later in the entertainment room, Mark sits watching T.V. with his cell mate and four other men watching a television program that appears on T.V. Seconds later, a young lady appears with the biggest smile in the world on her face. "Good morning everyone!" She says. "My name is Christy Billings and I am going to show you how to diversify your money using Godly principles. Is that alright with you today?" In unison, the audience responds.... "Yes!" "Okay, great!" Christy says. Mark nudges his cell mate. "That's her!" "What?" "That's Christy I told you about." His cellmate focuses his eyes to get a better look. "That's the girl you saved from being killed?" "Yes, that's her," Mark says. "The one you worked with, and grew up with from High School?" The cell mate asks. "That's the one," Mark says again. "Wow, it says on T.V. she is the owner of a Fortune 500 company, and a motivational speaker now," the inmate replies. "I knew she would do something special one day, I'm proud of her," Mark replies. "Hey, is she single?" The cellmate asks. Mark glances over at him staring. "Don't even think about it." The cellmate turns to Mark. "What?"

Back 2 Life

Made in the USA
Middletown, DE
20 September 2018